The WAKING

Dreams
of the
DEAD

The WAKING

Dreams
of the
DEAD

THOMAS RANDALL

BLOOMSBURY

NEW YORK BERLIN LONDON

Published by Bloomsbury U.S.A. Children's Books
175 Fifth Avenue, New York, New York 10010

Library of Congress Cataloging-in-Publication Data
Randall, Thomas.
The waking : dreams of the dead / Thomas Randall.—1st U.S. ed.
p.   cm.
Summary: After her mother dies, sixteen-year-old Kara and her father move to Japan,
where he teaches and she attends school, but she is haunted by a series of frightening
nightmares and deaths that might be revenge—or something worse.
ISBN-13: 978-1-59990-250-0 • ISBN-10: 1-59990-250-8
[1. Death—Fiction. 2. Nightmares—Fiction. 3. Supernatural—Fiction.
4. Schools—Fiction. 5. Japan—Fiction. 6. Horror stories.]
I. Title. II. Title: Dreams of the dead.
PZ7.R15845Wak 2009   [Fic]—dc22   2008030844

First U.S. Edition 2009
Book design by Nicole Gastonguay
Typeset by Westchester Book Composition
Printed in the U.S.A. by Quebecor World Fairfield
2 4 6 8 10 9 7 5 3 1

All papers used by Bloomsbury U.S.A. are natural, recyclable products
made from wood grown in well-managed forests. The manufacturing processes
conform to the environmental regulations of the country of origin.

For Fiddlestick's best friend,
Allie Costa

The WAKING

Dreams of the DEAD

PROLOGUE

Akane Murakami died for a boy she did not love.

Rain dotted the surface of Miyazu Bay and spattered the leaves of the trees on the shore. The night sky hung low with a gray blanket of clouds, as though at any moment it might tear open and spill down a deluge that would wipe all of Kyoto Province from the map. Akane felt no remorse at the thought. If Monju-no-Chie School vanished in a flood, erased from the earth by the fury of ancient gods or a mistreated planet, it would be better for her. Better, perhaps, for all of them.

She pushed her long, wet hair away from her face, fresh droplets of rain sliding under the collar of her shirt. Akane knew she looked a mess, but this did not trouble her. After all, who would see her out here on the shore of the bay, at night, in the rain?

The storm had soaked through her school uniform and it clung uncomfortably to her. At first she had plucked at it, but now she had become used to the cloth plastered against her body. The weight of her sodden clothes dragged at her, but Akane barely noticed. The rain fell and the wind made her shiver. No doubt this exposure would lead to a bad cold, but she was beyond caring.

Beyond caring about anything.

She had tried to be a friend to Jiro. Only a friend. He had beautiful, almost hypnotic eyes and strong hands from playing baseball. The girls at school fell all over one another trying to get his attention and Akane understood why, but she could not bring herself to fall in love with him. He made her laugh too much. Jiro was such a boy, so full of swagger and attitude. His parents had bought him a motorcycle for his last birthday, and his father had ridden it up to school one weekend so that Jiro could race it around and show off. They weren't allowed anything but bicycles at school, so that day, Jiro had been everyone's friend. Yet when he'd sat astride it, basking in the attention of the girls and other guys who envied him, he seemed so foolish.

Akane knew Jiro was no fool. He did well in school and had a talent for art that went far beyond the manga that she liked to read. His paintings took her breath away. But when others were around, he had to lift his chin and behave as though he felt he deserved to be the center of attention.

She teased him mercilessly. On his sleek red motorcycle that day, he had looked small, like a child pretending to be Akira, racing across the streets of some post-apocalyptic city. Jiro took her teasing shyly, smiling, when he would have been angry at anyone else. He spent time with Akane whenever he could, away from school and the other students. They walked along the bay and visited the ancient prayer shrines and wondered, together, about the ancestors who had lived on Miyazu Bay, who had lived and loved and shed blood there. They had talked about baseball and art and about books, for Akane loved to read.

Jiro became her closest friend, but she could never have fallen in love with him. In time, though, she understood why he behaved so differently around her than he did around other girls. Others had suggested it and Akane had always brushed their words away.

But tonight he had kissed her.

Jiro loved her.

Akane felt like a fool. She ought to have seen it, but even if she had, she would never have believed it. The look of hurt in his eyes when she had pushed him away, had gently explained that she did not think of him in that way, still stung her. She might not be in love with Jiro, but she cared for him deeply and hated being responsible for what she could only imagine he must be feeling now.

He had left her there, on the bay shore, as the rain began to fall.

Now she hugged herself and watched the sprinkling of raindrops upon the bay. The quiet of the storm held a beauty that made her hold her breath. The wind rippled across the water and rustled in the leaves of the trees, a gentle hushing sound that lent her comfort.

She did not want to go back to school. Not ever. But she had no choice. Soon, the soaking clothes and chilly wind would be too much for her and would drive her inside. Until then she would stay here, not far from an old prayer shrine where local people sometimes still burnt candles.

"I'm sorry," she whispered to the night and the storm.

For several more minutes she watched the rain fall and gazed at the dark, jagged silhouette of the black pines on Ama-no-Hashidate, the spit of land that jutted out into the bay.

At last she turned to make her way back up the long slope that led up to the school and her dormitory beyond. The rain had been falling hard for perhaps an hour and the slope had become soft and muddy underfoot. Akane slipped and fell to one knee, planting a hand to keep herself from sprawling face-first. Her knee squelched in the mud and when her hand struck the ground it squirted up to splatter her jacket.

She felt like crying. Instead, she found herself laughing.

As she climbed to her feet, she slipped again but this time did not fall. Already her shoes were ruined. Pushing her wet, slick hair away from her face, she looked uphill toward the lights of Monju-no-Chie School. Minutes before, she had wished it demolished, but now she felt grateful to see the glow of the windows. It would be warm and dry inside.

Off to her right, something squelched in the mud. Akane glanced in that direction and, at first, saw nothing. But then the darkness moved. Her breath caught in her throat as a patch of night deeper than the gray-black storm resolved itself, and then others began to appear in the storm around her. They reminded her, for just a moment, of the black pines outlined against the night sky on Ama-no-Hashidate.

"Who's that?" she said. "I was just coming back. I—"

4

The silhouettes gathered around her. Now she could see the rain trickling down their faces and they were close enough that she saw them, recognized them.

"He says he kissed you."

The girl who spoke the words had chocolate brown eyes and a round face that might have been lovely had it not been twisted with a cruel sneer. Her hair had been pulled tight in a ponytail, tied with a yellow ribbon.

"He says he can't ever love me because his heart is full of you."

Akane shook her head. She held up her hands, trying to explain. The girl slapped her so hard that the sound echoed like a whipcrack along the path. Akane drew a stunned breath and held a hand to her cheek, stepping back. But the girl followed her and this time struck her with a closed fist. The blow connected with the side of her head and Akane stumbled backward, slid in the mud, and fell. The rain-soaked dirt and grass was cold on her bare legs and as she slid, her skirt was dragged up. Akane reached to try to hold it down, hoping the girl would just go away now, satisfied with having humiliated her.

The first kick took her in the lower back. She shouted in pain, and then another girl kicked her in the jaw. Spasms of pain shot through her skull, and then the kicks and punches began to rain down upon her. In the dark and the storm and with her face now smeared with mud, she could not make out their faces anymore. One girl stomped on her right breast and Akane screamed. She felt a rib break. When she raised her hand to try to defend herself, a black shoe came down on her hand, snapping fingers.

Her mind shut down then. The blur of rain and pain, the storm of blows, swept her away on a wave of regret and confusion.

Fists bunched up in her long hair, fingers twining there, and then some of those dark silhouettes—those faceless shadow girls—dragged her down to the water. Hands gripped her, six or eight or ten of them, and hoisted her off the ground. Akane managed one last scream, ragged from where she had been kicked in the throat, and then they hurled her into the shallows just offshore.

Frantic, bleeding, and broken yet desperate, she tried to drag herself from the water. Rising up, she saw the silhouettes of those black pines and knew she faced the wrong direction. When she corrected her course, those other black silhouettes greeted her. A foot came down on her head, pressing her face under the water, into the soft bottom of the bay. Struggling, she gasped, swallowing dirt and detritus from the bottom and breathing in water.

Drowning.

The whole of Miyazu Bay seemed comprised of her tears. Even the sky wept as she died.

For a boy she did not love.

1

ℵ

"They're going to love you."

Kara glanced up from tying her shoes to see her father standing in the open doorway of her bedroom. He had always been tall and thin, so much so that her mother had sometimes called him "the stork," but dressed in a suit and tie, he had somehow lost his usual awkwardness.

"You look nice," Kara offered.

"Nice? That's the best you can do? I think I look dashingly handsome."

She smiled, arching an eyebrow. "Don't push your luck."

He stepped into the room, his expression turning serious. "Are you nervous?"

Kara rolled her eyes.

"Stupid question, huh?" her father asked.

"Very," she said, and then she relented, letting him see just how anxious she really was. "I'm going to screw it up. I know I am. I'm going to insult someone without even knowing it, or embarrass myself so badly I'll have to hide in the bathroom."

"So, pretty much like any other school year, huh?"

Kara launched herself off the bed to punch him in the arm. "That's not nice."

"No. But it's funny."

"It isn't a day for funny. It isn't a year for funny. Everyone in Japan is so serious all the time," she lamented.

"Not all the time. Just most."

Professor Rob Harper reached out to take his daughter's hands. Kara took comfort in his touch and looked up into his kind blue eyes. There were small laugh lines all around them—lines he'd earned—but it had been a long time since her father had really laughed. A long time for both of them. Come July, it would be two years since the car accident that had taken her mother's life and changed everything for the husband and daughter she had left behind.

"They're going to love you," he said again, more emphatically.

Kara sighed. "They're going to be polite. That's what Japanese people do."

A look of uncertainty swept across his face. He cupped her chin in his hands. "Hey. Tell me you're just having first-day jitters. Otherwise—if you've really changed your mind—we'll go home. Nobody says we have to do this."

Butterflies had been flitting around inside her since they had arrived in Japan and moved into the small house in Kyoto

Prefecture, both of excitement and panic, but they had never been as bad as they had gotten this morning.

"First-day jitters," she said. "I promise. Massive, gigantic jitters, but they'll pass. I feel like Alice in Wonderland. But I've been dreaming about this all my life, Dad, and I know it means a lot to you, too. I'm good. I'm going to be fine. You just have to promise me one thing."

Her father smiled. "What's that, honey?"

"Stop talking to me in English. You promised we'd only speak Japanese."

He slapped himself in the forehead. "D'oh!"

Then he stood a bit straighter. "My apologies, daughter. We've worked so hard, how stupid of me to forget."

"You have many things on your mind."

With a smile, he reached out and tucked an errant lock of her hair behind her ear. "See? You are ready. They're going to—"

She fluttered her hand dismissively. "Love me. I know. So you say."

"I need to get to school for the teachers' meeting. Are you sure you don't want to walk with me?"

"I'm sure. I want to arrive just the way the other students do, and that means without my father, the professor."

The new *professor*, she thought. *English language and American Studies. The* gaijin *professor.*

He bent to kiss her forehead. Some girls might have recoiled from such parental affection, especially at Kara's age. But she knew how fragile her father's heart was—just as fragile as her own—and she would never spurn him in that way. Kara might be sixteen years old, an age when a lot of her friends back home were doing everything in their power to get away from their parents, but all she wanted was to stay close to him. She only had one parent left, and she had vowed not to lose him.

"Enjoy the day," he said. "Live and learn."

Kara smiled. To most people, the phrase "live and learn" represented a rueful acknowledgement of mistakes they had made and the lessons that resulted. But Kara and her father had turned "live and learn" into their private mantra. The words held no regret for them. They were a philosophy. A way of life.

"Live and learn," she replied.

Her father gave her one final glance in which she could see his concern for her breaking through the hopeful, encouraging air he had put on for her benefit, and then he went out.

She listened for the front doors to slide open and closed, and then went into the small kitchen. They had cleaned up together after breakfast. Kara poured herself a small glass of water and sipped it as she tried to slow her frantic pulse. She breathed evenly, almost meditating, and found that it helped. For ten long minutes she paced the small house, rearranging items in the obsessive neatness they had achieved for the sake of local culture.

In front of the mirror, she unleashed her ponytail and then swept her blond hair up again, tying it back with a red elastic. Any time she caught sight of her reflection while wearing her uniform, she got a giddy feeling. Her school insisted girls still wear the sailor *fuku,* a navy blue sailor suit with white trim. The skirt came down to just above her knees and she wore a white blouse with a red ribbon tie underneath the jacket. Memories of *Sailor Moon* cartoons came to mind, making her smile.

Kara took her *bento*—the lunch box all the students used— and slipped it into her book bag, then went to the door. Taking a deep breath, she stepped outside.

A shiver went through her and goosebumps formed on her skin. If the school had been any further away, she would have gone back inside to put a heavy coat over her uniform. On the first of April—first day of a new school year—Kyoto Prefecture was still quite cold. Even so, the day was beautiful. The sunlight shone brightly on the small houses along the street. Miyazu Bay reflected back the blue sky with a purity that made her catch her breath. Kara had loved the house she had grown up in back in Massachusetts, but leaving an American suburb behind for natural beauty such as this was like waking up in some magical kingdom. She would endure almost anything to be able to wake up to this view of the bay every morning.

Taking solace from the day and from the view, she found a calm place within herself and started down the street toward the school, whose grounds sprawled beside the bay. Monju-no-Chie School looked more like a temple than any school Kara had ever seen. More than anything, it reminded her of the fortresses of warlords in the movies she'd seen about feudal Japan. Imposing, but it was much cooler than the almost industrial-looking schools they had seen in Tokyo and Kyoto City. Inside the walls of Monju-no-Chie, though, things weren't much different. Strict rules. Japanese propriety. Hard work.

Kara could live with that.

Actually, she'd been dreaming about it for years, romanticizing the country's history and mythology and spirituality at the same time as she ate up the new pop culture spreading across the world from Japan. Coming here had been a huge decision for both Kara and her father, a new beginning in a place they'd always talked about living, speaking a language they both loved. Nothing could make her forget her mother or loosen the tight knot of grief that her heart had become, but that loss had made Kara and her father realize that dreams should not be postponed.

They were starting over.

As she walked toward the bay, she stared at the terraced pagoda peaks of the school, and her heart began to hammer in her chest. Her throat went dry. Her new uniform skirt itched, her ribbon tie hung askew because she hadn't fastened it right, and her book bag felt heavy even though it was only the first day of classes.

Yes, she had wanted this for as long as she could remember, wished for it the way other girls wish to grow up to become princesses. But she hadn't given enough thought to what it would be like being the only gaijin girl—the only foreigner, the only westerner, the only American—at a private school with a view of the Sea of Japan. Made her feel pretty stupid, considering how many hours she and her dad had spent talking about it, but nothing could have prepared her, really.

The first few weeks, she'd felt like Dorothy after she'd just crashed her house in Oz. Adjusting to life in Japan had been hour by hour, an evolution—maybe even a metamorphosis— wandering around Miyazu City and the bay with her camera or sitting down by the Turning Bridge with her guitar. Now, with school starting, it would begin all over again. The gaijin girl. The few other students she'd met in town had been polite but not exactly welcoming. When she'd tried to talk to them about manga or music, searching for common ground, the conversations had been short.

They're gonna love you, her father had said, so many times. *Once they get to know you. Once school starts.*

Lonely and unsure, Kara had still found her love for Japan growing. Ama-no-Hashidate—the natural spit of land that connected the two sides of the bay—had a beauty like nothing else she'd ever seen. Whether on a perfect blue day or a cool, misty morning, the view transported her to another place, another age. And the city might not be Tokyo, but it came alive at night with music and color. During the day, the ancient places still echoed with the clang of swords and the chants of holy men.

She'd make it. Kara wouldn't allow herself to conceive of another possibility.

Picking up her pace, she strode down the street. Now

other students were streaming toward the school from all directions. A pair of girls ran past her in a grim race. Two boys stood leaning against a railing, talking excitedly about baseball. When one of them noticed her, he tapped his friend and their conversation stopped as they watched her walk by.

A trio of girls stood on the corner across the street from the arched entryway to the school grounds. They wore their skirts too short and had their hair done up in high pigtails. One of them wore voluminous, loose, white socks that bunched around her ankles, a style that had gone in and out of fashion for years. The other two were listening intently to the third, a tiny, petite girl whose features seemed far more mature, in spite of her size. She spoke earnestly to her friends, but when they saw Kara, the tiny girl whispered something Kara could not hear and all three of them giggled, hiding their smiles behind their hands.

Ignoring them all, she crossed the street and went under the archway.

Kara paused and glanced back at the other students she had passed. None of them seemed in much of a rush except for a boy with glasses, who careened down the street on his bicycle and under the arch.

Kara stepped aside as he rode past her. His expression was frantic, but he spared her a glance and a bright, brief flash of a friendly smile, which made her feel a million times better.

Monju-no-Chie School had been built perhaps two hundred yards from the bay, set on a slight rise. The main building faced northwest toward the neighborhood where Kara lived, so as she approached she had the perfect view. The grounds were elegantly groomed, the paths meandering as though never intending to reach their destination.

To her right, a long drive ran parallel to her path, toward the parking lot on the west side of the building. Jutting off to her left was a narrow, abbreviated road used as a scenic overlook; beyond that, a long stretch of uninterrupted bay shore that provided the school with an extraordinary view; and then thick woods that ran up the slope and bordered the school grounds to the east. Over there, between the school and the woods, was an ancient prayer shrine that had intrigued her the one time her father had let her go exploring the grounds after they had first arrived. She liked to think about the monks who might have brought offerings there and what spirit those offerings had been meant to appease.

With a few minutes to spare, she followed the gravel walkway that led around to the left, where the woods came closest to the school building. As she walked, she noticed a secondary path she had not seen before, trampled by years of student feet. It cut away from the gravel and down toward the edge of the bay. She followed it toward the water, shivering as she entered the shade provided by the trees. Up ahead, she saw what appeared to be another shrine, but it didn't look anything like the one she'd seen before.

Intrigued, Kara kept walking, hoping she was not already breaking some school rule. The bay lapped against the shore here and the view made her smile. She felt as though she could see the whole of the Sea of Japan if she concentrated enough.

As she approached the shrine, she noticed a scattering of flowers at the base of one tree. Descending the slope, she realized that there were other things there as well, drawings and photographs, small stuffed animals, and a Hello Kitty T-shirt. There were notes as well, many of them written to someone called Akane, and there were candles. At the center of this more recent shrine Kara saw a photograph. She crouched down to look at it, resisted the urge to reach out and touch it.

The dead girl had been very pretty. Just like back home, a teenager had died, and her friends had come out to this spot to remember her. For several minutes, Kara studied the things that had been left behind, but then she began to worry that others might see her and think she was intruding. Propriety was so important, and she didn't want to risk offending anyone because that would reflect badly on her father.

She turned back up the path, wondering how the girl had died. With a glance toward the flow of students making their way up to the school, and the way so many of them still gathered at the front steps and on the grass, she decided she still had a few minutes and went along the path that ran between the school and the woods to check out the ancient monks' shrine.

Someone had burned candles there recently. It was a peaceful spot, and she took a couple of minutes to try to force herself to de-stress. Her father said everyone would love her. That might be too much to hope for, but she told herself the opposite was just as unlikely. They couldn't *all* hate her.

Kara had never been so nervous.

She turned and stared up at the pagoda towers of the school, a fresh wave of anxiety crashing over her. She tapped the fingers of her right hand against her leg in time to a rhythm that played somewhere in the back of her mind. She chewed her lower lip, fidgeted with her ribbon tie.

"You'll be fine."

Kara glanced to her left and saw a figure standing in a shadowy, recessed doorway set into the side of the school building. At some point the door had been painted over, and whoever had done the job had painted the door handle and right over the lock. No one would be getting in that way, and it didn't look like anyone used it as an exit, either.

The girl who stepped out from that shadowed, arched doorway had her sailor jacket on inside out, revealing patches and badges she had sewn into the lining, some of which Kara felt sure said some pretty rude things in Japanese. Her hair was chopped short, a bit spiky and wild, and where it framed her face it hung several inches lower than at the back of her neck. In her left hand she held a cigarette, dangling it between two fingers.

It took a moment before Kara realized the girl had spoken to her in English.

"Do you think so?" she asked, in Japanese.

The girl lifted her cigarette to her lips and drew in a lungful of smoke, then let it curl out lazily as she replied, still in English. "It does not matter what I think. They will leave you alone. More alone than you want to be."

"How do you know?"

"That is what they do to anyone who is different."

"I would be grateful if you would speak to me in Japanese," Kara said, in that language. "My name is Kara."

"Sakura," the other girl said. With a great show of reluctance, she took a final puff of her cigarette and then crushed it out underfoot. Slipping off her jacket, she turned it right-side-out, then bent and picked up the cigarette butt, slipping it into her pocket.

"It's a pleasure to meet you, Sakura."

But the girl was no longer looking at her. Instead, Sakura gazed down toward the bay, or perhaps at the newer shrine—the one for the dead girl—which Kara could sort of make out from this distance, now that she knew where it was.

"Your Japanese is excellent, Kara," Sakura said, without looking at her. But she had heard, because she no longer spoke English.

Kara gave a slight bow of her head. She knew better than to thank the other girl for the compliment. In Japanese culture, to do so would be incredibly rude and arrogant, implying that she believed she deserved the compliment. Her bow would be the only acceptable show of gratitude.

Sakura offered a thin smile in return. "We should go inside."

They fell into step together. Sakura seemed very distant, as though she had forgotten Kara was even with her. The girl wore the rebellious attitude like a mask, but Kara had felt for a moment that beneath the sharp edges and hard looks there might be something else, that maybe she might have found a friend here. Now that hope began to diminish.

Sakura surprised her by speaking. "They haven't caught the killers."

Kara shivered and blamed it on the cold breeze off the

bay. So Sakura had been watching her while she was down by the bay, looking at the death shrine.

They rounded the corner to the front of the school to see many other students going up the front steps.

"That girl, Akane? She was murdered?" Kara asked.

Sakura stopped and looked back the way they had come. "Beaten, and then drowned. It happened in September. The police questioned every student and every teacher. No one knew anything. No one saw anything. But there were so many footprints in the mud that there had to be five or six of them, at least, so there are many liars here. And many killers."

Kara covered her mouth with one hand, horrified, wondering if her father had known about the girl's murder, and if so, why he hadn't said anything.

"Did you . . . did you know her?"

The breeze from the bay brushed away the slashed curtain of Sakura's hair, and for the first time Kara saw that as tough as she pretended to be, the girl was very pretty, her features almost delicate. Her eyes were the color of brass.

"She was my sister," Sakura said.

Then she walked on toward school and up the stairs, joining the orderly stream of students entering the building, leaving Kara staring after her and wishing she had worn her heavy coat after all.

The first of April felt awfully cold.

2

Monju-no-Chie School managed to be both traditional and progressive at the same time. Though tourists were not uncommon in the Miyazu City area, according to Kara's father, the school had only ever had a handful of gaijin students. Most westerners who attended school in Japan went to one of the international private schools that hosted students from all over the world, or immersed themselves in public schools in large cities.

The school still insisted on fuku sailor uniforms for girls and *gakuran* uniforms, a military-influenced style, for boys. Perhaps the nearness to the ports of Miyazu City helped explain the embrace of the naval dress. Not that Kara minded. The fuku might be itchy, but she thought the uniforms were really cute.

More than half of the students came from the Miyazu Bay area, and rode bicycles or took the train and then walked from the station. But Monju-no-Chie School had earned an excellent reputation, and privileged families from all over Kyoto Prefecture sent their children to live there. Boarding students resided in a second building located across a grassy sports field behind the main school.

Her father had given her the choice as to whether she would live with him in the small house the school had provided or in the dormitory with the boarding students. Maybe next year, if this grand experiment of theirs worked, she'd live in the dorm. But for now, she wanted to begin and end each day with her dad. Besides, she'd have a lot more in common with the students who came by train and bicycle than with the privileged kids who lived at the dorm.

Who are you kidding? You don't have anything in common with any of them.

Kara hurried up the front steps, merging with the flow of students. Sakura had already vanished inside the school, and though many of the boys and girls snuck glances at her, none of them seemed ready for conversation. Once again, she was on her own.

Just inside the door, a group of girls clustered around, sneaking shy smiles behind upraised hands, whispering to one another. Kara would have thought their gossip was about her, were it not for the immediate reaction they had to her passing. Most of the Japanese students were far too respectful to outright stare at her, but not these girls. They appraised her frankly, and the tallest girl—her shoulder-length hair veiling one side of her face—cast a dubious glance at her. She turned to her fawning friends and rattled off a snide comment.

"Look at the bonsai," the girl said. "Cut away and moved far from home. No roots at all. How long before she withers?"

The girls began to laugh, and Kara overheard the tall one's name—Ume.

She tried to breathe evenly, told herself to keep walking. How many times had her father reminded her how important this first day would be? She had studied local customs, understood that propriety ruled here. But this Ume girl had insulted her, and letting it pass would only make things worse in the future.

Kara turned on her heel and strode directly up to the girl, who must have been a *senpai*—a senior. Ume had either assumed Kara couldn't speak the language very well or didn't care that she'd been overheard. She looked down quizzically.

"Though she is cut away from where she grew, this bonsai is healthy and strong. She will survive, as long as she can keep her roots from being choked by weeds."

As soon as she had begun speaking, the girls had fallen silent and looked at her in surprise. Kara's Japanese was not flawless, but her father had been teaching her the language almost since she began to speak.

"*Oo jyozudesune*," Ume replied.

Skillful, a comment on her command of the language. She'd heard it a lot and understood that, though it might be a compliment, an element of condescension went along with it.

Kara bowed her head slightly. At home she'd have called the girl a bitch. But this wasn't home.

"Grow tall, bonsai," Ume said.

Despite her earlier rudeness, she had abruptly become

22

the most respectful, pleasant, and welcoming face that Kara had yet encountered.

"Have you chosen a school club yet?"

"Not yet," Kara said.

"If you like soccer, you would be welcome in our club."

The other girls looked surprised, even irked. As the other students continued to stream in through the main doors and gather in the corridor, Kara smiled thinly.

"I don't have the talent for the game. But I will cheer when you play."

Kara took a deep breath, reminding herself that not everyone would be like Ume. Japanese, her father had taught her, often consisted of saying things that were the precise opposite of what you actually meant.

She followed the flow of students into the *genkan*—a large, square, functional room lined with lockers. With so many voices speaking Japanese at one time, she found it impossible to interpret what anyone said. But that was all right. Since none of them were talking to her, she'd only have been eavesdropping.

All of the students were taking off their street shoes and stashing them in the lockers. From their backpacks, they all retrieved *uwabaki*—which meant "inside shoes," though they were really more like slippers.

A smile touched Kara's lips. Ever since her father had first told her about this custom, she'd thought it so strange, but sort of fun, too. The idea of all of the students wearing slippers made her think cozy thoughts of home—though there was nothing cozy about the genkan. The boys wore blue slippers and the girls pink. If there'd been even a single other American at the school, she could've made a joke about wearing pajamas to school, or carrying the dusty old teddy bear that sat in a box somewhere in storage back home. But she couldn't be sure the kids at Monju-no-Chie School would get the joke, or would think it was funny even if they did get it.

Still, it amused her enough. She had a smile on her face when she looked up and caught two boys watching her intently. Kara gave them a nod of recognition, and they grinned, one of them waving at her.

She let out a breath. *All right, so not every kid here is going to be nasty or bizarre.*

Bizarre meant Sakura.

Kara felt badly that she'd let herself start thinking negatively of the girl. She glanced around but saw no sign of her. With her hairstyle and attitude, the cigarettes and the patches and pins, Sakura was working hard to give off a rebel vibe. She might as well have tattooed *Tough Chick* on her forehead. But she'd been cool and accepting to Kara without putting up the walls that everyone else seemed to have built around themselves. So what if she seemed like trouble? Sakura's sister had been murdered. Grief could cause a person to do all kinds of things they'd never have done before.

Stashing her shoes in an empty locker, Kara leaned against it to put on her slippers. Now that the initial surprise of her arrival had rippled through the room and everyone had gotten a good look at the gaijin girl, they seemed to have gone back to their preparations for the start of the school year. She felt herself begin to exhale.

As strange as it all felt—Kara couldn't imagine any of her friends from home making it through an hour at this school without totally freaking out—an odd happiness began to spread through her. She and her father had talked about this adventure for years. It had taken her mother's death to make it more than a dream, and so the feeling was bittersweet. But Kara had vowed to herself that she would make her father proud, and be the girl her mother had always told her she could be.

I can do this.

Live and learn.

Someone bumped shoulders with her. She opened her eyes in time to catch the pained, embarrassed expression on the face of a tall, stocky boy with unruly hair.

"Excuse me," he said with a quick bow. "I'm very clumsy."

"We have that in common."

She'd said it only to make him feel better. The typical boy at Monju-no-Chie School was slender, even petite, compared to the guys Kara had gone to school with back home. To his schoolmates, the one who'd bumped her would seem like some kind of giant. She liked his face, and there was a sweetness in his eyes, but when he smiled, she felt a little tremor in her chest.

"My name is Hachiro," he said.

She smiled in return. "I'm Kara."

Hachiro nodded. "Yes," he said, in English. "It's nice to meet you."

Kara smiled. Most of the students here could speak English to some degree. When Sakura had done so, it had been because she'd assumed Kara's Japanese wouldn't be very good. Hachiro did it as a kindness.

"And you," she said in Japanese.

They walked together along the corridor, near the back of the herd of shuffling students. Kara had been concerned about finding her way to the morning assembly, but even without Hachiro, she could have simply followed the parade.

"I'm looking forward to having your father as a teacher," Hachiro said. "Last year we had several American scholars as guest speakers, but this will be the first American teacher we have for a full term."

"He's an excellent teacher," Kara said. "He always makes me want to learn more."

They entered the gymnasium, where lines were forming as the homeroom teachers gathered their students. Hachiro spotted his teacher and headed toward her line.

"I'll talk to you later, Kara."

"Bye," she said. She was sorry to part company with him. He really did have a great smile.

After a few seconds standing around feeling foolish, she figured out which of the teachers was her *sensei*, Mr. Matsui. With his white hair and square face, he would have seemed grim if not for his oversize glasses and the kind eyes behind them. Mr. Matsui took her in with a glance, gave an almost imperceptible nod, and then proceeded to treat her with the same dour disapproval he showed her classmates. Mr. Matsui turned his back on them and faced one end of the gymnasium, and all of the students followed suit.

The principal, Mr. Yamato, and several members of the

school's board of directors addressed the students from the front of the room. The sheer ordinariness of the remarks surprised Kara. So much of the culture in Japan felt entirely new to her, but it turned out that boring speeches were pretty much the same around the world.

Numb after only a few minutes of this, she stopped mentally translating and let her thoughts and her eyes wander. Two rows over, she caught sight of Sakura and stared at her until the girl felt the attention and turned. Kara gave her a tiny wave. Sakura smirked in a way that could have meant *Yeah, isn't this boring,* or *Oh, great, weird gaijin girl thinks she's my puppy now.*

Suddenly self-conscious, Kara turned her eyes front to find Mr. Matsui watching her with his eyebrows knitted together. His only comment was a stern throat-clearing; he couldn't quite manage a glower.

The voices of authority finished their declaration of the school's glory and the ominous drone about their expectations of their students, and then the assembly mercifully ended and the teachers led their charges to their homerooms.

Mr. Matsui's classroom—2-C—was on the second floor. Kara counted twenty-seven students in 2-C, herself included. Once again she found herself thrown off by the familiarity of the first-day rituals. Seats were assigned—her desk was third row, right in the middle—and then Mr. Matsui explained that each morning began with announcements and attendance. The class would rotate those responsibilities according to a schedule called *toban.*

When her teacher—her sensei—looked at her, she thought he might give her the toban duties for the first day, but instead he chose a girl from the front row named Miho. Though Miho's glasses were much smaller than Mr. Matsui's, Kara wondered if they were what made him choose the girl. Her long, black hair was pulled up on one side with a clip, and she sat stiffly, like she was in church. Kara listened to the names as Miho took attendance from a list the sensei had given her, but she knew she would forget most of them. One boy had dyed his perfectly combed hair a bronze color, and when Miho called his name—Ren—she blushed.

At last, the school day began.

At first, Kara liked the different structure of the school day. The students remained in their homeroom while, between classes, the teachers traveled. Mr. Matsui left them and a moment later the math teacher arrived. After math came Japanese—which, at this grade level, was mostly Japanese literature—and then science. There were no lab science classes on the first day and no gym until the second week, but those were the only classes that would require them to leave their homeroom.

Their books were kept inside the desks, and at the back of the classroom were lockers where they were expected to stash their lunches, jackets, and—on days when they had PE— gym uniforms. Between classes there were ten-minute breaks, during which the room became noisy with chatter and slamming lockers, but the minute the sensei arrived for the next class, all talking ended.

By lunchtime, Kara's back and butt were killing her. Sitting in one position for so long with just short breaks had become torture, and she understood that other than bowing and politeness, the first thing she needed to learn to get by in a Japanese school was patience. Once, at the age of ten, she had gotten food poisoning and her parents had brought her to a hospital, where a doctor had given her an intravenous drug to make her stop vomiting and fluids to rehydrate her. Lying there on the gurney in the emergency room for three hours had been the same kind of torment.

Fortunately, they had the whole lunch period to talk and move around.

The girl who sat in front of her seemed very nice, and the supercute guy to her right had beautiful eyes, but they were both named Sora, and Kara couldn't decide if that would be helpful or really confusing. Everyone moved their desks into circles so they could face one another and chat, and for a moment Kara thought she would be left an island unto herself, but both Soras gestured for her to join them. Nobody talked to her much, but to her relief she didn't mind.

Everyone seemed to have rice and *umeboshi*, which were pickled red plums, plus an assortment of other things. Kara could have asked her father to pack more familiar foods in her bento box, but it was important to her to live like other students, and so she had fish, rice, eggs, vegetables, and pickles. No umeboshi for her, but she could only go so far. For a girl who'd eaten peanut butter and jelly for lunch every day until the sixth grade, it would take some getting used to.

When lunch finished and bento boxes had been put away, it was time for English class. Kara's father—*Harper-sensei*, the students called him—did really well. They had discussed in advance how important it would be for him to treat her just as he did the other students, so their only communication consisted of a shared smile and a couple of questions that she answered after raising her hand. He seemed extremely happy, and Kara felt very proud of him. Yet once or twice, when he looked at her, she caught a glimpse of the wistful sadness that never left him for very long.

In his eyes she saw how much he wished her mother could have shared this with them. They both wished it. But there were some things that could never be, no matter how powerful the wish. Kara had learned that in the worst way—kneeling on the prayer rail beside the closed coffin at her mother's wake.

A shudder went through her. Death was a lesson she had never wanted to learn.

The thought reminded her of Sakura again. Could her sister really have been murdered here, on the grounds of the school? It seemed impossible that Kara's dad wouldn't have heard about it, until she gave it a little thought. They were in Japan. If a girl had died here, and if it was possible students were responsible, of course no one would want to discuss it because of the shame it would bring them. Besides, why would Sakura lie?

It's like Death's following me, she thought. She told herself how crazy that sounded, that no connection existed between her mother's death and the blood shed on the grounds of her new school. The car accident happened almost two years ago and halfway around the world. It couldn't have anything to do with the murder of a teenage girl in Japan.

But now that the thought had lodged in her brain, Kara couldn't shake the feeling that the shadow of her mother's death—the shadow that she and her father had moved from Boston to Kyoto Prefecture to escape—had reached out to touch her again. And if she let herself believe that, it was all too easy to believe that it would always follow her and touch her anytime it wanted, anytime she felt like maybe she could be happy again.

God, she thought as she tucked a stray lock of hair behind her ear, *morbid much?*

The last class of the day—in her case, art—was followed by the part of the Japanese education system that amazed Kara the most. Every day, when classes ended, all of the students took part in *o-soji*. The direct translation escaped her, but it meant the clean-up. The janitors at Japanese schools were maintenance staff only, fixing broken toilets and moving desks and that sort of thing. The students were the ones who picked up and collected trash, swept, cleaned the restrooms, and erased all of the chalkboards to prepare for the next day. She'd half-expected this to be done in a sullen silence, but everyone seemed to get into it, happy to be finished with the day's classes and more than willing to do their part with the clean-up. But o-soji was part of the layered hierarchy that defined Japanese culture. Junior students were basically the servants of the seniors, but the older students were responsible for mentoring the younger.

From everything she'd read, it seemed like corporate Japan—and every other sort of business—functioned on the same basic principle. Many occupations had a particular uniform, and they existed on a sort of ladder of respect. In a school setting, or even in business, she understood how everyone might benefit from the system. But already, in Miyazu City, she'd seen the way that some people further up in the hierarchy, like merchants, treated those whom culture dictated were beneath them—street sweepers and laborers, for instance—and it made her sad. That system was what made school so vital for Japanese students. Success or failure now could lock them onto a rung of the ladder they weren't ever likely to rise above.

Kara gathered up a trash bag and pulled it out of the can. Her art teacher, Miss Aritomo, stopped to compliment her on her Japanese.

Kara bowed. "I enjoyed art class today."

Miss Aritomo smiled. "Your father told me that you are a photographer. I would like to see some of your work."

"I'll bring some pictures in tomorrow," Kara said.

As Miss Arimoto walked away, Kara tied the top of the trash bag and carried it to the central staircase, where a bunch of students were sweeping up. In a classroom off to the left she spotted Sakura wiping down a blackboard. With a quick glance around to make sure no teachers were paying attention, she stepped into the room. In the central aisle, a girl pushed a broom like it was serious business.

"Hello," Kara said.

Sakura turned from the board and arched an eyebrow, looking at the garbage bag. "You could have found a better souvenir from your first day."

She kept up the tough-girl attitude—sharp edges and pitying looks—for several seconds longer, and then rolled her eyes.

"I'm teasing you, Kara. School might be more disciplined here than you're used to, but that doesn't mean nobody knows how to make a joke."

Kara laughed softly. "That's a relief."

"Things aren't nearly so serious in school clubs," said the other girl in the room, who'd stopped sweeping.

Now that Kara saw her face, her narrow features and round glasses, she recognized Miho, the girl who'd taken attendance in her homeroom that morning.

"This is my roommate, Miho," Sakura said.

Kara smiled at the thought of shy Miho and bold Sakura sharing a room together.

"I didn't realize you were boarding students."

Sakura ran an eraser over the chalkboard one last time. "Yeah. The forgotten ones."

"Forgotten?"

"By our parents," Sakura said, and though she smiled, her bitterness seemed genuine. "If they'd had a child murdered, most parents would probably have brought the other one home. Mine are trying to pretend it never happened."

A trickle of ice went down Kara's back. She knew she ought to say something but couldn't find the words.

"My parents haven't forgotten me," Miho said. She shrugged. "They just don't like me."

Sakura rolled her eyes again, grinning. "They love you, Miho. They just want to keep you away from gaijin boys."

Miho flushed and started sweeping again.

Confused, Kara looked at Sakura.

"She's obsessed with American boys. There were several she made friends with online. That would have been bad enough," Sakura explained, "but then she started to spend time with one she met in Kyoto. Miho's parents are very traditional. They want her to marry a Japanese man, to stay in Japan forever. If you'd been a boy instead of a girl, Kara, they'd probably have taken her out of here."

Kara didn't want to upset Miho, but she couldn't help herself. She turned to stare at the girl. "Really?"

She needn't have worried. As shy as Miho seemed, she gave a sort of helpless smile and shrugged again.

"Probably."

"That's extreme."

Miho nodded. "That's my parents."

"Go on, Miho, ask her," Sakura said.

Kara glanced from one girl to the other. "Ask me what?"

"Ever since she found out you were coming here, she's been hoping to talk to you," Sakura explained.

"About what?"

Miho glanced at the ground again. "American boys. If you have a boyfriend at home, or just boys you like."

Sakura and Miho looked at her expectantly.

"No boyfriend," Kara said. "But plenty of stories to tell."

Miho smiled like she'd just remembered it was her birthday.

3

By the time Kara left the school grounds for the short walk home, the afternoon shadows had grown very long and a crisp chill touched the air. It might officially be spring, but on the first day of April, the memory of winter still lingered. Once again she found herself breathless at the beauty of Ama-no-Hashidate. Late in the day, the pine-studded causeway had an almost mythical aura around it, as though if she went for a walk among those trees, she might encounter things that now existed only in ancient legends.

The day had felt even longer than she anticipated and Kara had been very tired when she left school. But with the cool air and the blue sky and the fading sunlight, she drew in deep breaths and felt like running. All of her preparation had paid off. The days would be hard work, but Kara knew now that she could handle it.

More than anything, she wanted to immerse herself in her

new home, to learn the streets and the houses and walk the shore of the bay, to go into Miyazu City and visit the shops, and to discover the history of local prayer shrines and festivals.

Unfortunately, she had homework.

But she'd have all year to explore, and she'd already made a start. Right now, school had to come first, especially since a lot of the students she'd met were also attending cram schools—*juku*—which meant that while she now headed home for dinner, they had gone into the city for more school. The idea made her shudder. Kara wanted to have the full experience of what it meant to attend school in Japan, but she understood now that it would be impossible. At some point, she'd return to the United States, either for her senior year of high school or for college. No matter what she did, she would never feel the kind of pressure that her classmates felt.

As she started up the path to the front of their small house, she smiled to herself. Cram school. The idea made her cringe. She'd live with the guilt.

"Hi, sweetie," her father called as she walked in.

Kara found him in the kitchen chopping vegetables. She dropped her backpack and gave him a short hug, picking up a slice of onion and eating it raw.

"Hey. How was your day?" she asked.

He took a sip from a cup of *sake,* then went back to chopping. "Good, but exhausting." Rob Harper grinned. "I'll never learn all of their names."

Kara crossed her arms. "Oh, come on. Don't give up already. It's only the first day."

"What about you?" he asked, turning to face her. He studied her intently. "Was it everything you hoped it would be?"

"Everything I hoped and everything I feared."

Her father looked at her in alarm, but Kara brushed his concern away.

"No, no, it was fine. I don't mean, like, utter disaster feared. It's just so weird being the only outsider."

"Were the kids that bad to you?" her father asked.

"Some," she said. "But I made a couple of friends today. At least, I think they'll be friends, given some time."

Picking up his sake cup, he nodded. "It's a start. What about school itself? Any trouble understanding the teachers?"

"Not enough to be a problem. I really like the art teacher. And I think I'm going to love learning social studies from a different perspective. Now if I can just figure out what club I want to join, I'll be pretty much set."

Her father turned on the stove and poured a bit of sesame oil into the pan. "Right, right," he said, chopping up garlic. "Did you see anything you liked?"

"Too many things." Kara took a step away as he dropped the garlic into the pan. "It's an interesting way to go about it, almost like a career fair. After o-soji, all of the clubs met in the gym, and I just kind of wandered around, talking to different people. It stinks that there's no photography club, but I guess I take enough pictures. I wouldn't mind doing judo or working on the yearbook. Miho, one of the girls I met today, does Noh theater, which is totally fascinating to me. But Sakura, her roommate, belongs to the calligraphy club, and that's pretty interesting, too. The only thing I'm sure of at this point is that I don't want to play soccer."

Her father sliced raw chicken on a dish, but he paused to brush all of the chopped vegetables into the pan.

"Why's that?" he asked as he scraped the chicken in as well.

Kara wrinkled her nose, only partially because of the smell of frying garlic. "Snotty girls. I mean, I guess they were okay. But you can always tell popular girls by their attitude. That requires zero translation. I couldn't stomach those girls at home, so I don't think I'm going to like the subtitled version any better."

Her dad blinked, brows knitting. "Meow?"

"Was that catty? I guess that was catty. But my cup isn't running over with regret." She shrugged. "Sorry. I'm not, like, a diva or something. But I don't want to be anybody's token gaijin girl. I'm a little odd, so I'll stick with the odd ones."

"Does that go for the boys, too?"

"Huh?"

"Just wondering if you met any boys today."

Kara arched an eyebrow. "None worth mentioning," she said, then thought better of it. "Actually, there was one—"

"Aha!" He pointed at her with the wooden fork he'd been using.

"No 'aha.' I'm not looking for a boyfriend. Hachiro was just nice to me. He's this big, friendly kid, sort of like a Great Dane puppy, already huge but hasn't grown into his size yet."

And, yes, great smile, pretty charming, she thought. She remembered the little jump her heart had given when Hachiro had smiled at her the first time, but she wasn't about to mention that to her father.

"Observant girl. You picked up a lot on your first day," he said.

"You taught me well." As her father took another sip of sake, Kara studied him. He did seem awfully upbeat after a long day. Drinking sake. He might even have been humming when she came into the house, now that Kara thought about it. "What about you? Anyone catch your eye in the teachers' room?"

Her father only smiled and reached for plates.

"Dad?" Kara prodded.

"Do you want some sake?"

Her mouth curled up into an *eeeew* face. Sake—nasty stuff. "You're dodging the question."

"I've already said you were observant."

Kara laughed and poked him. "Which one is it? No, wait. Is it Miss Aritomo? She's pretty and really nice. It's her, isn't it?"

Rob Harper nodded, surrendering before Kara had really begun the needling in earnest. "She's beautiful. But I barely spoke to her. And you know I'm not looking."

Kara's smile vanished. All the good humor, the excitement after their first day, was sucked from the room.

"Hey," her father said, reaching out to touch her face. "I didn't mean to—"

"There's nothing wrong with looking, Dad."

Kara's friend Anthony had lost his father to cancer when they were in eighth grade, and she had other friends whose parents were divorced. Most, if not all of them, had serious issues with the idea of their parents getting romantically in-volved with someone new. At first, she had felt the same way. But her father kept to himself too much, and when Kara thought about what her mother would have wanted for him, it gave her an entirely different perspective.

"She wouldn't have wanted you to be alone," Kara added.

He nodded. "I know," he said and bent to kiss the top of her head. "I know, sweetie. This is our new beginning, right? But it's only day one. I might need more time to adjust than you."

Kara forced herself to smile. "Who's adjusting? I'm freak-ing out."

The moment passed, and dinner was ready. Kara went to change—she made a habit out of dropping food on herself at the worst times, and she didn't want to stain her uniform. As soon as she returned, they sat down to eat. Kara had mas-tered chopsticks at the age of five, but she and her father had agreed that in their own house, they would use forks. Night came on, with even cooler temperatures, and Kara appreci-ated having something warm in her belly.

After dinner they cleaned up together. Her father went into the room he kept as an office to prepare for the following day's classes, and Kara retreated to her room to do her home-work. The events of the day were still fresh in her mind. Now that most of the morning's butterflies were gone from her stomach, she found herself excited all over again.

She'd been told to expect about two hours' worth of home-work a night, but since it was the first day, she finished in less than half that time. Her windows had been open a couple of inches to let in the breeze of the day, and she'd enjoyed the crisp air while she did her homework—it helped keep her awake. Now, though, she went and closed the one nearest her bed.

The window gave her a view of the school, and the bay shore. She could see lights across the water and a dark swath that could only be Ama-no-Hashidate. For a moment she admired the peaceful view.

Then she remembered what Sakura had said: her sister had been murdered at the water's edge. Kara's serene moment winked out, like a candle snuffed by an errant breeze. The place where Akane had died must be farther along the bay, on the school grounds, so Kara wouldn't be able to see the spot from here.

The thought troubled and intrigued her in almost equal measure.

She shook it off. Tragic as Sakura's loss might be, Kara couldn't let it ruin her appreciation of the delightful place where they had chosen to live. Miyazu City had its charms, chief among them the view of the bay and of Ama-no-Hashidate, which was considered among the three most beautiful locations in Japan. If Kara let this get to her, it would be a very, very long year.

Determined, she pulled on a sweatshirt. Her guitar called to her from the corner of the room, but she could play later. Right now, she wanted to explore, and she wasn't about to let the night, or tales of murder, make her afraid.

"Dad, I'm going for a walk," she said, at the door to his office.

He looked up from his desk, brow furrowed in momentary concern. Then he nodded. "All right. Don't go far."

Kara assured him she wouldn't and headed for the door. She stepped out into the night, burrowing a little deeper into her sweatshirt, and started walking, first thinking she might head to the Turning Bridge before her feet decided to stroll along the path toward the school. Maybe some of the boarding students would be outside. Could they go outside? The ones who went to cram school would probably just be getting back. If she became real friends with Miho or Sakura, or anybody else, she wondered what the rules were for socializing.

Still, the warm yellow lights in the distant windows of the school comforted her. As a little girl, she had been afraid of many things. Every noise outside her window might be a ghost, every creak of the house a thief who might try to steal her away. Her mother had stroked her hair and kissed her forehead, and always said the same words until they became a mantra.

"There's nothing in the dark that isn't there in the light."

Most of the time, her mother managed to convince her. But only *most* of the time. At sixteen, Kara still felt afraid sometimes, but she had to recite the mantra herself, these days. Her mother's death had stolen so many things from her, so many moments. Sometimes Kara missed her so much she couldn't breathe.

There's nothing in the dark that isn't there in the light, she thought as she walked along the path, forcing herself to taste the spring night air, to relish the beauty of the bay and the lights of the city.

A squeaking noise made her jump, but it was only an old man riding by on a bicycle. She smiled at him, but he didn't even seem to notice her.

Nothing in the dark.

A trio of boys marched up the path toward the front doors of Monju-no-Chie School like coal miners or factory workers headed home after a long day. Kara watched them approach, surprised to see them so serious outside of school. Boys were usually laughing about something; whether they were insulting one another for sport or talking about girls, they tended to amuse themselves. But not these guys. Kara didn't know the rules for students who lived in the dorm, but she doubted they were allowed to stay late in the city on school nights unless they were at juku.

Once more she felt grateful not to have the pressure the other students did. She couldn't imagine the stress of adding cram school—and that much more homework—to her current schedule. It had to be past nine o'clock, and these guys would have to do the homework from the regular school day plus whatever they had to do for juku. Once the teachers started piling on the work, that might be three hours or more a night, total.

"Excuse me?" Kara said.

The three boys had been so tired, or so focused on getting back to their rooms, that they hadn't noticed her. One of them even let out a small grunt of surprise, startled. Kara stood in the shadows off to the left of the front steps, hands in the pockets of her sweatshirt.

"What are you doing out here?" one of them snapped, angry or embarrassed.

"I'm sorry," she said. "I thought I would take a walk, but no one else is outside."

"It's late," one of the other boys said.

"I know. I just wasn't sure . . . I don't really know the rules yet. Are the students who live here allowed to have visitors in the dormitory?"

The one who'd spoken first, a short, doughy-faced guy, leered at her and waggled his eyebrows. "Why? Did you want to visit one of us, bonsai?"

Kara frowned. The piggish behavior bothered her, but not as much as the nickname. "Why did you call me that?" she asked, thinking of the soccer girls, and Ume, who'd been so bitchy at first and then tried to be nice.

"Everyone's calling you that," muttered the one she'd startled. "Bonsai. I wouldn't complain. It's not nearly as bad as some of the things they *could* be calling you."

"I'll try to keep that in mind. I'm sorry I bothered you," Kara said, half-scowling. She started to walk away.

"Bonsai!" one of the boys called. When she didn't turn, he tried again. "Kara."

She froze. They all knew her, didn't they? Everyone at the school, whether or not they'd ever even seen her face. She'd only spoken to a handful of her schoolmates, but every single one of them knew who she was. It creeped her out, more than a little.

"What?" she asked, turning to face the three boys again.

"No visitors are allowed in the dorm after eight o'clock,

44

except for other non-resident students. That's you. If you're part of a club or study group, you can stay until ten, and sometimes, if you get special permission, they allow non-resident students to sleep over with friends on weekends. But you'd only be allowed in the girls' wing. We have shared common areas, but you wouldn't be allowed into the boys' wing."

I'm heartbroken, Kara thought. But the guy didn't deserve sarcasm. His friend had been obnoxious, but this one had at least been polite.

"Thank you," she said.

His friends had already started tentatively up the steps, looking back impatiently. They behaved like she wasn't even there. Kara returned the favor, turning to stroll away from the school. She had gotten the answer she'd wanted. Living with her father would give her the best of both worlds. When all she desired was a quiet, safe place of her own in which to curl up, she'd find that at their little house. But if she made any real friends among the boarding students, they could hang out in the dorm as well.

She wasn't sure how it would work with local kids who attended Monju-no-Chie School. Walking around downtown or hanging out by the bay might work on the weekends, but she had a feeling she wouldn't be getting a lot of invitations for movie night. Study groups might be the only social life available during the week.

Maybe Miho and Sakura would end up being her friends, or Hachiro, but it was only the first day. Anything could happen. For now, Kara was on her own.

Strolling across the grounds, she found herself walking

once again along the path that led around the side of the school, near the woods. The dark, recessed doorway where Sakura had been hiding to smoke a cigarette before class seemed much darker now, and forbidding. But she'd come this way to take a look at the ancient prayer shrine at night.

She'd explored the area several times since they had moved to Japan, and she'd taken plenty of pictures. But at night, the whole world seemed different. The lights across the bay might be firelight or oil lamps; she could be seeing back across time. History always seemed to linger in the air. No matter how many computers the school had, what advances in technology the country might achieve, Japan always seemed an enigma to her. All of the engineering advances crafted by modern Japan seemed little more than a quaint mask of progress, and it seemed like the country's rich, textured history and traditions would always hide behind it.

She stopped to look at the shadows of the old shrine, moonlight filtering down through the branches above. Though part of it had been built from stone, the shrine had a wooden frame, and she knew the wood itself could not truly be ancient. Time and weather would have ruined it many times over the centuries, but someone—monks, maybe—had rebuilt it just as frequently. Even now, candles burned inside lanterns, and their ghostly light flickered with every gust of wind.

Kara took a deep breath. Somehow the shrine eased her mind. The monks who'd first built it, and the people who prayed here, worshipped very differently than she did, but she believed that they probably prayed for the same things she would. Peace and love, patience and courage. Those were things everyone needed, no matter what god they believed in.

A ripple of laughter came from behind her and she turned to see a quartet of figures hurrying up the walkway toward the front of the school. More students returning from cram school.

A tiny sound came from the shrine—out of the corner of her eye she saw something moving—and Kara spun, breath hitching, heart racing. But the small thing that moved out from the shadows and flowers of the shrine was only a cat.

"Oh my God," Kara said, lapsing into English. "You scared the crap out of me."

The cat arched its back and gazed up at her, eyes glinting in the light of the moon and the flickering candles. Kara smiled and knelt down, reaching out for it. She preferred dogs. Cats always had that imperious attitude, like they were the rulers of the world, and occasionally allowed humans to open a can of tuna for them and change their litter. She half-expected it to hiss or scratch, so she moved her hand slowly and was surprised when it allowed her to stroke its red and copper fur.

"What are you doing out here, pretty?" she whispered.

But already the cat seemed bored. It slid toward her, brushed against her legs, and then started down the path that led to the bay. To the right there were woods, and to the left, the neighborhood around the school and the road that led to Miyazu City. The school stood silently behind her, and down the gentle slope ahead, the water lapped against the shore.

The cat trotted toward the water and Kara followed, mainly for the serenity the bay provided. She needed to get back before her father started worrying about her, but first she wanted to enjoy the spring night and the moonlit bay for a few minutes. The cat seemed to have the same idea.

But Kara had another reason for coming down here. One that did nothing to soothe her. She'd been pretending to herself that this was only a stroll, to check out the grounds and figure out if anyone else liked to wander after dark. Though parents and teachers discouraged kids her age from dating—it got in the way of school—Kara knew that wouldn't stop teenagers. They might not be hooking up at parties, but there had to be at least *some* action going on with all the hormones swirling around.

But she'd known all along it wasn't just a stroll. And she didn't really expect to find anyone stealing kisses by the bay.

Not with the other shrine that had been put together on the shore of the bay, at the edge of the woods. Photos and stuffed animals and cards written in *kanji*. Bits of calligraphy. Flowers for a dead girl.

Did Akane come down here with a guy? Kara wondered. *Did whoever did it mean to kill her, or just bully her somehow, and she ended up dead?* Her father had warned her, even given her articles to read about the bullying that had become such a problem in many Japanese schools.

She'd wanted to think that anyone could have discovered Akane on the shore, maybe tried to rape her or something, and then killed her. A group of college students from the city. A fisherman. Anyone. And she supposed that was possible, but glancing around, it seemed unlikely. Who would come down to this spot except for students?

The question echoed in her mind, frightening her. Had Akane been murdered by her own schoolmates, and if so, had they graduated . . . or were there still killers at Monju-no-Chie School?

The cat shook her from her thoughts, brushing against her legs again before gliding down to the water's edge. The wind caused tiny waves that slapped the shore, and the cat darted away in surprise. As though annoyed, it cast a glance at the bay over its shoulder, then walked over to investigate the shrine Akane's friends had built in her memory.

Head low, sniffing the ground, tail swaying, it moved from a bouquet of decaying flowers to a pink pillow, sewn with silken hearts and ribbons. After a few seconds, the cat moved around the edges of the shrine.

Abruptly it hissed, arching its back.

Kara frowned, staring at it. The cat began to yowl and shake its head, and then it cried out the way she'd only ever heard cats cry while fighting. While injured.

It stiffened and slumped to the ground.

Kara's mouth hung open. "Kitty?"

The cat did not move. Not so much as a twitch of its tail.

Slowly, she walked over to where the cat lay on the ground. Its chest did not rise. Kara thought about dead things she had seen in the road, and she saw in the cat the same stillness, sensed the absence of life that she associated with dried, desiccated creatures, their fur or feathers flattened down like a rose pressed between the pages of a book.

She lifted one hand to cover her mouth, horrified, but quickly dropped it. That hand had touched the cat, and if it had some kind of disease, who knew what might happen to her? She needed to get home to wash up.

She shivered but could not turn away. Staring at the cat, she pushed out a foot and nudged it with the tip of her shoe. *Dead*. She hadn't really needed confirmation, but there could be no doubting it now.

Crossing her arms, she stared one last moment, about to turn away.

The tail twitched.

Kara yelped and jumped back, eyes wide, watching as the cat stretched, and then rose. Now she did cover her mouth, all fear of disease forgotten. It moved differently, lower to the ground, and it swung its head around and *looked* at her. At *her*. Its eyes glittered in the dark.

In the spot where it had lain dead a moment before, the cat let out a stream of piss. Kara wrinkled her nose, first in disgust, and then in revulsion at the rank stink that rose from the ground. She gagged, covered her mouth with the sleeve of her sweatshirt, and backed away. Maybe her first thought had been the right one: disease. Nothing healthy smelled like that. Nothing natural.

The cat looked at the shrine to Akane's life and death and hissed.

It darted at Kara. She cried out and staggered back, but the cat ran right past her, headed up the slope, toward the school.

On the short walk home, Kara broke into a jog and entered the house breathless. Her father had fallen asleep at his desk. Though she didn't want to wake him, she sat for a few minutes in that room, just to be near him, to feel safe. In her mind, Kara could still see the cat's eyes, the way it had stared at her, had noticed her. That look would haunt her tonight. She only hoped it didn't keep her from falling asleep. The sooner she got to sleep, the sooner morning would arrive. Sunrise, when it came, would be very welcome.

4

ॐ

The first drop of blood is in the genkan, where the students store their street shoes during the day. Kara notices it only because she steps in it, which is when she realizes she is barefoot. A rush of guilt shivers through her. If anyone comes and sees her walking in the school without slippers on, she will be in trouble. What would be worse, wearing her street shoes into the school or no shoes at all?

She slips on the blood, smears it on the floor. Frowning, she lifts her foot and stares at the bottoms of her toes, painted red.

Behind her, back at the entry doors, something moves and Kara flinches. She doesn't want to be here, but going out that way seems a terrible idea, so she walks deeper into the school. The lights are off, and yet she can see. On the stairs is an arrangement of candles and flowers, as though someone has set them up to create an atmosphere of romance, but all she can think is that it's a shrine.

To what, or whom, she doesn't know.

Something shifts at the far end of the hall to her left, in the shadows. For a long moment she watches, trying to make out what it is, and then, just as she turns her attention once more to the candles—which are in a new arrangement now, a new pattern spread all across the stairs—something darts across her peripheral vision, dark and low to the ground.

Kara stumbles up several steps, knocking over a candle. Eyes wide, she stares down at the melted wax as it pools on the step. Flame licks the wood and begins to spread. She reaches down to snuff it with her fingers, but when she touches the step, the wax and flame are gone. Instead, she touches something sticky and warm and red. Blood.

Soft laughter comes from behind her and Kara turns. A small parade of girls shuffle through the genkan. It must be them laughing—the sound comes from that direction—but still it seems unlikely, for they have no faces. No eyes. No mouths.

Trapped, for a moment Kara doesn't dare move up or down the stairs. Then a breeze flutters the candlelight and she glances around to find that the blood is gone and only a single, large candle burns at the top of the steps, as though to light her way.

With the rustle of laughter below, she starts up, away from those no-face girls. Her own breathing is strangely loud, echoing off the walls as though to smother her, and she can't stand being in the stairwell anymore.

At the top of the steps, she finds herself in the hallway of the house where she'd grown up, back in Medford, half the world away. This feels right, natural, and her fear abates. Down the hall, the door to her parents' bedroom is open and a butterfly of hope flutters in her chest.

Kara runs for that open door, not wanting to admit to herself what—or who—she believes she'll find in her parents' bedroom. The hall feels longer than it should, and at the end is a window she doesn't remember, with candles of various sizes and colors arranged on the sill, flames dancing.

She reaches the bedroom, grabs the frame, and turns to look inside.

It isn't her parents' bedroom at all. It's her homeroom, back at her old school. Lying across the desk is the body of a Japanese girl, her sailor fuku plastered against her body, hair matted with blood. But she has no face.

Kara screams and no sound comes out. A sudden terrible certainty fills her and she reaches up, fingers searching, to find that her own features are smooth and dry. No mouth. No nose. She no longer has eyes, yet still, somehow, she sees.

On a desk in the far corner, by the windows, sits a cat with eyes that flicker like candle flames. It watches her, arches its back, and then leaps to the floor. The cat begins to pad toward her, or so she thinks, until it stops at the teacher's desk and begins to lap at the blood that pools on the floor there.

Still silently screaming, Kara staggers backward, breath coming in gasps. Everything around her shifts, changing. Now the inner wall of the classroom is comprised of sliding doors, like in Monju-no-Chie School. She bumps into one, shoves it aside, and stumbles into the corridor. It isn't her home anymore. She's back at her new school, outside Class 2-C, and all she can think of is getting out.

Kara runs. She passes one classroom, but through the sliding doors she can see the shore of Miyazu Bay, water lapping over the legs of the desks, though this is the second floor. Quaking, she passes another classroom, and its walls and windows and desks are spattered with blood. No-face girls are collapsed on the floor and over desks like abandoned marionettes. A dead boy hangs from the ceiling.

She can't breathe and turns to run, but now there are cats at the top of the stairs. Too many of them. They move from the shadows, out of classrooms, and down the hall behind her, and then she is surrounded. Their feet leave bloodied red paw prints on the floor as they close the circle around her.

Again, she screams . . .

And wakes.

Kara drew in a gasp of air, as though she'd stopped breathing while asleep. Her heart hammered in her chest and she sat up, clutching fistfuls of her sheets as she stared around her bedroom. In the corners, shadows lingered. The light that filtered through the shutters over her windows cast only gloom into the room. Early morning, then, barely dawn. Too early to be awake, but she didn't dare lie down for fear she might fall back to sleep and back into that dream.

"God," she whispered, and swung her legs out of bed. "Not again."

Three days since school began, and she'd had the same nightmare for three nights in a row, disturbing her sleep. She ought to have been glad it was morning, but she still felt so tired that it might be worth risking more bad dreams if she could sleep a little longer. Or maybe not. The nightmare was awful.

She ran her hands over her face and got up, sliding back the shutters to have a look outside. Despite the gloomy light, there were very few clouds in the sky. When the sun stopped peeking at morning and came fully over the horizon, it would be a crystal clear day, warm and blue.

Kara stayed by the window, waiting for dawn to break and for the cobwebs of her dream to burn away. Already, only fragments of it remained, but it left her with the sensation that she'd been lost in the dream all night. Details changed, but certain elements had been consistent all three nights—the blood and the candles and the cats. The presence of her parents' bedroom and the feeling of expectation, like she might see her mother again, had been new this time, and it lingered with her. It felt like she'd lost something, though of course even if she had seen her mother, it would only have been a dream.

With a deep breath, she wrapped her arms around herself and watched the sun climb over the horizon. The morning light spread, and she began to feel better.

Then she remembered that it was Saturday, and a smile touched her lips, as though sunrise had spread within her. Yes, she had a few hours of school this morning, but the afternoon would be free. Miho and Sakura were taking her shopping in Miyazu City. After hearing about Akane's murder and the creepy thing with the cat earlier in the week—added to the stress of trying to adjust to her new life—no wonder she'd been so troubled. The dream had been haunting her all week, but her friends from home were fond of saying there was nothing a little retail therapy couldn't cure. Shopping was just what the doctor ordered. They'd walk all afternoon, get completely exhausted, and if she was lucky, there would be no dreams tonight.

No dreams tonight. She made it her mantra.

Or perhaps it was more like a prayer.

Pink lanterns were strung from the trees in Takinoue Park, where spring had just begun to blossom. Kara took a bunch of pictures, framing some of them diagonally because she liked her photos off-kilter. At home she would take pictures of her friends because they'd bug her until she relented, but Sakura and Miho seemed to understand that the camera meant something to her beyond just snapping tourist shots, and so they posed only when she asked them to get into the picture.

After school they'd taken the Tankai bus to Sanno-bashi, where only a few minutes' walk brought them to the park. Kara loved the Turning Bridge and Ama-no-Hashidate and had already photographed them endlessly, not to mention beautiful shots across Miyazu Bay, framing some of the islands in her shots, especially the misty rise of Mount Oidake on Kami Island. One day, she hoped to explore those places with friends. But today wasn't for sightseeing. It was a day just to be with the girls.

"Can I ask you something?" Miho said, adjusting her round glasses.

Kara lowered her camera. "Sure."

"We always hear about how much more time we spend in school than American students. Is that really true?"

"Well," Kara said, "back home, we don't have school on Saturdays, that's for sure. And the school days here are definitely longer. But in Japan, there are longer breaks between classes, and more art and physical education classes. We're probably not actually in class with a teacher that much more than in America, if you add it all up."

Miho nodded as though this satisfied some suspicion she'd already had. Kara had to know.

"Why do you ask?"

Sakura let out a derisive laugh. "I told her American boys are stupid. That they wouldn't be intelligent enough to keep up with her, but would expect her to act like she is even dumber than they are."

Miho glared at her.

Kara grinned. "You mean Japanese boys aren't the same way?"

"Exactly the same," Miho said.

"Not all of them," Sakura added quietly.

"Oooh, Sakura likes a boy!" Kara said.

Whatever vulnerability Sakura had just revealed vanished in an instant. Her cynical, tough-girl mask reappeared, and she winked at Kara.

"I like them all. Except American boys."

Miho glared at her. "You're evil."

But she couldn't keep the angry face in place for more than a few seconds, and then they were laughing. Kara's heart felt lighter than it had in days. She had never acquired a huge number of friends at home; she just didn't have that kind of personality. But she missed Dawn and Toni and Aaron, the kids she'd hung out with in her high school in Massachusetts. She'd kept in touch by e-mail, but she'd been gone three months and already it felt like they'd forgotten about her. Out of sight, out of mind.

Which meant she had to live in the now, with the people around her.

"Say 'cheese,'" she said, raising the camera.

Sakura and Miho grinned. "Chee-zu!" they both said.

Kara laughed. "It's 'cheese!' I'm not the one pronouncing it wrong."

"You're in Japan," Sakura told her. "We say 'chee-zu.'"

"Because *we* say 'cheese,'" Kara replied.

"Which is silly, anyway," Miho put in. "Why cheese?"

Kara laughed. "Fine. Explain 'chee-zu,' then."

Miho and Sakura glanced at each other, genuinely baffled, and Kara snapped their picture like that. She viewed the shot on the little screen on the camera and giggled, showing it to the girls.

"Who's evil?" Sakura said.

Miho crossed her arms. "Kara is evil," she said in English.

Kara nodded in appreciation. "Hey, that was pretty good."

"We need practice," Sakura said, also in English. "You should speak English with us."

"I need practice, too," Kara replied.

"We . . . ," Miho began, but switched to Japanese. "We should take turns."

Which sounded more than fair. For the rest of the afternoon, they moved back and forth between English and Japanese, correcting one another as politely as possible. They

59

were hungry and ate lunch in a small restaurant near the park. The girls were much more comfortable with gossip outside of school, and Kara learned the secrets—real or imagined—of some of the most popular students, not to mention some teachers. Some of the teachers she'd barely met, and some of the other students she'd never heard of, but Kara listened intently and laughed in all the right places.

Miho and Sakura weren't content to talk just about their own world, though. They wanted to know about her life in America, and Miho, of course, about every boy she'd ever kissed, or wanted to kiss. They had questions about fashion, shopping, and the house she'd lived in, and Kara happily filled them in. An older woman who worked in the restaurant joined in on the conversation at one point, wanting to hear Kara speak English.

"You should learn to speak Japanese-English," the woman said, "if you want us to understand when you speak your own language." When she saw the confusion on Kara's face, she went on. "The accent. If you speak English with a Japanese accent, it will be easier to understand you."

Kara bowed her head in gratitude for the advice. As the woman walked away, Sakura rolled her eyes.

"Don't listen to her," Miho said. "You need to speak American-English if we're going to learn correctly."

"Nothing to worry about," Kara replied. "It's hard enough to speak Japanese without trying to learn to speak English with a Japanese accent."

By the time they finished lunch it was after two-thirty, and

Kara knew she wouldn't be hungry at dinnertime. Still, her fish had been excellent and the plums delicious. And since she'd never be able to finish her dinner, it made total sense to her that they should get some candy at the little shop just down the street.

They rode the bus back into the heart of Miyazu City, eating their sweets and talking about nothing. A boy who looked old enough to be at university admired Sakura, apparently taken by the dramatic cut of her hair or the collection of patches and pins on her jacket, though Kara thought it just as likely he merely appreciated the shortness of her skirt. Many Japanese girls would have looked away, either with a shy smile or in an attempt to ignore him. The culture avoided bold eye contact whenever possible, but Sakura had her own style, and it involved challenging convention whenever possible. She gave the boy a withering stare that eventually forced him to turn away.

Kara and Miho shared a smile over that.

"You look tired," Miho said quietly, in English, adjusting the bow in her hair. "Are you feeling all right?"

The change of tone and subject was abrupt. Kara blinked and looked at her, but Miho's gaze was elsewhere.

"I haven't been sleeping well," she confessed, also in English.

"*Soudesuka*," Miho replied with a nod. "Sakura hasn't either."

The word meant something like *I hear you and understand*. Kara enjoyed how versatile the Japanese language was.

After a couple of months in Japan, shifting between the languages had grown difficult. If she was thinking in Japanese, it wasn't easy to switch to English.

"What haven't I been doing?" Sakura asked, moving across the bus to sit beside Miho.

Seeing them next to each other—the mousy, proper girl with her cute glasses and the wild child—usually made Kara smile at the contrast. But on the subject of sleep, she couldn't muster a smile.

Kara switched to Japanese, hoping they would stick with it. "Sleeping well. Why not?"

With a shrug, Sakura unwrapped a small candy and looked away from them. "I haven't slept well since Akane died."

"This is different," Miho said. Sakura ignored her, but Miho leaned toward Kara and whispered, "Bad dreams."

The words made Kara flinch, thinking of her own nightmares of cats and no-face girls and all that blood. A chill snaked up the back of her neck and she would have asked Sakura to elaborate, but then the bus slid to a halt and the doors opened.

"Let's go," Sakura said, leading the way.

The streets of Miyazu City looked nothing like an American or even European city. There were markets and shops everywhere, monks in white, police officers stopping bicyclists to see their riding permits, and tourists buying souvenirs of Amano-Hashidate. Some of them were embarrassingly American, one man even wearing a Hawaiian shirt and a cowboy hat, as though he had dressed up expressly for the purpose of becoming a caricature. Kara cringed at the sight of him, but nobody else seemed to notice, as though this man in his sandals and sunglasses was what they expected of Americans.

Don't be nasty, she thought. *He might be perfectly nice.*

Still, the shirt had to go.

They visited Miho's favorite dress shop, where a saleswoman seemed to adopt them as her personal mission, though none of them bought anything. Sakura dragged them into a bookshop, where she introduced Kara to her favorite manga and they both spent too much money, and then into a music store, where Miho insisted Kara pick out some American music for her. Since she hated J-pop—the bubblegum pop music a lot of Japanese kids liked—Kara was happy to oblige, grabbing the latest Alicia Keys and an ancient Nine Inch Nails, just for variety.

Outside a little store where Sakura had bought them each a spangly hair band and herself a pair of bright orange socks, they stopped for a break near a fountain. Kara thanked her for the gift, and Sakura seemed pleased.

"A keepsake of our day," she said.

Then her smile went away. She couldn't manage happiness very long. If Kara judged just by her appearance, she'd have thought it was part of the persona Sakura had crafted for herself, but she felt sure it had much more to do with Akane and the way their parents seemed to have just left Sakura here and forgotten about her. Maybe the girl felt like she shouldn't be happy.

The thought made Kara's heart hurt.

Sakura surprised both Kara and Miho by suggesting they

visit Temple Chigenji, which had been built by someone named Takahiro for his mother, who'd been a Buddhist saint.

"I didn't think you'd like history," Kara said.

"Just because I don't have respect for authority doesn't mean I don't have respect for the past," Sakura explained.

Standing in front of the temple, Kara felt exhausted. It had been a very long day.

"My mother would have loved it here," she said. "She never liked the idea of leaving home, living someplace so far away. But she would have loved it here. Sometimes beautiful places made her cry. I think Ama-no-Hashidate would have had her in tears. It feels like the top of the world . . . like you could sail north and find—"

Kara faltered. She'd been about to say *find heaven*, but she couldn't finish the thought. If that was where her mother had gone, Kara wished she would come back.

Miho touched her arm. "I haven't heard you mention your mother before."

"We know your father," Sakura added. "He gives too much homework."

Kara smiled, a twinge of sadness still in her heart. "He'll lighten up. He likes to put a scare into his students at the beginning of the year to make us take him seriously."

Both girls were still watching her but did not speak, as though waiting for her to go on.

At length, Kara glanced away. "My mother died in a car accident, almost two years ago. It's just the two of us, my father and me. She left us to take care of each other."

"But she loved you," Miho said.

Kara looked up to find a sad smile on the girl's face. She nodded.

Sakura did not smile. Her expression was hard, and her eyes difficult to read. But she met Kara's gaze.

"That's a treasure," Sakura said. "And you'll have it as long as you live."

Kara startled her with a quick embrace. By the time Sakura started to return it, Kara was already stepping away. The three girls looked at one another for a moment, and then the subject changed and they were talking about nothing and everything again, heading back along the street. Heading for home.

And they were friends.

Jiro had his window open, and the night breeze brought the powerful scent of cherry blossoms into his room. So strong was the aroma that he blinked in distraction and pulled his attention away from the television set. He spent too much time in front of the TV, his parents were always telling him. But the stupid game shows helped numb him.

Ever since September, when Akane had died, numb had been his goal. They'd been close friends—maybe even best friends—and he'd known that she didn't love him any other way. But his feelings for her had been so strong that it felt like love to him, or the way he thought love should feel. He still wasn't sure he knew what love really felt like, but no one else had ever made him so happy inside, so nervous, and so light-hearted, as though he could rise off the ground and fly.

Ume certainly never made him feel that way, and she was supposed to be his girlfriend. But then, he knew Ume had never been in love with him. She used the word, but Jiro didn't think she knew it was supposed to mean something more.

The light from the television flickered blue off the walls of his bedroom, the only illumination in the room except for what streamed in through the open window. He shivered. It was probably too early in the year to have the windows open so wide, but the chilly spring air felt good. All winter he had let himself shiver with the cold; it fit perfectly with how alone he felt. His best friend had been taken from him, and her sister, Sakura, wouldn't even talk to him. Every time she looked at him, he could see the blame there. But Jiro hadn't killed Akane. He would have given anything to have her back.

With a deep breath, he inhaled the aroma of the cherry blossoms. The scent was so strong it had gotten into his clothes, into the walls of the room itself.

He frowned. The odor was so overwhelming that it seemed weird. The nearest cherry trees were in a small park across the street, and there weren't even that many of them. Akane had loved the smell of cherry blossoms.

The light flickered again, but he glanced at the TV and realized it wasn't the odd game show that had caused it. Something had passed in front of the television.

Jiro looked around the room, confused. He was alone. It had to be just a trick of the light. With a shake of his head, he focused on the TV again and laughed at the absurdity there, as three women tried to drink some noxious brew. The one to drink it the fastest without vomiting would win. He began to feel queasy himself and changed the channel, searching for a

66

movie or something else to occupy his mind. He felt tired but wasn't ready to go to sleep yet. Tomorrow was Sunday, after all, and tonight he could stay up as late as he liked.

Outside his window, a cat yowled.

Jiro shuddered at the sound, then laughed at himself, startled by a cat. Still, when the cat's mournful cry came again, he felt a prickle of unease move up the back of his neck.

And then it let out a terrible cry, as though something had attacked it, and Jiro scrambled to his feet. His heart raced, pounding in his ears, and he stared at the open windows, waiting for the sound to come again. What had caused that cry, and why was the cat silent now?

He listened, but no other sound came . . . until he heard the tiniest mewling noise, like a newborn kitten or the sigh of something dying. Jiro didn't even like cats, but he had to respond. If the cat had been hurt, he wouldn't just leave it out there.

He started for the window but faltered at the sight of the dark silhouette that appeared on the other side, outlined in moonlight. Though he could not make out her face in the dark, the way the girl's hair fell on her shoulders and the way she cocked her head, the curve of her body . . . he knew her.

A breeze blew in through the window, her hair dancing around her face, and the scent of cherry blossoms grew even stronger. She beckoned to him and he went to her, feeling as though he must be dreaming.

They stood face-to-face in the light of the moon and the blue flickering from his television, he inside the room and she beyond the open window. She reached in to touch him and Jiro closed his eyes, weak with relief.

Her fingers closed on his throat, and relief blossomed into terror.

When she dragged him through the window, he did not even have the breath to scream.

5

Sunday morning brought a sun shower, the sort of thing that seemed only to happen in spring. Light rain fell outside Kara's window, beading up on the flowers that were blooming around the house, but the sun shone down in spite of the rain and the colors of the flowers were vivid. When, in mid-morning, the rain stopped, she was almost sorry.

She spent the morning with her father, cleaning up around the house and talking about the week they'd both had. He seemed glad that she'd made friends already, just as she knew he would be.

"What about you, Dad?" she asked while they were making lunch. "You've been thinking about this adventure longer than I have. Is it what you were hoping for?"

He took the question more seriously than she expected, brow furrowed in thought. Then, slowly, he nodded.

"So far, so good. It's certainly a big adjustment, and we don't have as much time together—"

"We're together all day!"

He grinned. "You know what I mean. With the long school hours, we're just busier."

"I'll try to ask more questions in your classes," Kara said.

Her father shook his head as he went to stir the chicken and vegetables they'd chopped into a frying pan. "We'll be fine. It's not just my adventure, Kara. It's ours. All of it."

She leaned against the counter. "Then you won't mind if I go over to school after lunch? I have a study date with Sakura and Miho."

With a fork, he split a piece of chicken in the pan to make sure it was cooked through, then looked up at her. "Like your father's ever gonna stop you from studying. Or from checking out what it's like to live in the dormitory. Go and have fun. Will you be home for dinner?"

"Definitely."

The first thing Kara saw when Sakura opened the door to her dorm room were the masks. There were three of them hanging on the far wall, to the left of the window, lined up one above the next like a totem pole. The top and middle masks were ugly, monstrous things, but the bottom one was the pretty, elegant face of a woman.

"Wow."

Miho looked up from the book she was reading. "English? You must like them." She smiled and sat up on her bed.

"They're amazing," Kara said. "Noh masks?"

"Yes!" Miho beamed.

"She collects them," Sakura explained as she closed the door. "Fortunately, she leaves most of them at home."

Kara admired the masks as Miho stood and pointed to them each in turn.

"The top one is Karura, a great bird of legend, who flies in four heavens and eats dragons," Miho explained, and now Kara saw that the green-painted mask did have a beak and a red crest so that it looked vaguely like a bird. "Next is Daikijin, Great Devil God, who protects festivals and ceremonies from evil spirits."

Kara blinked. The white and silver mask had been crafted with such care that its beauty was undeniable. But with its horns and shaggy mane and the sharp fangs in its wide-stretched, blood-red mouth, it was also ugly and frightening.

"It *looks* like an evil spirit," she said.

Miho frowned in disapproval. "You should not judge only by appearance."

Kara gave her a small shrug. "Of course. I meant no offense."

Sakura laughed. "Don't let her get to you. She loves those ugly things too much."

Miho shot Sakura an unpleasant look and then smiled and gave them a small shrug. "I can't help it."

"What about the bottom one? The woman?" Kara asked.

"That is Zoh-onna. She is not a goddess or spirit, only a woman of purity and serenity," Miho said.

Sakura sat on a cushion in the floor. "I always ask if there's one that is the opposite of those qualities. I'd like to wear that one."

The girls laughed. They were both in T-shirts and pajama bottoms, and seeing them like that gave Kara a relaxed, familiar feeling. She'd worn black jeans and a green hooded sweater and felt comfortable enough, but Sakura's silky-looking red pajamas and the cotton, very American-looking bottoms Miho had on—white and covered with the red and yellow S-crest that Superman wore on his chest—made her wish she'd worn pajamas as well.

Kara surveyed the rest of the dormitory room. There wasn't much more to see. The beds were wooden boxes with soft futon mattresses that unrolled for sleeping. At first she thought there were straw *tatami* mats on the floor but then realized the whole floor was tatami. There were a couple of big *zabuton* cushions on the floor. The two desks were tiny, and a slender laptop sat open atop one of them. There were bamboo sliding doors that must have been closets and two bookcases. One held mostly school books, but the shelves of the other were lined with manga digests.

"I can guess whose bookcase that is," Kara said, pointing to the manga.

"I'll let you borrow some," Sakura replied.

Miho crossed her arms. "Why not show her your art?"

Sakura's smile evaporated and, for the first time since Kara had met her, she shifted and glanced around awkwardly, unsure of herself.

"You draw?"

"She draws manga," Miho said. "She's really good."

"I'm not. I'm awful," Sakura mumbled.

Kara dropped down onto another cushion beside her. "I'm sure you're not. I'd love to see some of your art. But I understand if you don't want to show me today."

They were friends now, but they were new friends. Sakura's art clearly meant a great deal to her, particularly since she kept it mostly secret. She only shared it with people she trusted.

After a moment, she nodded and went to her bed, sliding out the drawer built into its wooden base. She withdrew a thick sketchbook and handed it over. Kara felt honored that Sakura would share this with her but didn't want to make a big deal out of it.

The three girls spent twenty minutes just flipping through pages and then looking at other drawings Sakura pulled from her drawer. To Kara's delight, she was really talented.

"Wow. Between this and Miho's Noh theater stuff, I feel like I have nothing to contribute. I don't do anything special."

Miho sprawled on her belly on the bed, ankles crossed, and poked her face between Kara and Sakura, hair falling across her glasses. "Don't say that. You are a photographer. And you told me you play guitar."

"Yeah," Kara said, "but you guys haven't heard me play or seen any of my pictures."

"We will," Miho promised. "And I'm sure you're very talented."

"And if you're not, we just won't be friends with you anymore," Sakura said.

Kara blinked, hurt, and then Sakura laughed. Miho whacked the top of her head and Sakura turned to attack her. Despite their obvious differences in personality and style, the two girls had become like sisters. Perhaps the way their families had cast them aside had made them closer. They didn't really have anyone but each other.

Sakura pinned Miho in about six seconds.

"I surrender," Miho said, and Sakura got up, pretending to react to nonexistent cheering from a nonexistent crowd.

"You watch too much television," Miho told her.

Sakura went to sit in front of the window. "You listen to too much bad music."

"Rock's been dead since before I was alive," Miho countered.

"I'd rather have resurrected rock rot my brain than pop candy so sweet it can rot your teeth."

Kara watched this back and forth like a tennis match, grinning in amazement. Miho had such a quiet demeanor during school, but here in her own room, she obviously enjoyed sparring.

"What do you think, Kara?" Sakura asked. "Rock or pop?"

Kara shook her head. "Oh, no. You aren't getting me in the middle of this. Besides, there are a thousand definitions for rock and pop. You'd have to play me some music to compare."

As Miho started for the laptop—presumably to play music—Kara held up a hand. "No, no. That wasn't an invitation."

Sakura laughed. "Okay. We'll leave you out of it, this time. But you'll have to play your guitar for us soon."

74

"That's a deal. Next time we'll study at my house. There's a lot more room there anyway."

Miho looked concerned. "You don't think your father would mind?"

"He'd be happy to have us there," Kara said.

Sakura sighed.

"You don't want to come to my house?" Kara asked.

"It's not that. You just said a terrible word," Sakura said.

Kara reviewed what she'd just said, fearing that she had somehow offended her friends. "What word?"

Miho threw a small cushion at Sakura. "*Study*. That is what we're supposed to be doing today."

"Right," Kara said. "I was doing my best to forget."

Reluctantly, the three girls dove into their studies. Most of their assignments for the weekend involved reading, and Kara still had math homework she had been avoiding.

They spent a contentedly quiet hour in one another's company, until finally Sakura let out a groan and stood. She walked to the window again and gazed outside.

"I need a cigarette. Can we go for a walk?"

Miho tucked a lock of hair behind her ear. "I ought to read these last few pages."

Sakura smirked. "The boys are outside playing baseball."

For a moment, Miho hesitated. Then she slipped a marker into her book. "I can finish later."

Kara laughed. "I thought you were only interested in American boys."

Miho glanced away, perhaps even blushing a bit. "That

depends on what you mean by 'interested.' My curiosity is like a—" She said a word that Kara didn't understand.

"What?"

Sakura kicked off her pajama pants and slid into a pleated skirt much shorter than the one she wore with her school uniform. She looked up. "A scientist who studies people."

"A sociologist?" Kara said in English.

Miho repeated the Japanese word and Kara stored it away.

"It's like watching animals in their natural habitat," Miho explained.

Kara smiled. "Then by all means, let's go watch the animals."

Sakura untucked her T-shirt, searched around for her cigarettes and lighter, and then went to the door.

"Miho, you're not coming?" Kara asked.

"She's coming," Sakura said. "She's just more proper than I am."

Kara smiled. At home, she and her girlfriends changed in front of one another all the time. It hadn't occurred to her to wonder, but now she realized that things might be different in Japan. Probably were. Or maybe Miho was just shy.

They waited for her in the hall, but a minute later Miho appeared in a cute blue dress from the downtown shop she'd taken them into the day before. She and Sakura put on light jackets, and they all went downstairs and out the back door.

On a secondary field behind the dorm, a group of boys had put together a baseball game. They were wisely batting away from the building, toward the tree line at the distant edge of the school property, but Kara still thought they were risking knocking out some windows. One foul ball spun backward off a bat could easily end the game with the shattering of glass. But she wasn't about to volunteer her opinion.

"Baseball club?" she asked.

Sakura nodded. "They're not good enough to be on a team."

But for Kara, it was nice just to see the game played. She had never been much of a baseball fan, despite the two World Series the Red Sox had won in recent years. Earlier in the week, Hachiro had been very disappointed when she didn't show as much enthusiasm for her hometown team as he did. He seemed to know everything about American baseball, so she wasn't surprised to see him playing the outfield.

Most of the boys wore caps with the school insignia, which she assumed was some sort of official baseball club thing. Hachiro wore a Red Sox cap. It surprised her. Sakura's hairstyle was one thing, but she didn't dare wear her pins or patches on the outside of her uniform or show her art to other students. As much as they might talk about their talents to Kara, her friends were no different from most Japanese students. They were taught that it was bad manners to stand out, except through academic achievement, and even that was frowned upon by some. But Hachiro grinned broadly out there on the field, proud of his Red Sox cap. It reminded her how much she liked his smile.

The guy up at bat hit one straight at the third baseman's

head. The kid playing third barely had time to raise his glove but somehow managed to catch the ball. The batter was out and Kara cheered.

Miho and Sakura looked at her.

"You picked sides already?"

Kara shrugged. "Hachiro's team is on the field. I have to cheer for them."

The two girls shared a knowing look and mischievous smiles.

"So you like Hachiro?" Miho asked.

Kara arched an eyebrow. "Nothing like that. He's very nice."

"Oh, I'm sure he's *very* nice," Sakura said, teasing her.

A moment later, a shudder went through Kara and she sensed someone standing beside her, a shadow blocking the sun. She turned to find that the soccer club girls had come to watch the game.

Ume gave her a dismissive look. "The bonsai likes baseball. What a surprise. A bunch of foolish boys trying to be something they're not. No wonder it appeals to you."

Kara took a deep breath, feeling herself blush. Back home, she knew girls who got into hostile confrontations all the time—they seemed hardwired for that kind of thing—but she'd managed to avoid fights or even grudges. Worse yet, she knew Japanese custom demanded she ignore or deflect Ume's animosity somehow. Just because this girl didn't care about how she was expected to behave, that didn't mean that Kara had to stoop to her level.

But the other soccer girls were whispering to one another

and doing that little smiling-behind-their-hands thing that annoyed the crap out of Kara. They were so happy with themselves, behaving like perfect little Japanese girls during school but full of quiet, malicious nastiness.

"If you're not interested in boys, I certainly won't judge you," Kara said. "It leaves more for the rest of us. And you have plenty of pretty girls to choose from."

The arrogant smile slipped from Ume's face. "I'm sure you've had your share of boys."

Kara felt her right hand clench into a fist. The implication— that she was some kind of slut—could not have been clearer.

"I ignore your taunts in school for my father's sake," she said, "but we're not in school now."

Miho slid her arm through Kara's and leaned over to whisper, "Don't let her make you do something you'll regret."

Kara glanced at Miho. Just beyond her, Sakura stood staring at Ume, jaw tight with anger or hatred, or both. She looked more furious than Kara felt. When Miho started to escort Kara away, she thought Sakura might not follow, that there might be some kind of fight after all. But Miho called to her to come along, and Sakura took a deep breath and joined them. In the midst of that tension, Ume did not so much as glance at Sakura. The queen bitch behaved like Sakura wasn't even there.

Some of Ume's friends called out, "Good-bye, bonsai" as they walked away, but Kara didn't turn around.

"Not worth it," Miho said softly as the three of them walked around toward the dorm. "Someday fate will punish her. She'll regret the way she treats people."

"You think?" Kara replied. "In my experience, girls like that just keep getting away with it."

Sakura gave a soft laugh. "Not forever."

"So she was trying to bait me?" Kara asked. "You think she wanted me to do something?"

"Of course. Your father may not blame you, but Ume's parents are wealthy. Her father is a diplomat, very influential. Who do you think would be blamed if you fought with her?"

Kara considered that, and what it would do to her father's position at the school. No matter how unpleasant Ume got, Kara would have to ignore her. She couldn't risk getting her father in trouble.

"I can't dishonor him."

"Exactly," Miho said. "In Japan, you must be careful of such things."

Sakura gave another humorless laugh. "I don't care if I shame my parents. I could hurt her for you."

"That's not helping," Miho scolded her.

Now Sakura's grin did have some humor in it. "I know."

"It's hard not to react to her. I was raised to speak my mind and stand up for myself," Kara said.

Miho sighed. "I would love to visit America someday."

"We'll go together," Kara promised.

"Not until I have a cigarette, please," Sakura said.

With her nicotine addiction leading the way, they went around the dorm, across the field that separated it from the main school building, and down the path between the eastern wall and the woods. Kara looked for the recessed doorway where she knew Sakura went to smoke. In anticipation, Sakura took out her cigarettes, tapped one into her hand, and put it between her lips. She produced her lighter and flicked its flame alive.

A scream tore across the school grounds and Sakura's hand froze. Kara and Miho exchanged a look and a second scream filled the late afternoon sky.

"It came from that direction," Miho said, pointing toward the front of the school.

They began to run. Sakura dropped her cigarette and vanished her lighter into a pocket. The girls hurried around to the front of the school to see other students rushing toward the bay shore.

Kara felt an unpleasant twist in her stomach and the back of her neck prickled with dread. People were gathering at the edge of the water, not far from the trees—not far from the shrine to Akane. A few of them had cell phones out, frantic conversations merging into a low buzz of chatter.

When the girls reached the shore, all they could do was join the crowd milling about the edge. Kara tried to listen to the mutterings of the other students, and she heard the Japanese word for "body" before an opening appeared in the mob and she saw two girls comforting a third, who wiped tears from her eyes. A pair of boys had taken off their shoes and waded knee-deep into the bay, peering down into the water.

Shouts and footfalls came from behind them now, and Kara glanced back to see other students coming around from the rear of the school, boys in their baseball caps and spectators from the game. Someone must have gone to get them, or else they'd been on the receiving end of cell phone calls. Word was spreading fast.

One of the boys in the water closed his eyes and took a step back from whatever they'd found.

"Stop that," the other boy said. "Help me."

He bent and reached down into the water, grabbing hold of something heavy. The other boy hesitated, but then a young teacher, Fujimori-sensei, pushed his way through the students, calling out *"doite"* as he made his way to the water's edge. He didn't pause to take off his shoes, and Kara felt sure someone must already have told him what was happening. Kara wanted to turn away, but she couldn't seem to manage it.

Mr. Fujimori reached into the water and helped the boy drag the body onto the shore. The dead boy's face was bloated and pale, and his clothes squished as they set him down. He wore no shoes, and for some reason that detail was the thing that snapped Kara out of her mesmerized state. She swallowed hard, covered her mouth with a hand, and turned away.

As she did, she saw Sakura's face, etched with horror and a kind of panic.

"Jiro?" Sakura said.

Kara blinked. Jiro? She knew that name. Pale and puffy, she had not recognized the dead boy, but if it was the same Jiro, he was a friend of Hachiro's.

Miho stepped up to Sakura and took both the girl's hands in her own. "Are you all right?"

Sakura shook her head. "I dreamed it," she whispered, eyes wide with shock. "I dreamed he was dead."

Mr. Fujimori had his cell phone out now and was calling the police. A voice rose above all of the mutterings and questions and crying.

"Jiro! No!"

The crowd parted to let Ume through. Hachiro followed a few feet behind her, looking numb and lost. But Ume clutched at her clothing and twisted her hair as she stood a few feet away from the dead boy. Then she screamed, tears spilling down her cheeks. Several of the soccer girls tried to pull her away and Ume slapped the one nearest her, screaming at her to get away. The girls backed off, but Mr. Fujimori moved to block her view of Jiro's corpse.

Ume shook her head from side to side, sobbing in her grief. Her whole body trembled as she tried to get by the teacher. Mr. Fujimori attempted to hold her, but Ume brushed him off and fell to her knees. The bay water gently lapped the shore. The corpse's legs were still in the water, and it shifted slightly with the ebb and flow.

Kara could never have predicted something so horrible, but she found herself regretting her exchange with Ume. The girl was so distraught, so inconsolable, that she wished she could take the words back.

But then Ume exploded. She leaped up and turned on the crowd.

"Sakura!" she screamed, running into a cluster of students. She pushed her way through half a dozen others. "This is your fault, somehow. You did this!"

Miho and Kara put their hands up to stop Ume, but the girl stopped short. She shook as she pointed an accusatory finger at Sakura, who stunned Kara by beginning to weep.

Mr. Fujimori grabbed Ume by the shoulders and physically moved her away from the crowd, along the shore to a place where he could try to calm her, speaking in kind, quiet tones.

"Why would she say that?" Kara asked, turning to Sakura. "What's she talking about?"

But Sakura could only shake her head, unable to reply. After a moment she stepped away from them and fled back toward the dorm.

Miho looked at Kara, hesitated a moment, and then opened her hands in apology and went in pursuit of her roommate.

Kara could only glance around at the other students, lost for any explanation. No one paid any attention to her, and she felt more than ever like the bonsai Ume had named her. Hachiro stood by Jiro's body, looking stricken, but Kara didn't know what to say to him. Though her books were still in the dorm, the only place she wanted to be now was at home.

She didn't belong here.

"We should never have come."

Rob Harper sat on the small sofa in the living room, holding his head in his hands. With a sigh, he leaned back and stared at his daughter, eyes wide with a dawning realization.

"I should get you out of here."

Kara's mouth dropped open. "No, Dad," she said, sitting next to him.

"Seriously, honey. This is starting to seem like a very bad

idea." They were speaking English tonight. The things they were discussing, what they were feeling, were too raw to take the time to translate.

She took his hands in her own and sat with him. In jeans and an old green sweater, he ought to have looked right at home, just Dad. But the lines around his eyes had started to deepen and he looked tired. The worry etched into his face didn't help. He looked older to her.

Kara nudged against him and he put an arm around her. She pushed her face to his chest, listening to his heart. Perhaps two minutes went by, but they felt like forever to Kara. At last, she spoke up again.

"They call me 'bonsai.'"

Her father blinked. "What?"

"Bonsai. Like the tree. Cut away from where it belongs and planted someplace else."

"Who calls you that?"

Kara shrugged. "Some of the girls. But it doesn't really bother me. I kind of like it, really. Not the girls. There are some real bitches, but you find them everywhere. It's almost comical how stereotypical they are, thinking they're special when they're just like a million other girls. I mean, I've kind of taken the 'bonsai' thing to heart. That's me. I'm a bonsai. But bonsai grow, and people think they're beautiful and special and they take them into their homes. I *have* been cut away from where I came from and planted someplace else. And sometimes that means I'm going to be awkward or uncomfortable and feel like I don't belong—"

"Kara," he started.

She held up a hand to forestall any interruption. "But that doesn't mean I want to leave. If anything, it makes me want to work harder, not at fitting in but at just living, at—what's the word?—*thriving*, in my own way. It's important to stay and see this through."

Her father shifted, studying her as though seeing her for the first time. "A boy died, Kara. And there was another—a girl back in the fall. The school administration won't talk about it, but Miss Aritomo says she was murdered."

Kara nodded. "I know. Her name was Akane. She was my friend Sakura's older sister. But, Dad, think about what you're saying. We're going to run home because of this? It creeps me out, yeah. I feel a little sick, actually. But would we have moved out of Medford if the same thing happened back home?"

"Of course not, but—"

"What? What's different?" The question silenced him, and Kara knew what he was thinking. "I know you want to take care of me."

"That's my job."

Kara took a breath. There were so many things she could have said: that he couldn't have prevented her mother's death, that life didn't work that way, that he could not be with her every second. But they'd had many such conversations after the accident that killed her mother.

"We're supposed to take care of each other, remember? That was the deal," she said.

His smile was weak, but it was there.

"This has nothing to do with me," she told him. "And we shouldn't jump to conclusions. It's terrible, but Jiro could have killed himself. Or it could've been an accident. Don't panic just yet."

He took a deep breath, then pulled her toward him, kissing the top of her head.

"Okay," he said. "But no wandering by yourself for a while. Honestly, honey, I've been a little worried about you anyway. You haven't been eating much, and you've been looking kind of tired."

"I am tired. But I'm a teenager. We're supposed to sleep twenty-three hours a day."

He chuckled. "All right. But I'm going to keep an eye on you."

"I wouldn't have it any other way."

She stands on the shore of the bay, the lights along Ama-no-Hashidate like stars against the darkness of the water and the black pines on that spit of land. The bay ripples and Kara steps into the water, unable to resist. Something brushes against her ankle and she looks down.

The corpse that drifts there stares up at her with her mother's face.

Kara doesn't run. Her chest aches with grief, a physical pain that is all she's ever known of sorrow. Her throat closes and she feels tears burn the edges of her eyes, but when she reaches up to wipe them away, she finds only smooth skin.

No eyes. No mouth. Once again, she has no face.

Under the water, her mother's corpse begins to move, but this time it is not the wind-driven ebb and flow of the bay that shifts the cadaver's arms and legs. No, the body moves under its own power, rolling over onto its knees, naked back rising, slick and wet and gleaming in the moonlight.

Mom? she says, but has no mouth to speak the word.

The corpse rises, but the long hair is too black and the body too thin. She lifts her head and the face has now changed. Her mother's features are gone, replaced by brown eyes and high cheekbones that could almost be Sakura's. Yet it isn't Sakura, either.

Which is when Kara realizes that Akane has risen from the bay. She has never seen the girl, but it can only be her. The resemblance to Sakura is too strong. Kara reaches out a shaking hand, thinking of the horror Akane had endured here on the shore of the bay, but the dead girl arches her back and hisses, baring sharp, tiny teeth. Her eyes have changed. They have the slit cruelty of a cat's eyes.

And she starts out of the water.

Kara cannot scream, but she can run. She turns back toward the school and catches sight of something moving over by the trees . . . by the shrine the other students have built to remember Akane. In amongst the photos and flowers and messages prowl a dozen cats. As Kara glances at them, they freeze and turn toward her.

Look at her. Notice her.

Again she turns to run, but abruptly she is no longer by the bay. Instead she runs along the corridor inside the girls' wing of the dormitory. A door stands open on the left side of the hall, just ahead, and a terrible knowing fills her, for she recognizes immediately whose room this is.

She only sees the blood as she begins to slip, and then she

falls, scrambling along the floor of the corridor in a long puddle of blood that smears her hands and face, mats her hair, and stains her clothes. When at last she stops sliding, trying to get up, knees and hands slipping in the sticky blood, nose full of the terrible stench, she raises her head and finds that she is right outside Sakura and Miho's room.

The door hangs wide open.

Sakura lays on the floor on bloodstained rice mats, a thousand tiny claw marks slashed into her face and chest, arms and legs and throat. She stares at Kara with a single, blind, dead eye. The other is missing, leaving a dark crater behind, claw marks around the edges.

Sitting atop Sakura's corpse is a cat with copper and red fur.

It purrs happily.

Kara woke with a scream, then lay in the dark, heart pounding, waiting for the sounds of her father rising. But the house remained quiet, and after a few moments she rose and went out into the hall, opened his door, and peeked inside. He lay in his bed, sound asleep. She tried to tell herself that her scream had been short and not as loud as she'd imagined. Or that it had been part of her dream, and she'd not screamed at all upon waking.

The alternative, that he'd slept right through her terror, was too awful to consider.

6
卍

It rained all morning that Monday.

Kara tried her best to shake off the trauma of the weekend, but the whole school remained haunted by Jiro's death.
In the breaks between classes, students talked in low tones.
A couple of girls in Kara's class even cried after Japanese History. But when there were teachers in the room, no one had
an opportunity to ruminate on death. Maybe the teachers
worked them extra hard on purpose that day, or maybe it was
simply that, now that the first full week of school had arrived,
it would always be like this. The teachers were merciless.

Kara had to work hard to keep focused. As grim as the
day was, nobody could help Jiro now. The rain let up for about
half an hour, and she thought the sun might actually make an
appearance. Then it began to pour harder than ever, the rain
pelting down with such force that the noise of it hitting windows and walls and the roof of the school made Yuasa-sensei

raise his voice. The sensei asked Ume to turn on the lights in the classroom. Outside it had grown dark as night.

At lunch, Kara opened her bento box and discovered a small, folded piece of paper, stained with the juice of the shredded steak and peppers her father had packed for her. She unfolded it to discover a short note in his messy scrawl. *Have a good day*, it read. *Love, Dad.*

Six simple words, and yet they made her feel so good. And less alone. Smiling, she folded the note and slipped it into her jacket pocket.

The one thing she couldn't shake, though, was her concern for Sakura. Ume had gone a little nuts yesterday, which could probably be forgiven, since Jiro had apparently been her ex. But clearly something simmered underneath all of this that no one had bothered to share with Kara. She didn't understand the dynamics. Ordinarily she wouldn't mind, but she had found a friend in Sakura and she wanted to be helpful and supportive, which was difficult without knowing the whole story.

On the other hand, she also knew it was none of her business, and she'd have to live with that.

After lunch, the principal called an assembly in the gymnasium and spoke to the students, discussing Jiro's death in only the most peripheral ways, as if he had passed away in his sleep or something equally innocuous. A counselor spoke next, announcing that appointments would be available to anyone who wished to come in to discuss their feelings about the tragedy.

When the assembly ended, the principal announced that

all afternoon classes were canceled. After o-soji, the day students would be allowed to go home and the boarders back to their dorm. But he also noted that most club meetings scheduled for the afternoon and evening would still take place, so Kara thought the gesture of canceling classes seemed pretty pointless.

Mr. Matsui, her homeroom teacher, approached her in the corridor after the assembly.

"Today is your turn to help with the girls' bathroom on this floor," he said, smiling oddly.

Kara caught herself before she could make a sarcastic remark, but the expression of dismay on her face must have been clear, for the teacher chuckled softly.

"Don't worry. I have given you a reprieve until next week. You can sweep classrooms today."

She bowed in gratitude, relieved but also curious.

"Sensei, I am thankful, but why would you do this?"

Mr. Matsui glanced around. Students were moving busily through the halls, preparing to perform their tasks for o-soji. No one was paying them any attention. His brown eyes narrowed behind his glasses, his square head inclining toward her.

"You may be used to working hard in school, but I thought you might need time to adjust to cleaning toilets."

Kara smiled. "You're very kind. Honestly, I would prefer never to clean a toilet. I suspect everyone feels that way. But I don't want to be treated differently just because I'm not Japanese."

He studied her, smile slipping away. Serious as his expression became, she felt his approval.

Mr. Matsui bowed. "An admirable choice." He arched a graying eyebrow. "Report to the girls' bathroom, then."

She returned his bow and hurried to her duties. For the first four or five steps, she felt proud of herself and grateful to Mr. Matsui. By the sixth step, all she could think about was cleaning toilets, and she began to wish she was the kind of person who would have accepted Mr. Matsui's gesture. He had done it out of kindness, but if she didn't like people being cruel or ignorant toward her because she was different, she didn't think people should treat her better because of it, either.

The door to the girls' bathroom swung open as Kara approached, and Miho came out lugging two bags of trash.

"Hi," Miho said, stopping in the hallway. She made a face. "Listen, I wanted to tell you I'm sorry for running off yesterday. I didn't want to leave Sakura on her own—"

"It's okay," Kara interrupted. "I understand. Or, I guess I do. As much as I can, since obviously there's a lot going on around here that I don't know, with Sakura and Ume and all of that."

Miho started to reply, probably to apologize, but Kara held up a hand.

"No, no. It's just an observation. I'm not upset about it. I'm new, and we don't know each other that well yet. It's okay."

Miho looked unsure. "Really?"

Kara smiled. "Really."

"So, what are you doing for o-soji? I've already got the trash, so . . . oh, no. Don't tell me you have toilet duty?"

Kara executed a deep, theatrical bow.

Miho laughed and shook her head at the same time. "Well, the good news is that after today, you won't have to do toilets again for months."

"The worst part is that I sort of volunteered for it."

"What?"

"A long story," Kara said. "I'll explain later."

She opened the bathroom door. Miho started down the hall with her garbage bags. The door had started to swing shut when Miho called back to her, and Kara propped it open with her hand.

"Yeah?"

"You only have a week left to decide what club you're going to be in," Miho said. "Miss Aritomo will be doing a presentation for new members at Noh Club today. You should come."

Kara thought about it. She'd done some research online over the weekend about Noh theater, mainly because Miho had already suggested she join the club. Some of it seemed really interesting, though it sounded like a ton of work.

"Okay. I'll come."

Miho beamed.

Kara sat with Miho in the middle of Miss Aritomo's classroom, listening to the art teacher talk about the Noh theater club. The woman spoke with contagious passion, eyes alight with a love for her subject. *No wonder Dad has a crush on her*, she thought. Petite and very pretty, Aritomo-sensei had a quiet intelligence and a bright smile, and Kara had yet to see her in an outfit she didn't envy. Today she wore a simple white blouse and beige skirt, but the cut was so stylish that she looked like she'd just stepped off a runway.

Any time Miss Aritomo's name came up, Kara's father got a certain look in his eyes, a glimmer of a grin that he couldn't hide. He might not even know how attracted he was to her, but Kara knew him too well to miss it. She'd seen him grieve and, though he had laughed a lot as well in the past two years, when things were quiet, he often got a lost, distant look in his eyes that she could never seem to erase. He might not think he was ready to fall in love with someone else, but every time she saw that glimmer in his eye, Kara made a wish that it could happen for him.

As for Noh theater, Kara found everything about it fascinating. As an art form, it dated back seven hundred years. The masks, the costumes, and the precision of the performances all seemed to her to reflect the magic and mystery that Japan represented in her heart.

Miss Aritomo had welcomed them all and seemed very pleased to see Kara, which made her feel good. She had spoken briefly about the origins of Noh theater and the respect that its greatest practitioners received, as well as the seriousness with which all those involved approached their work.

"In total," Miss Aritomo told the gathered students, "there are only about two hundred and fifty Noh plays."

Kara raised her hand. From the surprise on Miss Aritomo's face, she realized she probably should have waited until the end of the presentation to ask questions, but her hand was already up.

"Yes, Kara?"

"I'm sorry, Aritomo-sensei, but didn't you say that Noh theater had been performed for seven hundred years?"

Miss Aritomo nodded. "That's right."

"And there are only two hundred and fifty plays?" To her, it seemed like Noh theater could be no different from novels, with millions of stories to be told.

The teacher smiled. "It is a precise art form, not something that can be created quickly. But you are right to question the number. Over the centuries there were certainly many more, but still not as many as you might imagine. Only specific kinds of stories have ever been considered appropriate for Noh theater, so the number of works is naturally limited."

Then she had shown them a long scene from a Noh play entitled "Aoi no Ue" on DVD, and Kara had watched, breathless. Like the limitations on form and story, the slow movements of the performers interested Kara a great deal. The skill involved impressed her as immense, similar to the discipline in ballet. What she had gleaned from a quick online search on Sunday morning did not begin to communicate the strange, dreamlike beauty of the actual performance, which in this case had something to do with exorcising the spirit of one woman from the body of another. It seemed most Noh plays had something to do with gods or monsters or spirits.

So weird, she thought, watching that ten-minute scene. *In the U.S., ghost stories get no respect, but here, it's high art.*

While watching the DVD, though, Kara caught several members of the Noh club—boys and girls—sneaking dark looks in her direction. These weren't soccer girls, obviously, since they were in the Noh club. It wasn't Ume's clique but other students Kara didn't know yet.

She brushed it off, trying to ignore it, but the longer it went on, the more she began to feel unwelcome.

"One element of Noh theater that many find interesting is the solitary preparation of the performers," Miss Aritomo explained toward the end of the presentation. "Unlike most theater, Noh performers work in private. The actors and singers practice independently, only joining all of their efforts together for the actual performance, which adds to the challenge but also introduces a spiritual, ritualistic element that we will discuss in future meetings."

Something struck the back of Kara's head. She grunted and turned around, even as she heard the ping of metal on the floor. A five-yen coin rolled a few feet and then fell over.

Someone had thrown it at her.

Several of the club members would not look at her. Others stared at her in curiosity or defiance, as if to say, *What are you going to do about it*?

"Kara?" Miss Aritomo asked, "Is something wrong?"

She considered speaking up but knew it would get her nowhere. Nobody would admit to having thrown the coin, and no one would tell on whoever had done it. She was an outsider.

"I'm sorry," Kara said, bowing her head. "Something buzzed around my head. It must have been a fly."

Miss Aritomo gave her an odd look. "All right. Let me know if any other flies trouble you."

Again, Kara inclined her head.

When Miss Aritomo began to speak again, Kara risked a glance at Miho, who sat in the next row, one seat up. The quiet girl might not come to her own defense, but the glare she cast back toward the kids sitting behind Kara was withering. It made Kara feel a little better, but not much.

After the club meeting ended, she and Miho went downstairs and waited for Sakura outside in the rain. They hid in the arch of the doorway on the side of the building, where Sakura usually smoked. The rain had lightened, but still they were thankful for the overhang of the roof and the recessed door.

"What did you think?" Miho asked, in English.

Kara blinked, taking a moment to switch her brain back into English. "It's cool."

Miho smiled at the Western slang. "Cool, yes. Very cool."

"But I don't think it's for me."

"Don't . . . ," Miho started, and then switched back to Japanese. When she was upset, the effort it required for her to speak English made her impatient. "Don't let them stop you from joining. You'll enjoy it. And those idiots will leave you alone once they know you. They'll get used to you."

Kara leaned her head back against the door, staring out at the rain, wondering what was taking Sakura so long. She sighed and looked at Miho. Raindrops had beaded on the girl's glasses, but Miho had not bothered to wipe them.

"I won't get used to them. I'm sorry, but I just don't think I can be a part of that group. I understand why you love Noh theater so much. I want to love it, too. The costumes and masks are amazing and it seems so . . . ." She didn't know the

Japanese word for *ethereal*. "It feels almost like a dream. And I adore Miss Aritomo. She's really sweet. But if I'm around those people, I don't think I'll be able to love it, Miho. It's pretty clear I'm not welcome there, maybe because I'm a gaijin and Noh is such an ancient Japanese tradition. But the reason doesn't really matter. I don't want to stay where I'm not wanted."

Maybe calligraphy was the way to go after all.

"I'm sorry," Miho said. She looked disappointed but did not try to change Kara's mind.

"Me too."

The girls stood in the recession another few minutes, just listening to the sound of the rain.

"This is strange," Miho said.

"What is?"

"Sakura never takes so long. She likes calligraphy, but that doesn't stop her from being the first one out the door when the meeting is over."

"Maybe it isn't over," Kara suggested.

Miho shook her head. "No. They never go on this long."

The tone of her voice, even more than the words, told Kara that Miho was worried. The way Sakura had been behaving the day before, in the wake of the discovery of Jiro's body—she might just be feeling oversensitive. Maybe Sakura had just wanted some time alone.

They set off together, walking around the front of the school. Most of the juku students and those who didn't live on campus would have left immediately after their club meetings. Half a dozen guys and girls gathered a short way down the front walk, standing under umbrellas, probably talking about whatever meeting they'd just come from.

Kara glanced down toward the bay but didn't see anyone near the water. With the storm, she couldn't even make out the location of the shrine that had been created for Akane.

"Let's try inside," Miho said.

But none of the students they encountered had seen Sakura. Kara spotted Mr. Matsui and asked him, but he also shook his head.

They walked to the room in the eastern wing, at the farthest, rear corner of the first floor, where the calligraphy club had its meetings. Two girls remained in the room, though no teacher was present. They worked quietly on a large piece of parchment, practicing the sweep of the brush over paper, one girl seeming to guide the other.

"Reiko?" Miho asked.

Both girls looked up. The older one reacted, lowering her gaze a moment before focusing on them again.

"You're looking for Sakura?" Reiko asked.

Miho nodded.

"Do you know where she is?" Kara asked.

The girl shook her head. "Not exactly. In one of the classrooms, I think. But I don't think you should interrupt them."

"Them?"

Reiko's eyes widened a bit. "Oh. I'm sorry, I thought you knew. It's really creepy. The police are here. They took her out of our meeting to talk to her about Jiro."

Kara knew her mouth was hanging open and how foolish it must have looked, but she couldn't get it to close. Her heart began to pound and she felt her face flush. She and Miho turned to each other, but it was obvious that neither of them had any idea what to say.

The police were here. What did that mean? Had somebody listened to the accusations Ume had made the day before? Did they have a reason to? Kara hated the questions, but she hated not having the answers even more.

"Poor Sakura," Miho said, at last.

"Yeah," Kara agreed. But in the back of her mind, she was also thinking, *Poor Jiro.*

That night, Kara sat at the small desk in her bedroom, staring at her computer screen. The rain had stopped but the clouds had never gone away, and now—long after dark—the air still felt chilly and damp. She wore a hooded woolen sweater, the sleeves pulled down over her hands, leaving only her fingers uncovered.

Her doubts had returned full force. She hated the emotional seesaw she'd been on the past few days; that just wasn't the kind of girl she wanted to be, some emo drama queen. But she didn't know how else she was expected to react to the ugliness moving to Japan had brought into her life.

Had she made the wrong friends? It seemed so. At first she'd felt such sympathy for Sakura, but now all of this death and brutality had come too close.

A lot of the guys she knew at home listened to Led Zeppelin, though the band had broken up when their parents were little kids. Still, they wore the T-shirts and scribbled lyrics on their notebooks. She knew plenty of the songs herself, and most of her guy friends were torn between whether "Stairway to Heaven" was the best or worst rock song ever written. Kara was on the fence, but the lyrics came to her now.

There's still time to change the road you're on.

Could she switch gears now—switch friends, even? Would others accept her?

That's not the question, Kara, she thought. *The question is, do you want to?*

She didn't.

Weird as all of this stuff with Sakura was, the girl had been the first person under the age of thirty to be nice to her in Japan. Kara liked her, and she liked Miho as well. Maybe they hadn't known each other long, but no way was Sakura capable of killing someone, even by accident. Kara felt guilty for even considering such a thing. She couldn't turn her back on a friend just because things were getting weird and nasty.

Feeling lonely and far from home, she'd replied to a bunch of e-mails that had been sitting in her in-box from her friends back in Boston, and then surfed the net for a while, reading about new movies and new music. She downloaded some tunes and browsed the Facebook and MySpace blogs of some of her friends.

She'd lulled herself into such a state of online oblivion that when the little Instant Messenger window popped up on the left side of the screen, she blinked stupidly at it a second before registering who the message was from.

Hi. You're up late, Sakura had written, in Japanese.

Kara had been typing and reading in English, and her skill with written Japanese was not in the same league as her talent with speaking the language. She did her best.

So are you.
Can't sleep.
Neither can I. Are you okay?
Not really. But I will be.

Kara paused before she replied, pushing up the sleeves of the sweater she'd put on to warm her against the chilly spring night. She didn't want to intrude if Sakura didn't want to talk about it. But there was no way the girl would have IMed her this late without expecting her to ask.

What happened with the police?
It sucked. And Miho said you were upset. Do you think I'm a freak now?

Kara stared at the screen, fingers paused over the keyboard, cheeks flushed with guilt.

No. I've just been worried about you.
☺ *Thank you. The past two days have been hard enough without having friends turn on me. Ume, that bitch, told the police they should talk to me about Jiro's death. Some of her friends said the same thing.*
Why would they believe that? Kara wrote.

I don't know if they did. But it's their job to check it out, right?

So what now? Kara asked. *Are your parents going to come?*

Are you kidding? The police called them, and all they wanted to know was if I was being charged with a crime. I guess that's what it would take to get them to pay me a visit.

Kara felt sick with anger at the callousness of Sakura's parents. Their older daughter had been murdered, and they'd abandoned their youngest child to grieve on her own. She wondered if Sakura had always dressed and acted like such a rebel, or if it had all come about after Akane's death. The wild child thing was really a facade—no matter what attitude she presented to the world, it wasn't like she was some party girl, drinking and doing drugs—and Kara would have bet that Sakura had put that persona on like a mask after her sister's death.

As she was typing a reply, another message came in from Sakura.

I've got to get some sleep. Thanks for not thinking I'm some serial killer. ☺

Kara deleted what she'd been writing and started over, signing off with a simple, *Good night.*

No bad dreams, Sakura wrote.

Kara stared at the words. Bad dreams. On Saturday, the day they'd gone to the park and shopping, Miho had mentioned something about Sakura having nightmares, and Sakura had seemed on edge about it. Kara had been having terrible dreams herself, things that troubled her deeply. Now she wondered exactly what Sakura had been dreaming about.

What do you mean—she started to write.

But then Sakura logged off for the night, leaving Kara to stare at the screen and wonder.

Tired as she was, suddenly the idea of sleep unsettled her. A line from Shakespeare whispered across her mind.

For in that sleep, what dreams may come?

Tuesday passed by in such ordinary fashion, mostly a blur of teachers' voices, studying, and the whispers and glances of other students, that Kara could almost forget how scary and weird things had been getting. She hadn't slept well the night before, but if she'd had any nightmares, she didn't remember them.

During o-soji, she got to sweep the stairs with Hachiro and two other students. At first it was awkward just being around him. He and Jiro had been close, and she didn't know what to say to comfort him. Kara had liked Hachiro from the moment they'd met. He was a big, friendly guy, smarter than he wanted people to see. Though she wasn't looking for a boyfriend, there was something really charming about him.

She still had until Monday to decide what club she would join but had pretty much decided to go with calligraphy, so she gave herself the rest of the afternoon off, went home early, and made dinner for herself and her father.

That night, she went to bed thinking that maybe the dark cloud that had been hanging above Monju-no-Chie School had passed.

In the early hours of Wednesday morning, long before dawn, Kara woke up screaming, tears and sweat on her face.

Her father stumbled in, half-asleep. She sent him back to bed, insisting that she was fine, that it was only a bad dream. And perhaps it was. But even as pieces of the dream slipped from her mind, gone forever, the echo of it remained. She lay in bed with her back to the windows and her legs drawn up beneath her, and only managed to drift off again when she saw the sky begin to lighten outside.

7

卍

On Wednesday morning, the world seemed to hold its breath.

No rain fell, no spring showers or storm clouds. On the contrary, the sun rose on a pristine day, the sort that almost demanded rambling along the shore of Miyazu Bay in quiet contemplation. Blue seemed insufficient an adjective to describe the sky. Instead of the bright, vibrant color that crowned perfect spring days, that morning the sky had a dusting of white over blue; not clouds, but the sort of crisp air that spoke more of mid-winter sunrise.

Kara kissed her father good-bye and went out the door, backpack slung over one shoulder, a small blue bow in her long blond hair. She started to whistle but faltered. Whistling, singing, anything that didn't involve walking to school was beyond her today. Her eyes burned from lack of sleep.

A wind had come through in the night and seemed to

have blown away the bad aura that had hung over Miyazu City for the past week or so. Despite her exhaustion, Kara felt a little better, as though the air was fresher and just breathing it in could cleanse her, and maybe keep the nightmares away. What a relief that would be.

Meanwhile, she had to make it through today. She would focus on the weekend, on having some time away from school. On Saturday afternoon, she'd already promised herself she would go down to the Turning Bridge and play guitar and sing, just shaking off the dust that had been settling on her spirit of late. She had hardly played guitar at all since school started.

And maybe there would be other plans as well. The one good dream she could recall from the previous night had involved Hachiro. At first she had dreamt they were walking together in the rain in a city that seemed sometimes to be Boston and others to be Miyazu. Then, somehow, they were swimming in a lake, or maybe the bay, laughing and splashing each other. He seemed even bigger in her sleeping imagination, like some kind of Goliath, and he had touched her face. She'd laughed, getting all shy, and looked down at herself in the water.

Only then did the dream-Kara realize they were swimming naked.

Sheer embarrassment had woken her, and then she'd seen the clock and realized somehow she had turned off the alarm. Twenty minutes later than she'd planned, she had stumbled out of bed to the shower.

Under the hot spray of water, she grinned at herself. How strange to still be embarrassed about something that had only happened in a dream. But then the dream of Hachiro began to slip away, and she started to recall the nightmares that had come earlier in the night. Slivers of those dark dreams flitted like ghosts at the back of her mind, tainting what remained of her one happy dream.

But it had gotten her thinking of Hachiro and how a walk along the bay with him might make her smile. She focused on those more pleasant thoughts as she walked to school, shoes clicking on pavement.

Nearby she heard the creak of a rusty bicycle chain and the rumble of a car engine. Someone tooted their horn not far away. None of it had anything to do with her; they were the sounds of any city. Kara kept to the side of the road, going over homework in her mind, making sure she was on top of things for her classes.

Three boys in Monju-no-Chie School uniforms rode by on their bikes, racing.

"Good morning, Kara!" one of them called, in English.

Surprised, she studied their backs as they pedaled toward school. The boy glanced over his shoulder and she recognized him as Ren, the spiky-haired kid in her homeroom.

Kara raised a hand to wave, but he'd already turned back around, bending to make up for the moment of distraction, still trying to win the race against his friends. Up ahead, other students congregated in front of the school.

Ren's greeting had lifted her spirits. Her eyes felt heavy, and she knew she was moving slower than usual this morning. But tonight she would sleep, she promised herself. Early to bed and too tired to dream.

At home, her mother had kept a Native American dream catcher hanging from the lock on her bedroom window. Kara wondered what had happened to that dream catcher. More than likely it had ended up in a box in storage, but she wished she had it now.

Curt, angry voices snapped her from her reverie.

"Are you calling me a liar?"

"I didn't say that. But I think drawing attention is a mistake—"

"You think? No, you don't think. Little mouse, you're not worthy to share the air I breathe, and you want to tell me how to behave?"

Kara couldn't help staring. She kept walking but slowed down as she passed the two girls on the corner, not far from the freestanding arch that marked the entrance to the school's grounds.

A furious Ume had her hands balled into fists at her sides as she menaced Maiko, one of the soccer girls in her clique. As nasty as Ume was, one thing she had said was true: the girl was a mouse in comparison.

The argument accelerated until Kara couldn't understand more than a few words of their rapid-fire Japanese. They were simply speaking too fast for her to translate. Then Ume glanced up and saw her watching, and it stopped abruptly.

"You! Ugly gaijin witch, what are you looking at?"

Kara flinched, not in fear but in astonishment. Ume had been a total bitch from day one, but she had been calm and collected, vicious in that quietly devastating way popular girls had perfected all over the world. This behavior went way beyond that. Her father referred to loss of temper on this scale as "going apeshit," and Ume had definitely reached that point.

Eyes front, ignoring the two girls now, she picked up her pace and hurried toward school. As she walked away, she heard one last snippet of the argument.

"We both just need to sleep," Maiko said.

Ume practically snarled her reply. "I don't want to sleep," she said. Her voice cracked on the last word, brittle and almost hysterical.

The words echoed in Kara's mind as she lined up outside of school and then went inside. In the genkan, she put her street shoes into her cubby and slipped on her uwabaki, lost in thought.

Shuffling to the morning meeting, she started looking around at the other students. Sakura had been looking exhausted and frayed the past couple of days, but under the circumstances that was no surprise. And Kara herself looked like hell in the mirror this morning. Good thing that—dreams about Hachiro notwithstanding—she wasn't really searching for a boyfriend.

But Ume and Maiko had both looked frazzled this morning as well. Ume's hair had been perfect last week. The girl had the poise and skin and bone structure of a porcelain doll. But Kara remembered thinking recently that Ume looked tired, and today the girl looked like she was unraveling. Her clothes needed ironing and her shoulder-length hair had been put up in twin clips, as though she couldn't be bothered to do anything else with it. Maiko didn't look much better.

As Kara glanced around the gym while Principal Yamato

talked, she saw other students who looked ragged around the edges. Ume and Maiko hurried into the back of the room, almost late, but Kara spotted other members of their clique. As a group, the soccer girls did not smile. Most had dark circles under their eyes. A couple of the boys looked equally tired.

Hachiro leaned out of his line and caught her eye, offering a smile. Kara could muster only a halfhearted grin in return, but she felt a strange sense of relief to see that he looked happy and alert. Whatever sickness had begun to affect so many of the students—it had to be a sickness, didn't it?—Hachiro seemed not to have caught the bug.

Maybe they're just not sleeping, Kara thought.

She frowned. Could it be that simple? All of them, just not sleeping?

All of them having nightmares.

Troubled by this thought, she studied them again, more carefully this time. Several of the soccer girls caught her staring and made unpleasant faces, but no one said anything or made rude gestures. They didn't want to get in trouble.

When they were dismissed, and Mr. Matsui was leading them to the classroom, Miho caught up with her.

"Are you all right? What was going on in there?"

"I'm okay," Kara said, brow still furrowed in thought. "Just more bad dreams. And I'm starting to think they're . . ."

She couldn't think of the word in Japanese.

Miho supplied it. "Contagious?"

Kara shot her a look as they walked up the stairs. "Exactly. How did you know that's what I was going to say?"

Adjusting her glasses, Miho shrugged. "I don't know. I'm

fine. The only reason I haven't been sleeping that well is because of the bad dreams Sakura's been having. But I've heard other people talking about it in the dorm."

"That's weird."

"You've been having them, too?" Miho asked.

Kara nodded. "I wonder what they're all dreaming about?"

But then they were walking into class, and Mr. Matsui cast an admonishing glance at them and they had to drop the conversation. Kara took her seat. Ren said good morning to her again and she waved. When he wished Miho a good morning as well, she blushed so hard her whole face went a shade of deep pink. As much as she talked about only liking American boys, Kara thought the bronze-haired Ren was a definite exception.

Ume's friend Maiko sat in the front left corner of the room, beside the windows. Mr. Matsui called on her for toban, the morning attendance and announcements. The girl pursed her lips, as though she might be thinking about telling him off, but she obviously thought better of it. She stood and took the notebook from him and went to the front of the class.

Barely lifting her eyes from the book, Maiko took attendance.

When she got to Kara's name, she paused and looked up. Again, she seemed about to speak, but then shook her head and returned to her task. Kara had no idea what the girl had on her mind, but something was troubling Maiko deeply.

For the rest of the day, Kara tried her best to focus. By early afternoon, she had to accept that her best would not be good enough. Even the breaks between classes, when she could get up and chat with Miho and get a breath of fresh air by an open window, didn't seem to help. Half of what she'd heard today had gone in one ear and out the other. Her notes were a mess. Between the distracting thoughts that kept popping up in her mind and the way her whole body seemed to just hang wrongly on her bones, exhaustion dragging her down, she felt that if she had to spend one more minute sitting on the hard wooden chair, she would scream.

When her father came in to teach his class, Kara wanted to run up and hug him. But he was Harper-sensei in the classroom, not her dad. Still, he smiled at her, and a few times he gave her looks of parental concern, obviously noticing that something was wrong. That alone was enough to restore her spirits a little. Besides, just because she was American didn't mean she would automatically pass American Studies.

As the clock ticked away the afternoon—the end of the school day still seemed far away—she glanced out the window. An old cypress tree grew near the school, thriving and alive. The wintry cast to the sky had receded and now only pure blue remained.

Her father was discussing the three branches of American government, and she forced herself to pay attention. But as she pulled her gaze away from the window, she saw that Maiko had her head down. Exhausted as she was, Kara's first reaction was envy. The thought made no sense. The moment her father saw that the girl had fallen asleep on her desk, she would be in big-time trouble. He had explained to Kara that the code of conduct at the school was very strict. At home, he might have let something like that slide, but he would have no choice but to punish her in some way. Harper-sensei would give her an extra assignment rather than make her sit on her knees in the hallway as some teachers would do.

At her desk, Maiko began to shiver, as though she was cold. Still asleep, head on her arms, she gave a tiny gasp, then a low murmur. Kara narrowed her eyes, staring at the girl. Then Maiko began to whimper in her sleep, and she understood.

Maiko was having a nightmare, right there in class.

Kara trembled, skin prickling with goose flesh. Just the thought of her own nightmares made her pulse quicken.

Most of the class was looking at Maiko now. Kara's father had ignored her as long as he could, but now, at last, he started walking toward the sleeping girl's desk. All Kara could think about was that whimpering—what was Maiko dreaming about to cause her to make that sound?

Her father tried to shake the girl awake. Kara couldn't watch. She looked away, glancing toward the door to the hall.

A cat stood poised just beyond the open door.

Kara jumped in her seat, heart racing, staring at the feline. For a second, she feared she might be dreaming, that if she turned and looked at her classmates again, the girls would have no faces. The cat had red and copper fur, and she had seen it before . . . had seen it fall to the ground amid the remembrances left at the shrine for Akane, down by the water. It had collapsed as though struck by lightning, and she'd been sure it was dead before it had gotten up and darted off into the woods.

For several seconds, Kara and the cat just stared at each other.

It opened its jaws in a silent hiss, back arching. Kara froze rigid, breath catching in her throat.

Maiko gave a yell as she woke. Several kids in the class laughed, though most remained silent, fearing some punishment themselves. Kara turned to look at Maiko, saw the confused look on the girl's face, and the relief—she might be in trouble, but at least she was no longer trapped in that dream.

Or maybe she is. Maybe we all are, Kara thought, turning back toward the door.

The cat was gone.

It undid her. Kara took a long, shuddering breath and brought both hands up to cover her face, rubbing at her tired eyes. She opened her hands as though playing peekaboo, and still the cat was nowhere to be seen.

She half rose, ready to rush from the room, to search out the cat, to find out who it belonged to and what the hell it was doing here, and why it haunted her dreams. But then she saw her father staring at her, brow furrowed in consternation and concern, and she sat back down.

The class dragged on forever. Kara fidgeted in her chair, not hearing a word, not able to focus at all. She watched Maiko in case she fell asleep again, studied her classmates to see if any of them looked tired, and every minute or so her gaze strayed nervously to the doorway. The frisson of fear that had prickled her skin had not receded at all.

When her father finally slid the door closed, trying to get her attention back, that only made it worse. Without being able to see into the corridor, she could easily imagine the cat still there. She knew all of this was paranoia and sleep deprivation, but knowing didn't help. She needed to get out of school, to go home and get some rest while the sun was still up. It would be worse after dark.

When at last the class ended, her father beckoned for her to follow him out into the corridor. Today he'd worn a dark jacket and black tie, and Kara flashed to her mother's funeral, to a vision of her father standing beside her grave in grim funeral clothes. He wore something similar every day to teach at Monju-no-Chie School, but the comparison had never occurred to her before. Now she'd never be able to erase it from her mind.

"What's going on with you?" he asked in English. They'd agreed on no English in school, but there was less chance of being overheard this way.

"Nothing," she said. "I'm fine."

"*Kara.*" His tone said it all—she wasn't fooling either of them. "You looked like a deer in headlights in there. You're either scared of something or you're on drugs, and it damn well better not be the latter."

She looked at him, forced herself to focus on his eyes, and then she took a deep, shuddery breath and let it out in a long sigh. Her back and shoulders and neck were knotted up with tension, and she felt the muscles relax.

"I haven't been sleeping well. I think . . . I don't think I'm the only one. I was getting freaked out in there, but I'm all right."

He looked dubious. Kara took his hands in hers and squeezed.

"Really, Dad. I'll be okay. I think everyone's on edge 'cause of what happened to Jiro. The weirdness is like a cloud around here. It'll blow over."

He had to get to his next class, but it was obvious he was reluctant to go. Finally he nodded.

"Okay. But you really need sleep, kiddo. I've got some Ambien. I know you don't like to take that stuff—"

"Are you kidding?" Kara said quickly. "I'll make an exception."

Her dad smiled. "All right. I'll see you later. If you start getting really antsy, just tell the teacher you're sick and come find me."

Kara would never do that. They had to fit into the culture of the school, and Japanese students at Monju-no-Chie School weren't about to beg off class unless they were throwing up or too weak to get out of bed. Their parents weren't going to coddle them, either. Her father would lose some of the respect of his peers if she behaved that way, and more if he seemed to condone it. She wouldn't do that to him.

"Sure," she lied.

Her father headed off to teach his next class and she went back into the room, glancing around first to make sure there was no sign of the cat. It made her feel a little better to know she would be able to sleep that night.

But not much. Whatever the weirdness was, it was just as contagious as the dreams. The more people had trouble sleeping, the more irritable they got. That was only natural.

But that didn't explain the cat—the same creature that she'd dreamt about—showing up just as Maiko had been having her nightmare, almost like the cat knew. Or as though it had brought the nightmares to her itself.

Calligraphy made Kara feel a thousand times better.

At first, listening to the teacher—Kaneda-sensei—she had thought it might be the most boring thing she would ever do. The gray-haired, fiftyish woman had a slow, drowsy voice, like some of the baseball commentators back home. Nothing made her fall asleep faster than when her dad would put on a Red Sox game on an August afternoon.

She'd also been on edge, wondering if the members of the calligraphy club would freeze her out the way the Noh club members had. And some of them had looked at her with disdain when they saw she was attending the meeting. But Sakura introduced her to some of the girls, and there were several kids from her homeroom in the club, including Ren and the female Sora. Ren teased her, slowly pronouncing the Japanese names for the special paper they used—*hanshi*—and the different brushes, but his teasing was so good-natured that Kara could shoot him a halfhearted icy stare and then laugh, which seemed to set everyone at ease.

What really helped, though, was when they actually got down to work. Kaneda-sensei stopped to show her brushstrokes several times, and she encouraged Sakura and the other members of the club to help as well. It was her first time even attempting calligraphy, and though she knew she couldn't possibly be writing the kanji characters correctly, the process alone felt therapeutic. As she practiced different characters, following the order of brushstrokes carefully, she found her anxiety slipping away with every swath of black ink.

Japanese art all seemed to combine precision with beauty, but she had not seen the value in that precision with something like Noh theater. She admired it, yes, but couldn't imagine doing it herself. Calligraphy was different. Working with the ink and brush seemed almost like meditation.

When the meeting ended, she knew she had found her club.

Afterward, Sakura and Ren walked out with her, the two of them involved in a conversation about their favorite manga that sounded almost like a completely different language to her. They talked artists and ink thickness, and when they discussed the actual stories, they spoke about the characters and places as though they existed in the real world.

Kara had already decided she liked Ren, but seeing the way he could distract Sakura from her troubles, she liked him even more. She only hoped that his interest in Sakura didn't extend beyond friendship, because that might break Miho's heart. As much as she dismissed the idea of dating Japanese boys, and only wanted to talk about American guys, it was painfully obvious that Miho had a crush on Ren. Kara made a mental note to talk to Sakura about him; she wouldn't want to hurt her roommate without even realizing it.

"Why didn't you two join the manga club?" she asked as they went into the genkan and changed into their street shoes.

They exchanged a look and a laugh.

"Matsui-sensei guides the manga club," Sakura said.

"So? He's very serious, but he's nice enough."

Ren shook his head. "Not if you don't like baseball. He really would like to guide the baseball club, but since he had to settle for the manga club, he only wants to talk about baseball manga. We met in manga club last year and switched to calligraphy together."

Kara couldn't help the insinuating smile that touched her lips. "Really?"

Sakura rolled her eyes and whapped her on the arm. "It's not like that. I'm not Ren's type."

The two of them shared another look and a laugh at what must have been a private joke between them. From Sakura's tone, Kara got the implication. Miho would be very depressed if she found out that Ren was gay. Kara wasn't going to be the one to tell her.

"Let's go," Sakura muttered. "I need a cigarette."

They said their good-byes to Ren and went out through the front doors. The shadows had already grown long. Kara wondered how she would feel about being in school during the worst winter months, when she would be arriving shortly after sunrise and heading home after dark. Winter would be very long. Fortunately, it was far off, and they had all of spring and summer stretching before them.

"You and Miho really have to come over for dinner one night," she said as they headed around to Sakura's smoking spot.

"Your father really wouldn't mind?" she asked.

"I'm sure—," Kara began but stopped mid-sentence.

The soccer girls were there, gathered around like some 1950s gang waiting for a rumble. She knew a lot their names, now. Chouku. Hana. Reiko. In their sailor fuku uniforms, they looked like a real-life version of something out of one of Sakura's favorite manga.

Ume started toward Sakura. Maiko grabbed her arm, trying to hold her back. Ume shook her off. A couple of other girls murmured hesitations, glancing around, worried there would be trouble and they would be caught up in it.

"Sakura . . . ," Kara began.

But she had no more luck than Ume's friends. Sakura stormed toward her smoking spot. A couple of spiky-haired boys, obviously friends of Ume's, were standing in the recessed doorway, but they did not try to help or interfere. They were there just to watch. They smiled.

To Kara, they all looked tired.

"You're going to stop!" Ume jabbed Sakura in the chest with one long finger.

Sakura scoffed. With her jagged slash of hair and sleepless eyes, she actually looked dangerous, like she might at last be just as wild as she always tried to appear.

"Stop what? Breathing? Sorry, I'm not going to make it that easy for you."

"You know what I'm talking about," Ume said, almost snarling, stepping in close.

Kara tried to separate them.

Ume slapped her hand away. "Don't touch me, bonsai. This has nothing to do with you."

Kara looked around at the other girls and the boys

watching from that recessed doorway. They all looked ragged and on edge. She thought about her own behavior earlier, and the way Ume had sniped at Maiko that morning, and she knew, suddenly, that things could turn very ugly here. Not just ugly—violent.

"Maiko," she said, turning to the other girl.

But Maiko looked away. None of them would meet her gaze. Some glared at Sakura expectantly, waiting for a fight, practically salivating over the possibility. Others looked like they wished they were anywhere but here, as though they thought maybe Ume was acting a little crazy but didn't want to be the first to say it.

"You are going to stop," Ume went on. "I don't know how you're doing it, but you're putting these things in my head." She spread her arms to indicate the others. "In all of our heads."

A terrible smirk appeared on Sakura's lips. "Oh, I get it now. You're having dreams, too, aren't you? Bad dreams."

"See!" Ume said, triumphantly, pointing at her again and turning to the others. "I told you! She admits it."

"She didn't admit anything," Kara said. "A lot of us are having bad dreams."

Ume stepped in close to Sakura. She was taller and glared down at her. "It isn't just in dreams anymore. Some of us . . . we've seen things while we're awake, too." Her voice dropped almost to a whisper. "Things that shouldn't be there."

Maiko took a step closer to them. But instead of menacing, she was pleading. "What did you do, Sakura? Is it some kind of drug? Or did you poison us? Please, you have to stop." Her bottom lip quivered. "I'm falling apart."

Maiko sounded so full of despair that Kara couldn't help feeling badly for her.

"You're haunted," Sakura told Ume. She glanced around at the others. "You're all haunted, as you should be. None of you should be able to sleep."

Kara stared at her. What the hell was she talking about?

Ume laughed. Nobody else did.

"I knew your sister was crazy, but I didn't realize you were just as bad," Ume said.

Her mistake had been in getting so close.

Sakura slapped her, open-handed, with such force that the sound echoed off the stone wall of the school. As Ume reeled away, Sakura followed. Grabbing a fistful of her hair, she punched her in the face hard enough that blood squirted from both nostrils.

"Jesus, cut it out!" Kara shouted and grabbed Sakura by the arms, hauling her backward.

Sakura managed to launch a kick that hit Ume in the gut. The taller girl fell to her knees and vomited in the grass. As she wiped puke and blood from her lips, the two boys by the door began to cheer and the other soccer girls started for Sakura. Even the ones who had seemed unsure before looked like they had made up their minds now. They were going to take Sakura apart.

"Stop it!"

They all turned to see Miho and Hachiro coming around from the back of the school and running toward them. Hachiro had been the one to shout.

"What's wrong with you? All of you?" Miho asked, rushing to help Kara escort Sakura away.

"Do you want to be expelled?" Hachiro shouted at the others.

He stayed there, warning them all not to follow, and nobody did. Maybe because Hachiro had been so close to Jiro, maybe because they trusted him, or perhaps just because of his size, they all listened to him.

Except for Ume.

"I'm not haunted!" she cried after them.

"Yes, you are," Sakura whispered to herself.

Miho and Kara walked on either side of her, around the front of the school building and down the street. Kara didn't know where Miho was leading them, but at the moment, anywhere was better than here. It was a miracle none of the teachers had come out during the scuffle. They were lucky it had been so quick. But the headmaster would hear about it soon enough.

"Are we going for candy?" Sakura asked, softly.

Miho smiled. "Yes."

"You're going to give me sugar after that?"

Kara glanced at Miho. "Is that a good idea?"

"For her, yes. For us, maybe not so much."

They all laughed, just a little. But as they walked, Kara kept stealing glances at Sakura, until finally the other girl shook her head.

"You want to ask, so ask," she said.

"Fine. What was all of that about?"

All trace of humor left Sakura's face. "I don't know for sure if Ume was involved in Akane's death. But if she didn't kill my sister, I think she knows who *did*. They think I'm doing something to them, but they're wrong. I haven't done anything."

She stopped and looked at Miho and Kara. "It's Akane. She's haunting them. Her spirit's still here at school, still lingering where she was murdered. I hope she drives them all mad."

Sakura walked on.

For a few seconds, Kara and Miho only stared after her, wide-eyed. Then they set off after her. Someone had to stay with her.

But all the while, Kara thought about what she and Ume and Maiko had said about their bad dreams. Kara hadn't even known Akane, but the nightmares were haunting her as well. She thought about mentioning this, explaining to Sakura that it proved she was wrong. Even if she believed in ghosts or spirits, if Akane really was haunting Ume and the others, the spirit wouldn't bother with a girl who'd been living halfway around the world when she was murdered.

Then she thought about the cat she'd seen in school that day, and her dreams, and how badly Sakura seemed to need to believe Akane's spirit still hung around Monju-no-Chie School, and she decided to keep quiet.

There would be time for logic and reality-check questions another day.

For this afternoon, there would be candy.

8

Mid-morning on Thursday, while she was supposed to be paying attention in her history class, Kara couldn't stop thinking about Ume and Sakura's behavior the day before. Not even twenty-four hours had passed, and she was already sick of watching her back, waiting for whatever Ume might do in retribution.

At least Kara had gotten some sleep. Her father had given her Ambien. She didn't like taking the pill—it made her feel groggy in the morning, and she didn't want to have to rely on medication in order to get some rest—but at least she'd been able to sleep, and she hadn't dreamed at all, which was a major bonus. This morning she felt more alert, more aware, and only now did she realize just how much her restless nights had begun to wear on her. As bad as she had looked—the dark circles under eyes, her sallow face—she'd felt even worse.

Today she found herself more able to concentrate, and

that meant a focus on recent events that she hadn't been able to manage earlier in the week. What seemed surreal and impossible just the day before now seemed vivid and credible. Others were having bad dreams—Ume and the other soccer girls, some of the boys they hung around with, Sakura, and Kara herself. But Miho claimed she hadn't been troubled by nightmares, that only Sakura's sleeplessness had interrupted her slumber.

So where were the connections?

Sakura claimed Ume had something to do with her sister's death, and that Ume and her friends were being haunted. Despite the cat and the terrible dreams she'd had, Kara couldn't bring herself to believe that. But clearly, something was troubling them all. Ume thought Sakura had drugged them, but that seemed not only improbable but ridiculous.

Kara had no answers, only questions. Foremost among them was how she fit into the whole scenario. She had never known Akane. If Ume was right and Sakura had done something to them, why would she include Kara? She wouldn't. And if Akane had decided to haunt Ume because the girl had been involved in her murder, again, why haunt Kara as well?

None of it made any sense. And, as much as she thought the girl was a shallow bitch, Kara didn't think Ume capable of murder, or even of being an accomplice without falling apart. Sakura had lost her sister; it made sense that she couldn't be objective.

But maybe she's half right, Kara thought. *Maybe Ume knows who did it. Maybe they all do, and what's haunting them is guilt.*

Not that Sakura would talk about it. Neither she nor Miho had elaborated any further on the reasons for the animosity that seethed between Sakura and Ume. After the clash with Ume and her friends, going to buy candy had seemed like a silly thing to do, but Kara had seen it as almost a last supper. After all, as soon as Ume reported the violence, Sakura's punishment would be swift. Ume's friends would support whatever version of the truth the girl wanted to put forward. Kara had no doubt that Sakura would be expelled, or at least suspended.

She glanced at the clock and wondered how long before Sakura would be called in to see the headmaster. Had it already happened? If not, then why not? If there weren't any repercussions, that meant Ume hadn't reported the assault. And the only explanation for that was that she was planning some other form of retribution.

Someone knocked lightly on the door.

Every student in the room turned to look, but Joken-sensei completed his thought before surrendering command of the classroom. Looking perturbed at the interruption, he went to the door and slid it open.

Through the gap, Kara caught a glimpse of Mr. Matsui, which surprised her. He must have had a class to teach, so what was he doing out in the corridor?

Joken-sensei stepped into the hall and the two men spoke in low voices, not quite a whisper but not loud enough for the students to hear more than muffled inflections.

Oddly, it was Mr. Matsui who poked his head back into the classroom.

"You will be on your own for several minutes. Misbehavior will not be tolerated. See that you conduct yourselves properly until Joken-sensei returns."

Without further comment, he withdrew, sliding the door closed.

For perhaps ten long seconds, the class remained silent, staring at the door and at one another. Then a current of murmurs swept the room as they began to wonder aloud about what had just happened. Had Joken-sensei had some sort of personal emergency, a terrible message Mr. Matsui was delivering? Or—given the grim expression on Mr. Matsui's face— had he been called away to handle another school crisis?

A terrible feeling came over her.

Sakura, she thought.

Kara turned to find Miho watching her, just a few desks away, and she knew the concern in the other girl's eyes was reflected in her own. Joken-sensei looked the part of the venerable old professor, with his white hair and bushy eyebrows and narrow glasses, and he clearly had a position of great respect among the faculty. If Sakura were about to be expelled or disciplined in some way, it made sense that he'd be called away.

But what about Matsui-sensei?

Kara shook her head at Miho. She didn't think this was about Sakura after all.

Other guesses were discussed in low tones. Kara glanced around, then her gaze landed on the door. She wondered where her father was, and if he'd been pulled out of his class as well.

"Do you think there's a fire or something?" a boy asked.

Ren turned toward the kid, rolling his eyes. "Don't be stupid. They'd evacuate us, not close us in here."

"Definitely," Kara said. "Seems to me they don't want us going anywhere."

Most of the class looked at her then.

"You think something's going on they don't want us to . . . ," Miho began, but her words trailed off as understanding dawned on her face, followed by sadness.

Ren swore. "Do you think they found someone else?"

That silenced everyone. Nobody wanted to believe it. The grief of Jiro's death was still very fresh, but it was awful enough as an isolated incident. If they were being kept in class because another student had been killed . . .

Kara stood and went to the door.

"What are you doing?" someone snapped.

"Sit down," a boy named Goto said, angry. "We'll all get in trouble."

Kara took a breath and slid the door open a few inches. No one shouted at her from the hall; as far as she could tell, there was nobody in the corridor to notice her. Off to the right, she heard voices from the direction of the stairwell, and heavy footfalls, but not coming toward her.

She slid the door further open and looked out into the hall. At the eastern end of the corridor, Miss Aritomo leaned against a window, looking down. When the art teacher began to turn to scan the hall for activity, Kara pulled back into the classroom and shut the door.

"Something's going on outside," she said.

Several students got up and headed for the windows. Maiko, who sat in the front corner, was the first one against the glass. Half a dozen others followed, and then Miho, Ren, Kara, and both Soras joined them.

"You idiots," Goto chided them. "What are you doing?"

Nobody answered him.

From her seat, a girl asked, "Do you see anything?"

At first, Kara didn't. The field behind the school and the dorm off to the right of the property and the trees in the distance were undisturbed. But then she noticed movement in her peripheral vision and looked down and to the right. At the far corner of the building, several teachers stood on the pavement of the parking area, necks craned as they stared up at something.

"Oh, no," she started to say.

"The teachers are down there," Ren said at the same time.

Maiko fumbled with a latch and slid open the window in front of her. For once, Goto said nothing. When Kara glanced back at him, she even thought he had shifted in his chair, as if he wanted to get up and join them but didn't dare.

"Someone's up on the roof," Maiko said. "A girl."

That got them all standing, rushing to the window in a clatter of desks and chairs and falling books. Kara was jostled and nudged and she nudged in return, feeling a little sick even as she did so, hating that they were all so desperate to watch the spectacle unfold. Was it horror or fascination or excitement that made them all so determined to *see*? She didn't want to know the answer.

Maiko hung halfway out the window, with a couple of

girls holding onto her so that she didn't fall. She twisted around, looking up at the far corner, trying to get a glimpse of whoever stood at the edge of the roof.

Through the open window, they could all hear the teachers' voices now, shouting and calling to the girl on the roof.

"Can you see who it is?" Miho asked.

But Maiko didn't need to reply. The teachers began to call out a name, and they all knew, then.

"Hana, no!" they shouted. And, "Hana, wait!"

Though she wasn't a boarding student, Hana was one of Ume's friends—one of the soccer girls.

Maiko drew back inside the classroom, one hand over her mouth. She backed up until she stumbled over her own desk and sat hard on her chair. Her eyes were rimmed with red and she looked ill, but her sickly appearance wasn't new. Maiko had already admitted that the nightmares were making her fall apart. This could only make it worse.

The girl looked right at Kara, returned her stare. Then Maiko gave an awful, brittle little laugh.

"Am I awake?" she asked, her voice very small.

What terrified Kara was the look on the girl's face. Maiko really didn't know.

More shouting drifted in from the open window. Kara leaned against the glass, looking out at the teachers. Even at this distance, she saw the sudden change in their faces.

Mr. Matsui actually screamed.

Hana plummeted, without any screams of her own, and when she struck the pavement, she crumpled like a discarded rag doll, bones giving way.

There were shrieks inside the classroom. Miho reached out and took Kara's hand and they stood together. Ren turned from the window, wiping tears from his eyes.

Everyone looked at Maiko.

Who gazed out the window, not seeing any of them, expression entirely blank.

"I wonder how she got up there," Maiko said quietly, in a tone that suggested not horror but envy.

"When I decided to come to Japan to teach, I never imagined anything like this," Rob Harper said. "I know bullying is an epidemic here, but this kind of ugly stuff feels so American to me. I guess I figured I was leaving it behind."

Kara sat on the floor just outside the closed door of her father's classroom, knees drawn up beneath her. Inside, he and Miss Aritomo were talking quietly, and though it was obvious they thought otherwise, she could hear almost every word.

"I wish I could disagree, but suicide has become more common here in recent years," Miss Aritomo said.

Mr. Matsui appeared from his classroom down the hall, glanced up and down and caught sight of Kara. He gave a bow of his head and she returned the gesture. Mr. Matsui walked toward her but turned to go downstairs, no doubt to some kind of gathering of teachers and administrators.

Otherwise, the upper floor seemed deserted. There were police in the building, and there must be plenty of them outside, and the faculty were scattered all over the place, but the students were gone. They had been kept in their classrooms for nearly two hours—through lunch, though no one in Kara's room seemed to have much of an appetite—and then they had all been dismissed. The boarding students had been the first to be allowed to leave. Only when they had departed, in an orderly fashion, of course, did the day students get the go-ahead to leave.

There would be no o-soji. And the homeroom teachers informed their classes that school had been canceled for the following day, which was Friday.

Kara wanted to go home. And not to the small house she and her father had rented near the school. *Home.*

Instead, she was the only student still at the school.

Her thoughts drifted, her mind numb, and she wouldn't even allow herself to think about Sakura or Akane or Jiro—any of it. She rocked a little, impatient, wishing her father could leave now.

Hana had been nothing to her except another sour-faced, jeering girl who took Ume's lead and sneered at the little gai-jin bonsai. But the idea of anyone throwing themselves off the roof, hitting the pavement so hard that their bones gave way in an instant, collapsing like a house of cards . . . The idea was hideous.

She couldn't stop wondering why Hana had done it. Maiko had said that she was falling apart because of the nightmares and her inability to sleep. Had the same things driven Hana off the roof?

Kara pushed her palms against her forehead. *No more.*

In her father's homeroom, he and Miss Aritomo lowered their voices. Kara listened harder. The only reason for them to quiet down would be if they didn't want to be overheard. She should have granted them some privacy, but curiosity beat courtesy, and she put her ear close to the sliding door.

"How can you be so certain there's no connection between Hana and the boy who was killed this weekend?" Rob Harper asked.

"There can't be," Miss Aritomo said. "They knew each other from school, of course. But the school isn't very big; it makes sense that they would know each other. Hana killed herself, Rob. No one pushed her. Half of the teachers saw her jump."

"And that boy, Jiro, drowned. Two suicides, by students who knew each other? It could have been some kind of lovers' quarrel."

Miss Aritomo did not reply at first. Kara could feel the weight of her silence, even through the door.

"What is it?" her father asked.

"Jiro may not have committed suicide."

"That's not what I was told."

"Probably because your daughter is a student here," Miss Aritomo said. "They wouldn't risk the other students finding out the truth . . . or worse, their parents."

"Or they didn't tell me because I'm a gaijin."

"That's possible, too."

Her father sighed. "So the boy was murdered?"

"The police have not been able to say for certain," Miss Aritomo replied.

"That's why they're still saying he drowned?"

"Jiro *did* drown, but from what I've heard, that isn't the only reason he died," Miss Aritomo said. "When they found him, he had been . . . most of his blood was gone."

Kara flinched, trying to process that. She stared at the door.

"How is that possible?" her father asked.

"The police are suggesting that he might have been bleeding into the water," Miss Aritomo said.

"That doesn't make any sense," Kara's father said. "That much blood doesn't just *leak* out. He'd have to have been dead before he went into the bay, but that doesn't work, either, because Jiro couldn't have swallowed water if he was already dead. Drowning wouldn't have been part of the cause of death, unless whoever did it had some way to drain his blood—or pump it out, or something—while he was *in* the bay. That's insane."

"Yes. I do not understand how it is possible. But now you see there can't be any connection between Jiro's death and Hana's suicide, unless she was in love with him and killed herself in grief."

Kara couldn't listen anymore. Head spinning, she stood and knocked on the door, cutting off the conversation inside.

"Come in," her father called.

She slid the door open. Her dad and Miss Aritomo looked at her with a mixture of guilt and suspicion, as though they'd been caught in something illicit. That look made Kara think back to a moment she'd barely noticed in their conversation.

The art teacher had called her father by his first name, sort of an intimate thing in Japan for a man and woman who were only colleagues.

"Hi, honey. Sorry to keep you waiting," her father said. "Actually, it's good that you knocked. We're supposed to be downstairs by now, I think."

"I saw Matsui-sensei going down," Kara said. She glanced at Miss Aritomo and gave her a small bow. "I don't want to be any trouble. I know there's a lot going on. But I'd really rather not sit around an empty school waiting, and I know you don't want me going home alone. Would it be all right if I go over to the dorm and hung around with Miho and Sakura until you can leave?"

Her father considered for a moment, and then nodded. "I'll come and get you. What room are they in?"

Kara told him, and then the three of them walked down to the first floor together. She hugged him good-bye and went down to the genkan to put her street shoes on.

Outside, all but a single police car had departed. In her mind's eye, she pictured what the parking lot side of the school would look like. At the back corner, there would be police tape. On the pavement would be smears of blood, the school waiting for permission to wash it away.

She went the other way, around the side where Sakura always went to smoke, where they'd run into trouble the day before. The spot where Hana had died might not be as awful as she imagined it, but then again, it might be worse. Best to just avoid it completely.

Even as she walked across the field between the school

and the dorm, Kara didn't turn to look. But there were plenty of students who were. At least twenty kids—boys and girls both—were outside the dorm, sitting on the stairs or just standing around, some of them pretending to play catch. They all seemed to be moving in slow motion, mesmerized by death.

It startled Kara to see Miho sitting on the steps by herself, staring across at the school, the sun glinting off her glasses. Of Maiko and Ume and Hana's other friends, there was no sign.

"Where's Sakura?" Kara asked as she sat down next to Miho.

"Upstairs, watching TV."

"I guess she thinks she knows why Hana did it?"

Miho looked at Kara. "Because she was haunted. Yes. I'm really worried about her. She doesn't seem sad, or even surprised."

Kara wanted to tell Miho about the conversation she'd overheard between her father and Miss Aritomo, but with so many people around, now wasn't the time. Instead, she asked a question, keeping her voice low.

"I still don't understand," Kara whispered. "What aren't you telling me, Miho? I know what Sakura said about Ume, but what's the connection between Jiro and Akane?"

Miho studied Kara's face, then glanced around at the other students who surrounded them and shook her head.

"It's not my story to tell."

9

卍

The warm, white sand gave way under Kara's bare feet, sifting between her toes. Her shoes dangled from the fingers of her left hand. In spite of the sun and the blue sky of that Saturday morning, the air had a chill that made her glad she'd worn a turtleneck this morning, but her jacket was unzipped. On the bay side of Ama-no-Hashidate, the thick black pines provided shelter from the wind that swept in off the Sea of Japan.

Loosely translated, Ama-no-Hashidate meant "bridge in the heavens," but Kara liked specifics and preferred the more literal translation, "standing celestial bridge." From the mountain overlooking the bay—accessible by cable car—the view was even more magnificent. The two miles of serpentine sandbar, with its pine trees only edged with white sand, were set off against the blue water.

According to local lore, for more than a thousand years, people had been visiting Ama-no-Hashidate and experiencing it in a way that Kara thought was just weird. You were suppo-sed to turn your back to the view, then bend over and look at Ama-no-Hashidate through your legs. From that perspective, the dark spit of land against the blue water looked like a bridge across the sky.

Supposedly.

"I tried it once," she said.

Hachiro had been walking beside her, hands stuffed in his pockets. She felt like some kind of Hollywood pop tart with a bodyguard. Hachiro towered over her. Yet for all his size, Hachiro had a gentleness that set her very much at ease.

On Friday, they'd had no school. A terrible stillness had settled on Monju-no-Chie School and on the entire area, as though everyone connected with the school held their breath and didn't think it was safe to exhale yet. Maybe they were right, but Kara had to exhale.

This morning, she'd planned to come down to Ama-no-Hashidate and play her guitar by the Turning Bridge. Instead, she had left her guitar at home and walked over to the dorm, hunted down Hachiro, and asked him to come with her. He'd agreed instantly, and as they'd walked to the Kaitenbashi— the Turning Bridge—and across to Ama-no-Hashidate, he'd lightened her spirits, talking incessantly, making her smile the way he always did.

Until his words ran dry.

Jiro had been his good friend, so it made sense that there would be a limit to how long Hachiro could pretend he wasn't grieving. Kara thought that her quietness probably also made him nervous. For her to ask him to accompany her this morning had been a very un-Japanese thing to do. She liked the way it made her feel, and if Hachiro was off balance, not knowing quite how to handle it, she didn't mind very much. His utter lack of smoothness and cockiness charmed her, and given the way her expectations about life in Japan had turned out, she wasn't in the mood to worry about fitting in.

"Tried what?" Hachiro asked.

"Hmm?" She glanced at him, saw him studying her curiously. "Oh, the whole 'viewing heaven's bridge' thing. I didn't care that I looked silly, since everyone else was doing the same thing. But I didn't see it. To me, it just looks like an upside-down view of the sandbar, and it made me dizzy as hell."

Hachiro laughed. "You're not much of a romantic."

Kara cocked an eyebrow. "You'd be surprised."

He gave her a befuddled look and glanced at the pine trees as though he'd never seen anything so fascinating. Shoes in hand, Kara started walking again, and Hachiro fell into step beside her. Her free hand brushed his and for a moment, as though by instinct, his fingers curled with hers, then set them free.

"It's hard to believe this is just a sandbar," she said nervously.

"Just a sandbar?" Hachiro said. "It cuts off the bay from the sea! There are thousands of pine trees out here! It's hardly just a sandbar. Ama-no-Hashidate might be the most beautiful place on earth!"

Kara smiled. "It sounds like you're enough of a romantic for both of us."

The words disarmed him. Hachiro had no idea what to make of her, and Kara liked that just fine. She found herself wishing she had brought her guitar after all.

"I suppose this is a bad time to ask if you've decided you don't like Japan," he said.

Kara shrugged and kept walking. "I don't know. I can separate Japan from what's happening at school, as crazy and upsetting as it all is. When I was eleven years old, a younger kid who rode the bus with me just didn't show up at the bus stop one morning. The principal got everybody together and explained that he'd been born with a heart defect, and that he was dead. It seemed almost ridiculous. How could this kid be dead? He was in the fourth grade. But we went through it as a community. It's different here. It's like, students on one side and grown-ups on the other, trying to pretend this isn't all as ugly as it seems.

"I'll say this: of all the different things I fantasized about living in Japan, this is something I never imagined. I know I can't judge how much I like this country while this is all happening. So right now, the jury is still out."

Hachiro nodded thoughtfully. "What about before, when you first got here?"

Kara thought about that. She and her father had come to Japan to start over, to leave behind all the painful reminders of her mother's death and build a life that she would have wanted for them. But now death had thrown a terrible shroud over their new home. She wasn't ready to have that conversation with Hachiro, was she?

No. Stick to school, she told herself.

"I love the people, and it's beautiful here. I don't even mind being 'bonsai.' But there are so many kids at school who barely acknowledge my presence, who won't talk to me or really look at me, and I'd be lying if I said that didn't bother me. Most of the time, I can ignore it. And I've made friends, so it's not that I'm a total outsider. But I hate being judged just for being gaijin. If they'd talk to me and then decide to hate me, that'd be different. At least they'd be hating me for me."

Even as the words came out of her mouth, she knew it sounded like whining. How many kids did she know back in Boston who'd been discriminated against in the same way, just based on their sexual preference or the color of their skin? Far too many.

"They'll get used to you," Hachiro said.

"It's all right. They probably won't, but it isn't as if they're the kind of people I want to be friends with anyway."

Hachiro nodded. "I understand that. I'm starting to realize there are people who are my friends that I don't want to be friends with."

Kara paused and looked out at the bay. Hachiro came to a stop behind her, but he didn't move to her side.

"You mean Ume?"

Hachiro didn't reply. When Kara turned, she saw the contemplative expression on his face.

"She's one of them," he admitted without a trace of a smile. "I'm starting to wonder how well I know a lot of the people I thought I knew."

Kara began to reply, but Hachiro cut her off.

"No," he said. "That's not true. I've been wondering that for quite a while."

Four feet separated them, but without taking a step, she felt that the space between them had vanished. The sun felt warm on her face and she could smell the detergent her father used to wash her sweater.

Hachiro might really be as good a guy as she'd hoped.

"Can I ask you something?" Kara said.

"Of course."

"Sakura thinks her sister is haunting Ume and the others. She and Miho think that Ume knows who killed Akane. But when I ask them why they think that, they won't tell me anything else. So what is it? Why would they think that?"

Hachiro didn't look away, and she was grateful for that. But he cocked his head and regarded her a moment as though sizing her up anew, seeing more deeply into her than he had before.

"Maybe we should start back," he said. "We could get something to eat."

"Does that mean you're not going to answer me either?"

"No. It just means that we're halfway across the bay, and I'm getting hungry."

Kara smiled. "All right."

They turned together and started back along the sand and she switched her shoes to her right hand. The water lapped against the shore, but otherwise the world had become eerily silent. The boats out on the bay seemed very far away.

"Last year, Jiro was Ume's boyfriend. That's why I know

her and her friends a little better than other people. They wouldn't have paid any attention to me except that Jiro and I are . . . were friends."

He paused, and she could feel a wave of grief emanating from him. Kara wanted to make his sadness go away but didn't know how to begin.

"Akane, though . . . she was beautiful, and always seemed to be lost inside her head. Something about her was just different, and fragile. For months, she and Jiro were best friends, and Ume hated her for it. And then Jiro did something stupid."

Kara's stomach gave a little twist. "What?"

Hachiro didn't look at her. They kept walking. "He told Akane that he loved her."

"And Ume found out?"

Now he stopped and turned, and his eyes were dark. "I don't know. She might have."

Kara pushed her hair away from her face, that sick feeling spreading.

"What did Akane say? To Jiro, I mean, when he told her he was in love with her?"

Hachiro sighed. "What you'd expect. That she loved him as a friend. The worst thing a girl can ever say to a guy."

Kara took that in. "Do you think Jiro would have hurt her?"

"Jiro's dead. And I don't care who wants to say it might be suicide. He wouldn't have killed himself. To some people it might look like he did kill Akane, and did it out of guilt, but I know—"

"I believe you," Kara interrupted. She didn't want to tell him about the conversation she'd overheard between her father and Miss Aritomo—that would feel like a betrayal of trust—but she couldn't just say nothing.

"You do?" Hachiro asked, surprised.

"I do."

"Good. So Jiro didn't kill Akane, and then someone killed him."

"So do you think Ume could have done it?"

Hachiro gave a curt shake of his head. "No. I can't imagine it. The police talked to everyone, and they think it was random. Someone walking by the bay that night attacked her."

"But they never arrested anyone."

"They never had any suspects that I know of. No witnesses. I don't think they knew where to start. Anyway, Ume's not strong enough to have hurt Jiro, and I have to think whoever killed Akane also killed Jiro. Otherwise, there are two killers out there, and that's pretty hard to believe."

Kara nodded, but she didn't know what to think. Ume and her friends might not be haunted by a ghost, but their nightmares wouldn't let them sleep. Hana had killed herself. And Ume had enough guilt to accuse Sakura of drugging or poisoning her.

Tonight, she would be spending the night at the dorm, in Miho and Sakura's room. The school allowed boarding students to host day students for sleepovers on the weekends before or after a holiday. This weekend didn't qualify, but her father had called the dorm director Friday afternoon to ask if, under the circumstances, the rule might be bent. It would be good for the students to be able to share their feelings about the tragedies of the past two weeks, he'd said.

The dorm director had agreed, earning Kara's father many hugs.

As odd as Sakura had been behaving, Kara had been a little unsure about how much she was looking forward to the overnight. Now her anxiety began to build. She didn't want to take Ambien tonight, and she knew bad dreams would plague her. Psychology wasn't the culprit here, she felt sure. How long would it be, she wondered, before someone else fell apart to the extent that Hana had?

"Is this why you asked me to come out with you today?" Hachiro asked, a look of badly disguised disappointment on his face.

"No," Kara assured him. "It isn't. I just thought it would be nice to take a walk. We both needed to clear our heads. I'm sorry I got us onto such unpleasant topics."

"That's all right," Hachiro said. "It would be impossible to pretend we're not thinking about them."

"Exactly. Anyway, on to happier thoughts. You mentioned lunch?"

His eyes lit up. Hachiro was still a growing boy, and he needed to be fed. And Kara found that she was getting pretty hungry as well.

They walked along the shore of Ama-no-Hashidate, headed back to the Turning Bridge. Several times, Kara thought Hachiro would take her hand, but he never did.

"There is one other thing that's kind of troubling me," Hachiro said.

"What's that?"

"Earlier, you mentioned the nightmares that everyone's having, how you can't sleep?"

"Yeah?"

Hachiro didn't look at her. "Jiro was having them, too. He talked about his nightmares all the time. Akane was in some of them. He said she had no face."

10

卍

Blue light washed over Kara's face. She breathed deeply, feeling the rise and fall of her own chest, vaguely aware of her surroundings. Then some tiny internal alarm sounded and she opened her eyes wide.

Sakura had a small book light on, and she lay in her bed reading a manga. Miho stood by the DVD player, putting a disc back in its case. The movie had ended.

"How much did I miss?" Kara murmured, pushing herself up to a sitting position on the futon the girls had set out for her.

Sakura looked up from her manga, her short blade of hair a kind of curtain obscuring one eye. "Most of *Kiki's Delivery Service* and all of *Nausicaa*."

Kara scowled at her. "No way. I saw most of *Kiki*. And you didn't . . ." She looked around for a clock and instead stared at Miho. "Tell me you didn't really watch *Nausicaa*."

Miho tried to keep a serious face, which must have been difficult enough in her flannel Hello Kitty pajamas. But the girl was a terrible liar. She smirked.

"No. *Kiki* just ended. So much for our Miyazaki marathon."

"We got through two movies," Sakura said. "Tonight, that's a marathon."

They'd wanted to watch movies tonight, just to clear their minds, and had agreed on nothing violent. All three of them loved the films of Miyazaki, who had become perhaps the most successful director in Japan while making only animated films. Kara had vetoed *Howl's Moving Castle* because she'd seen it too recently, and they had all seen *My Neighbor Totoro* far too many times, so they had started with *Spirited Away*.

In truth, Kara had exaggerated for how much of *Kiki's Delivery Service* she'd been awake. She had to have missed at least the last half hour. But the upside was that in that time, nothing unpleasant had visited her dreams.

"We are such party girls," she said.

Miho nodded in mock seriousness. "We are troublesome. All the drugs and sex. We're bound to end up in jail."

"Or dead by eighteen," Sakura muttered with her usual sarcasm.

Kara and Miho blinked at each other. Another time, that might have been funny. But not now.

"Oh, shit, I'm sorry," Sakura said, looking up. She set the manga on her bed, a stricken expression on her face. "I can't believe I just said that."

"You didn't mean it like that," Kara said.

Sakura smiled, grateful for the instant forgiveness. Laughter came through the walls from the room next door. Kara returned the smile.

"Thanks for letting me sleep over."

Miho slid the DVD onto a shelf. "Thanks for coming. We'll do it again, too. Sometime when there aren't clouds hanging over our heads."

That made all of their smiles falter.

"Time for lights out, you think?" Sakura asked. "Or should we put something else on? Maybe something with cute American boys to send Miho off to dreamland."

"I think I'm too tired," Miho said. "But I can sleep through anything, so I don't mind if you two want to put on something else."

Kara looked at Sakura. There were dark circles under her eyes and a wildness in them that seemed different from the rebellious nature she'd recognized the first time they'd met. Sakura smiled thinly, and an understanding passed between her and Kara—neither of them expected to sleep well tonight. Yet Sakura almost seemed eager.

"It's all right. We'll have all day tomorrow," Sakura said. "Let's go to sleep."

"Should I turn out the lights, then?" Miho asked.

Kara looked at Sakura again, and then nodded. "Sure."

And then they lay in the dark. The girls slept with a window open, and the night air crept across the floor, making Kara nestle under the blanket they'd given her.

She'd fallen asleep during the movie, but now she couldn't

even close her eyes. In the darkness, she stared up at the ceiling. She had told the girls about her walk with Hachiro but had been waiting for the right moment to broach the subject of their conversation. The moment had never come, unfortunately, and now—even though Sakura and Miho had both avoided talking about Hana or Jiro or Akane or even Ume—Kara couldn't go to sleep with her questions unanswered.

"Jiro was having the dreams, too."

"What?" Miho asked, turning on her side.

Sakura raised her head from the pillow, her brass-colored eyes gleaming in the dark, hair spikier and wilder than ever. "What dreams?"

Kara searched for her eyes in the dark. "Hachiro told me Jiro had nightmares about Akane, but in them, Akane had no face."

Sakura flinched and glanced at Miho.

"I've had dreams like that, too," Kara went on. "Girls with no faces. And Akane coming up out of the bay," she said, relieved to be speaking the words aloud. "And one night, I was down at the water, near the . . . the shrine people made for her, and I saw this cat."

As she told the story of watching the cat walk over the shrine and drop dead, only to stand up again a moment later like nothing had happened, she watched both girls' eyes widen.

"Akane," Sakura whispered. "I told you guys."

Sakura seemed almost pleased, and the thought made Kara shiver.

Miho stared at her, then turned to Kara. "It might just

have stumbled. It might have laid down. I know I wasn't there, but if it got up again, Kara, it wasn't dead. I've been trying to tell Sakura that Akane's not haunting anybody, and that story doesn't help. Anyway, I haven't had any dreams like that."

"I know," Kara told her. "But Sakura has."

Sakura hesitated but finally nodded. "Ever since school began," she confessed. "And they keep getting worse. When I wake up, I'm not just afraid, I'm angry, and all I can think about is Akane, and missing her and grieving for her starts all over. Every night."

Miho shot her a look of heartbreaking sympathy. "I'm so sorry."

"But why am I having them?" Kara asked. "I wasn't even here."

"I don't know," Sakura said. "Maybe because of that night with the cat. But I do know why Ume is having them."

Kara didn't have to ask. Sakura had made it clear that she suspected Ume knew more about Akane's death than she was telling.

"Do you really think your sister is haunting us?" Kara asked, thinking of all of the no-face girls in her dreams and the terror she felt when she awoke from them.

"Not just haunting."

Miho stared at her. "No, Sakura."

Kara turned to Miho. Suddenly she looked far too old to be wearing Hello Kitty pajamas. " 'No' what? You think Akane's doing more than haunting?"

Miho exhaled, seeming to deflate into surrender. "Sakura

thinks it is Akane's spirit, taking revenge. She thinks a ghost killed Jiro and drove Hana off the roof."

Kara stared at her, then looked at Sakura again. "I'm sorry. Dreams or no dreams, I can't believe that. I don't believe in ghosts."

Sakura laughed. "You're in the wrong country, then. Japan is full of all sorts of ghosts."

"I don't mean to be cold, but Akane can't come back and take revenge. She can't come back at all. She's dead, Sakura. Dead and gone," Kara said, wondering at the emphasis in her own voice, and at the fear.

Sakura lay her head back on the pillow, staring up, and from that angle Kara could no longer see her eyes.

"Then how do you explain all of this?" Sakura asked.

"I can't," Kara replied.

"That's right. You can't."

Kara still had questions, but the conversation clearly seemed over. The other girls lay in the dark, not speaking, waiting for sleep to arrive. While Kara felt trepidation at the thought, she realized now that, nightmares or not, Sakura looked forward to her bad dreams, for in them, however briefly, she could be reunited with her sister.

Within just a few minutes, she heard Sakura's breathing deepen and the slow rhythm of sleep overtaking her. Perhaps ten minutes passed, and then she glanced at Miho, who lay on her side with her eyes closed and seemed also to have fallen asleep easily.

How they could simply shut off the conversation and not

want to talk it over, try to figure out what was really going on, Kara did not understand. Perhaps they were simply afraid and in denial.

Kara frowned, noticing an odd, sweet smell in the room. A flower smell. It took her a moment to place it—cherry blossoms.

The scent grew quickly until it was almost overpowering, like hugging an old aunt who wore far too much perfume. She glanced around to see from where the odor might have come. In the dark, gleaming with moonlight, the Noh masks on the walls were hideous and unsettling. Kara felt like they were watching her, laughing at her. She rolled onto her side, turning toward Miho . . .

. . . who lay in bed, not asleep after all. Her eyes were open and her breath came in quick sips. She stared, face contorted with such fear that Kara gasped, chilled, heartbeat quickening. Her skin prickled with terror and she didn't want to turn, did not want to see what had so frightened Miho.

But she forced herself to look.

The cat sat just inside the open window, on the wide sill, its copper and red fur raised in hackles.

It hissed, long and slow, and it watched them with human eyes. After that first night, by Akane's shrine, Kara had told herself she had imagined those eyes . . . the dark eyes of a girl . . . eyes that reminded her of Sakura's.

"Do you," Kara managed, her voice ragged. "Do you see it?"

Miho did not reply, and when Kara looked at her and saw tears glistening on the girl's face, she knew it had been the stupidest question she had ever asked.

The cat arched its back. It hissed again, jaws opening wide to reveal fangs like a serpent's, long and yellow and glistening wet, as though with venom.

Miho screamed.

Kara joined her, as though she had needed that confirmation of her terror, that permission to lose control.

They scrambled from beneath sheets and blankets and clung to each other, moving toward the door.

"Sakura!" Miho screamed. "Sakura, wake up!"

Startled by their screams, Miho's roommate nearly fell out of bed. But when Kara looked back to the open window, only the moonlight remained.

"What happened?" Sakura demanded.

"You saw it," Kara whispered to Miho, holding the girl's hands in her own, the two of them huddling together. "You saw it, right?"

Miho nodded. "Yes. The eyes. Oh, the eyes."

Kara looked to the window again. The cat had really been there, and now it had gone.

But to where?

Something woke her.

Kara opened her eyes and inhaled sharply, as though surfacing from deep water or a nightmare. Yet she couldn't remember any dreams at all. The events of that night had been terrifying enough.

Shifting slightly on the futon the girls had put out for her on the floor, she looked out the window. Morning still only hinted around the edges of the sky, just beginning to glimmer with the onset of dawn. The smell of cherry blossoms had vanished from the room, but her memory of that powerful scent lingered.

Drawing the blanket tighter around her, she closed her eyes but soon discovered that sleep would not be quick to return. Early or not, she felt entirely awake.

With a sigh, she opened her eyes again, and then remembered the impression she'd had a moment ago that something had woken her. Kara lay there and listened to her surroundings. Miho snored lightly but Sakura slept in silence, so much that Kara had to turn and watch her a moment to make sure she hadn't stopped breathing. It took a moment before she confirmed the rise and fall of her chest.

As the sun rose, a gray-blue hue spreading across the sky, the wind picked up. She could hear it rushing by outside, but the windows did not rattle. The old dormitory building creaked a little, but she heard nothing that could have stirred her, not even footsteps padding down the hall outside on the way to the bathroom.

Listening to the gentle sounds of the morning, she felt her eyelids growing heavy again and let them close. Even if she couldn't fall back to sleep, she wasn't ready to get up yet, and she didn't want to wake her friends.

Her body rocked back and forth. Kara felt herself swaying. The motion entered her subconscious and she dreamed herself in a small boat atop undulating water, the rolling waves tilting her side to side.

Kara.

The sea became rougher.

"Kara."

She moaned, the boat and the waves vanishing. Vaguely aware of some reality intruding upon her peace, of hands shaking her, she curled in upon herself, limply batting at the offending grasp.

"Kara, wake up!"

Her body felt heavy and cramped, so tired, but she forced herself to open her eyes. Squinting against the sunlight that washed into the dorm room—and how did it get so bright?—she glanced up to see Miho bent over her, a stricken expression on her face. Without her glasses, she looked almost like a stranger.

In the back of her mind, she felt a spark of worry. What had upset Miho so much? But she still felt tired and sluggish and closed her eyes again.

"What time is it?" she asked.

"It doesn't matter. Just wake up," Miho said.

The urgency in her voice finally made Kara throw off the gauzy blanket that sleep had wrapped around her brain. She blinked rapidly and looked at the window again. Last time she'd awoken, it had barely been dawn. From the look of the sky, hours had passed.

It took her a moment to realize that she and Miho were alone in the room. Sakura had gone.

"What's happening?" she asked.

Miho bit her lip, tucked a stray lock of her silky hair behind one ear, and shook her head. "I don't know," she said. And then, in English: "Something bad. Something really bad."

Footfalls raced past the room out in the corridor. Down the hall, someone shouted. Kara sat up and saw that the door stood open a few inches. Voices came to them from elsewhere on the floor, too many speaking for her to make out many specifics, but she heard something about a doctor and an ambulance.

And she heard weeping. Sobbing.

Two girls hurried past the door, whispering to each other.

"Miho, tell me," Kara said, rising to her feet and reaching for her jeans. She slid them on and zipped them, then went to the door, but Miho didn't follow.

"Chouku is dead."

Kara caught her breath. Chouku was one of the girls on this floor—one of the soccer girls. The police could say all they wanted now about suicide or about how none of these things were related, and the school administration could try to pretend nothing really was wrong in order to save face, but nobody would believe that now.

"Is it murder?" she asked, her voice soft, cracking on the last word.

Miho nodded, gesturing toward the door. "Sakura is out there. I don't want to see it again."

From somewhere in the distance, beyond the walls of the dormitory, Kara could hear the high-pitched keening of an ambulance siren. She hesitated a moment, looking at the shattered Miho, and wondered what would become of her friends. Would this, at last, force Miho and Sakura's parents to pay attention to them? To come and see their daughters, and maybe take them home? Selfishly, she feared such an outcome. But for their sake, she hoped so. Sakura had been crumbling for days, brittle from lack of sleep and her lingering grief over Akane. And now Miho seemed frayed to the point of breaking.

Kara pushed her hands through her blond hair, snatched a rubber band from Sakura's desk, and tied her hair back in a ponytail. She pushed the door open and stepped out into the corridor.

Most of the doors on the floor were open, girls in pajamas and nightgowns standing, framed in their horror, looking further along the hall toward a cluster of students crowding outside a door four rooms down. Girls wept, some with their hands over their mouths. Others whispered to one another. One girl—Chouku's roommate, Kara figured—sat on the tile floor, long legs drawn up beneath her. The sobbing Kara had heard before came from her. A statuesque, athletic-looking girl, she was only vaguely familiar to Kara. They did not share class or an after-school club, so she would only have seen her in the morning or during o-soji.

Another girl sat cross-legged in the corridor in front of her, holding the weeping girl's hand in her own. Perhaps because she wore purple pajamas with butterflies on them and sat hunched over, hair falling across her face, it took Kara a moment to realize this was Ume.

Further along the hallway, at the top of the stairs, Sakura leaned against a balustrade and watched all of the shock, horror, and sorrow unfold. She had no tears and no fear. *No, for her there's only satisfaction,* Kara thought.

She shivered, horrified at herself for even considering such a thing. And then she wondered why the thought had come to her, and if it had arisen because that truly was what she saw in Sakura's face. Not for a moment did Kara believe Sakura wanted anyone to die, but the girl wouldn't mourn, either.

Unseen, or at the least ignored, Kara made her way down the hall past the pale, drawn residents of the dorm until she came to Chouku's room. Ume and Chouku's roommate didn't even look up at her.

"They're all over her," a voice said from inside the room, frantic and on edge. "Yes, everywhere. And I think she's like the other one. So pale."

Kara entered the room.

The only person alive in that small chamber was Miss Aritomo, the art teacher. She faced the window, her back to Kara, her cell phone clapped to her ear, and at first she didn't notice that anyone had entered.

Chouku lay on her stomach on the bed, a sheet covering her up to her shoulders. Spots and streaks of blood marred the white sheet, but Kara saw no other sign of blood anywhere in the room. The girl lay totally inert and her flesh was a bluish-gray, verging on white, almost as though she—like Jiro—had been dredged up from the water. Yet she had died here, in this room, and only last night. For her to have gotten so pale, so quickly . . . there had to be another explanation.

I think she's like the other one, Miss Aritomo had said.

Which made Kara think of the conversation she'd overheard between the art teacher and her father, about Jiro's body being drained of blood.

"I don't know what kind of animal, but I'm telling you,

they look like bites to me," Miss Aritomo said firmly to whoever listened on the other end of her phone call.

The teacher reached over, back still to Kara, and lifted the
sheet, providing a quick glimpse of Chouku's naked corpse. All
over her body, from heel to calf to back to throat, there were
hundreds of tiny punctures, arranged in half circles like the
bite marks of a small animal. She had to have been bitten dozens of times, and yet the only blood in the room was smears
on her pale flesh and spots on the white sheet.

Kara gasped.

Miss Aritomo turned, lowering the sheet, and her face
grew stormy with anger.

"What are you doing? Get out of here!" she snapped.

Kara backed up quickly, bumping into the door frame,
and stepped into the hall.

"And close the door behind you!" Miss Aritomo said.

Kara pulled it closed, glancing around to see that all of
the girls in the corridor were staring at her now, including
Ume and Chouku's roommate.

"Sick freak," Ume said, in clear English, her lip turning up
in disgust. "What does she want from us?"

Kara stared, confused, and then realized Ume wasn't
talking about her. Slowly, she looked up. Sakura still stood by
the stairs, arms crossed in defiance now, and she met Kara's
gaze with her own.

Burdened by the weight of the other girls' attention, Kara
focused straight ahead. She walked over to Sakura and bent
to whisper in her ear.

"Can we go back into your room? We have to talk."

Sakura narrowed her eyes and gave Kara a cautious look, as if trying to decide yet again whether she could be trusted.

Kara rolled her eyes. "Just come on."

She turned and started back along the corridor, weaving through the gaggle of grieving, horrified girls. Sakura followed, and when she passed outside Chouku's room, Ume spit on the floor by her feet. Surprisingly, Sakura made no attempt to retaliate or even speak to her.

Miho had shut the door, forcing Kara to knock.

"Who is it?"

"It's *us*."

The door opened quickly. Kara led Sakura into the room and Miho shut the door again behind them. Miho leaned against the door, arms crossed protectively over her chest, and chewed her lower lip expectantly. Sakura went to gaze out the window for a moment, perhaps listening to the escalating volume of the siren from the approaching ambulance, and then flopped onto her bed. Her eyes were unfocused, gazing at some bit of nothing in the middle of the room.

Seconds of awkward silence ticked away with Kara standing roughly between the roommates.

"You both saw her?" she asked.

Miho nodded and glanced away. She wiped at one eye and Kara thought her lip might have quivered.

"Not much to see," Sakura said.

"You're wrong," Kara told her.

She described what she had seen when Miss Aritomo lifted the sheet, and the conversation she had overheard between the art teacher and her father.

"The only blood I saw was on the sheet," Miho said.

Kara threw up her hands. "That's what I'm saying. Miss Aritomo was even saying something on the phone about how it reminded her of 'the other one.'"

Sakura frowned, staring at her. "What 'other one'?"

"You're not making sense," Miho said.

"I can't believe I forgot to tell you about this. There never seemed to be a right time, and then last night I didn't remember, and I've been so damn tired that—"

"Tell us what?" Sakura prodded. "Speak!"

Kara took a breath. "The other day I sort of accidentally eavesdropped on my father and Miss Aritomo. I kind of thought it was a romantic thing and I didn't want to interrupt them—that would be weird—but then they started talking about Jiro and the investigation into his death, and . . ." She shuddered with revulsion. "All the blood had been drained from his body."

"That's not funny," Miho said.

"I'm not trying to be funny. I'm completely serious. So, just now, when she said Chouku's body reminded her of 'the other one,' she had to be talking about Jiro. This isn't a nightmare. This is real. Maybe there's a"—she tried to find the Japanese word for *rational* in her memory but couldn't—"maybe there's an explanation for this that will make me feel ridiculous later for how much this is scaring me. But I can't imagine what it could be."

Sakura sat up, perching on the edge of the bed, elbows on her knees, and stared at Kara. "What are you suggesting?"

"Come on! The nightmares. The bite marks all over

165

Chouku. She and Jiro both drained of blood. Haven't either of you ever seen a vampire movie?"

In the silence that followed those words, Kara felt her face flushing with heat and knew how pink her cheeks must be. If she'd been in a joking mood, she'd have made a little cricket noise. But she had run out of jokes.

Miho spoke first.

"You're serious," she said, as though suggesting the impossible.

"Totally!" Kara replied. She hated the way they were looking at her, but she wasn't about to back down. "You didn't see the bites all over her body. Fine. But what's happening here is . . . it's not natural. You can't deny that. The dreams alone are proof of that. All of us having these dreams, not being able to sleep, the terrible things in our nightmares? That crap is just not normal."

"We're not all having the nightmares," Miho said quietly.

Kara snapped, "Yes, I know. You don't have them. Good for you!"

The girl blinked, obviously stung, and Kara felt guilty—but not so much that she was prepared to drop it.

"Miho, you saw the cat last night. You admitted it to me."

"What cat?" Sakura asked.

Kara and Miho studied each other, each waiting for the other to explain.

"There's no such thing as vampires," Sakura said.

Kara shot her a dark look. "Are you serious? In this country, people still believe in everything. There are ancient prayer shrines all over the place. People still respect the old gods, even if they don't pray to them anymore. The Japanese take their legends very seriously."

"There are no vampires in Japanese legend," Miho said. "Not in myth, not in Kabuki, not in Noh theater."

Kara sighed and turned toward the window. The ambulance siren had ceased, which meant the EMTs would be in the building by now, on their way up to Chouku's room.

"Fine," she said with a shake of her head. "Then you tell me what's going on."

"I've told you both," Sakura said, her voice even and emotionless. It scared Kara how detached she'd grown. Grief had forced her to shut down.

"It's Akane," she went on. "The police never did anything to punish her killers. They could never prove anything. She's come back to make them pay."

Kara studied her eyes. "You can't really believe that. I'm sorry, Sakura—really sorry—but Akane is *dead*."

"I never said she wasn't," Sakura said. Then she stood and went to the door. Miho moved out of the way. Sakura looked back at them. "I've been studying them, trying to figure out who else was involved. I think the ones who are crying the most are probably the other killers, or at least they were there. Chouku's friends. Ume's friends. I'm going to go and watch them, to see if I can narrow it down."

With that, she went out into the hall and left the two of them standing there, staring at the open door.

Miho closed it quietly and turned to look at Kara with frightened eyes.

"She's really scaring me," Miho said.

Kara nodded. "Me too."

Miho took a deep breath and let it out. She bit her lip, shook her head, clearly struggling to make sense of her thoughts.

"What?" Kara urged.

"I said there were no vampire legends. But there *are* stories about other things . . . things that are *like* vampires," Miho said. "One of them, the *ketsuki,* appears in the form of a cat."

11

卍

I don't know the whole legend of the ketsuki," Miho went on. "It's some kind of demon spirit, I think. There's an old Noh play about it. But from what I remember, it takes the form of a cat and it drinks blood."

Kara couldn't breathe, staring at her. The memory of the bite marks all over Chouku's naked body remained vivid in her mind, but somehow even worse was the memory of the cat standing in the open third-story window the night before. Her skin prickled.

"You saw it last night," Kara said. "Where could it have gone? The door was locked."

Miho rubbed the back of her neck, head bowed, hair spilling around her face like she wanted to hide but had nowhere to run. "The window was open, though."

"Oh, Jesus," Kara whispered, walking over to the window.

She searched the sill for any sign that what they'd seen had been real—a few shed hairs, some paw prints—but found nothing. Still, they had *both* seen it. "If you saw it, too, then it couldn't be a dream."

A long silence ensued, the girls lost in their thoughts, until their reverie was broken by a knock on the door.

Miho shot a quick, frightened look at Kara. But it was morning, and there were so many people around—if all of this wasn't their imaginations running wild, some kind of evil cat spirit wasn't about to come knocking on the door.

Kara nodded to her. Miho took a breath and opened the door.

Rob Harper stood on the other side, worry lining his face. When he spotted Kara, he let out a relieved breath and walked in, snatching her up in his arms. She hadn't been picked up in a long time and it felt simultaneously wonderful and humiliating.

"Dad, I'm okay," she said.

He gave a soft chuckle and put her down, the relief draining from his face, replaced by a deep frown.

"When Miss Aritomo called, I had all kinds of awful thoughts," he said in English. "But then she said she'd seen you. I came right away."

"So it was you she was talking to before?"

Her father nodded. "When you came into the . . . into the dead girl's room? Yes. I wish you hadn't seen that."

Kara sighed. "Me too."

They'd been speaking English, but now her father looked

over at Miho. "I'm sorry," he said in Japanese. "I didn't mean to ignore you. I was just—"

"I understand, sensei," Miho said, executing a polite bow.

Kara's father had completely forgotten such formalities, but now he returned the bow. Then he looked at his daughter.

"The police are here. They want to talk to everyone—"

"They can't claim this one is a suicide," Kara said, also in Japanese, not wanting to be rude to Miho, though a flash of anger sparked in her.

"No, they can't," Rob Harper agreed. "I spoke to them, gave them our information, so if they want to talk to you later, they can come find you at home. Right now, I'm taking you out of here."

Kara hesitated, glancing at Miho.

"I'll be fine," Miho said. "Sakura will be back soon."

But Kara wasn't worried about Miho talking to police. She was worried about later, when night fell again. Sakura had gone over the edge with her obsession and her grief, and she had been having the nightmares, just like all of the dead kids. Maybe Miho was safe because she hadn't had the dreams, but maybe not. What the hell did any of them really know about the demon that preyed on Monju-no-Chie School?

Demon? Kara thought. *Seriously?*

But she found that she *was* serious. The word had sounded faintly ridiculous when Miho had spoken it out loud, but in Kara's head it sounded all too real and plausible. Her nightmares had leaked out into reality, or at least that was how it felt. The cat had been real. It had been there, looking at them, perhaps trying to choose its next victim. For some reason it had moved on to another room, another girl.

How close did we come to dying? Kara pictured Sakura's body sprawled facedown with all of those bite marks on her flesh and felt panic rising. She thought of claws in her own skin, teeth puncturing her.

"Stay at our house tonight," she said to Miho.

Her father shot her a curious, confused look. But Kara pressed on.

"You and Sakura should stay with us tonight," she said. "It isn't safe in the dorm, Miho. We were lucky last night. It could have been any of us."

But maybe not you. Why not you? Why don't you have nightmares? Kara thought Sakura's certainty that it was her dead sister Akane back from the dead to take revenge was crazy. But she'd already established a connection between everyone who had been plagued by nightmares and all of those who had died. If Ume really had killed Akane, and her friends had helped—or at least known about it—then they were being targeted. Jiro had been indirectly responsible because he'd spurned Ume and fallen in love with Akane. And Sakura might be visited by the dreams because she was Akane's sister.

Which explained why Miho didn't have the nightmares.

But it didn't explain why Kara *did* have them.

"Dad," Kara said, "just one night. I don't want to leave them here."

"What about the rest of the students?" her father asked.

Kara tried a smile but knew it must look broken and desperate. "We can't fit them all in our house."

Her father relented. "If Mr. Yamato doesn't object, it's fine with me. I'll find out."

She hugged him and kissed his stubbly, unshaven cheek. He must have thrown on his clothes after Miss Aritomo called, no shower, no shave. But he'd never looked better as far as his daughter was concerned. Her dad had come to the rescue.

Miho and Mr. Harper bowed to each other again.

"I'll call you later," Kara told her. The girls shared a short embrace.

"I'll see if I can find that Noh play," Miho said.

Kara nodded. "Good."

Her father led her out of the room. In the corridor, some of the girls had retreated into their rooms, though most of the doors were open at least a fraction. Police and EMTs crowded the third floor, along with teachers and several school administrators. Ume had closed her door.

Kara followed her father to the landing, but voices from the common room off to her left drew her attention and she looked over to see Sakura seated in a wooden chair, being questioned by two policemen. The girl wore torn pajama pants and a T-shirt upon which she had painted some kind of calligraphic message. One of the cops stood, arms folded, glaring down at her and the other sat in a chair opposite Sakura, sleeves rolled up, leaning forward and speaking to her quietly. To Kara, they looked absurdly cliché, the living embodiment of every movie's good-cop/bad-cop routine. But if she'd been sitting in that chair, she suspected she'd have fallen for it completely. Under the intense gaze of the cross-armed detective, the kind tones of the other would have been welcome.

Sakura seemed unfazed. She sat rigidly, back straight, chin up, studiously ignoring them both. As Kara paused to stare into the room, Sakura spoke quietly, a perfunctory reply to one of the questions that Kara couldn't hear.

"Kara, come on," her father said, in curt Japanese.

Hearing this, the detectives both turned toward them. The intimidating one scowled, strode over, and shut the door with a bang.

"Kara," her father said, taking her by the arm.

"Dad, they don't really think Sakura could have killed Chouku, do they?"

"I couldn't begin to tell you what they think. I just know I need to get my daughter out of here and home safe."

His tone made her look up at his face. He brushed the hair away from Kara's eyes and cupped her cheek in his hand. She wanted to ask him what he meant by "home" but knew that was a conversation for later.

"All right. Let's go."

They started toward the top of the steps, only to be halted by Miss Aritomo, who came down the corridor after them. Kara assumed she'd been in Chouku's room talking to the police.

The dynamic chemistry between her father and the art teacher crackled in the air, an unmistakable energy. As Miss

Aritomo closed the distance between them, both of them wearing looks of profound concern, Kara had the impression they were about to embrace. But then Miss Aritomo brought herself up short.

"Harper-sensei, Yamato-san would like to speak with you for a moment before you leave," she said.

Kara felt her father hesitate; he glanced at her.

"Go ahead," she said.

"Are you sure? I really just want you to get home."

"I could go—"

"No. I want you with me," he interrupted. "Would you mind waiting just a few minutes? I promise I'll be right back."

"It's fine," Kara said. "But I don't want to stand around here. Can I wait out front?"

Her father frowned, weighing the request. But with so many cops and teachers going in and out of the building, there wasn't much chance of anything happening to her.

"Stay by the stairs," he said, then threaded back down the jammed corridor with Miss Aritomo.

The second floor buzzed with chattering students, some of whom were visibly upset, even weeping, but others who seemed only morbidly curious. A trio of boys stood on the steps, daring one another to go up. Kara passed them without meeting their eyes and hurried down to the lobby, longing for the sun's warmth and a breath of fresh air.

As she strode across the foyer, someone called her name and she turned to see Hachiro coming down the steps after her.

Kara waited for him. "Hi."

The sadness in his eyes broke her heart. He had known Chouku well, and his face showed all of his pain. Jiro had been his best friend, and now this. Today the sweetness that usually lit up his face had been replaced by a grim expression that made him seem far older.

"Hello, bonsai," he said, trying to keep a light tone between them.

Kara reached for his hand. "I told my father I would wait outside. And I feel so cold, I need the sun. Would you walk with me?"

Hachiro nodded, clutching her hand, and accompanied her, holding the door for her. When they stepped into the sun, Kara felt some of the tightness in her shoulders relax and the ice in her gut began to thaw.

Side by side, they looked out across the green field that separated the dorm from the school. Though the air was very chilly, the vivid blue sky spoke of another perfect spring day.

"I can't believe it," Hachiro said.

Kara looked at him, squeezing his hand. "It's true. I . . . I saw her."

Without warning, her hands began to tremble. She took a long, quavering breath and tried to say more, but no words would come. Hachiro looked at her, his eyes very old suddenly, and instead of asking the questions that he must have had, he took her into his arms and held her while she shook.

"Something awful is here," Kara whispered against his broad, strong chest. "Something evil. I know that sounds crazy—"

"No," Hachiro said flatly. "It doesn't. Not at all. I think you may be right."

On a huge wicker chair in the corner of her father's bedroom, Kara curled up and delved into the pages of *Sense and Sensibility*, desperate to lose herself. The era conjured by Jane Austen's writing had always been the most effective retreat from thoughts she wanted to avoid and emotions she hoped would go away. The words lulled her, wrapped her in cleverness and longing and the concerns of another age.

Her father had been back to the school twice that day and on the phone half a dozen times in between. Even now he was in his office with the door closed, and though she could hear the occasional muted tones from the other room, she could not make out any specifics.

When he came out of the office and down the hall, pausing to regard her from the open doorway to his bedroom, Kara kept reading to the end of the paragraph before she looked up. The real world—and the surreal world that had begun to intrude upon it—was not welcome. She tried to communicate that to him silently, to let him know that for just a while she wanted to pretend that nothing was wrong. But he was too preoccupied with the panic at school to notice her wordless pleading.

"The board of directors has closed the school until further notice," he said.

Kara held her page with a finger. "Good. I don't know if . . . I mean, hopefully they'll catch whoever did it. But it's all just too much now. They can't expect the students to be able to focus."

"I'd like to think that was part of the decision," her father said, "but I'm sure it was mostly pressure from the parents. The day students won't be coming in tomorrow, and a lot of the boarding students are going home, at least for now. Some parents have apparently already begun to take their children out of here."

"Already?" Kara said, glancing quickly at her clock. An hour or so to go before dinner. If Miho's or Sakura's parents came to get them, would they even stop to tell her they were leaving?

"People are afraid."

They have reason to be, she thought. *Or some of them do.*

"What about us? What are we going to do?" Kara asked, curious but grateful that she had her father. She could survive just about anything as long as he was around. Her mother's death had shattered her, but she still felt fortunate to have one parent who loved her instead of two living parents who barely remembered she was alive, like Sakura's and Miho's parents.

"I'm not sure yet. Tomorrow I'm going to talk to Mr. Yamato and find out how long he thinks the school will be closed. If it's more than a couple of days, I thought I'd take you down to Kyoto, get us both out of here for a while."

"That sounds nice."

But her father's eyes were troubled. "I don't want you over at the school after dark."

Kara frowned. "What about the other kids, the ones whose parents won't come for them right away?"

"The other kids aren't my daughter."

They both recognized how grim the conversation had become. Kara could see that her father wished he could take it back, or at least lighten his words with some humor.

"I didn't mean that as harsh as it sounded," he started.

Kara shook her head. "No, Dad. It's okay. You don't have to worry about whether or not I'll take all this seriously. I take it wicked seriously. I'm not going to be hanging around the school much, even during the day. At least not on my own."

This time, he really did smile.

"What?"

"You said 'wicked.' Speaking Japanese so much, it's been a while since I've heard that. Makes me a little homesick."

"Right now, what wouldn't make you homesick? But Harpers aren't the type to run away, are we? You always say that."

Her father came to crouch by the chair, one hand on her knee, locking her gaze with his own. "If it means keeping you safe, I'll run as fast and far as our legs can carry us."

Kara smiled and her father kissed her forehead before he rose and left the room. She dipped back into Jane Austen but had only read a couple of pages when she heard someone knocking at the front door.

"I've got it!" Kara called, unfolding herself from the wicker chair and hurrying out through the living room,

She opened the door to find Miho, alone, on the stoop. In black pants and a dark gray jacket, she seemed almost swallowed by the dark. She'd pulled her hair back into a hasty ponytail and carried a backpack, which Kara figured contained her pajamas and a change of clothes for tomorrow. Night had fallen, and Miho cast a nervous glance over her shoulder at the darkness behind her.

"Hey, where's Sakura?" Kara asked, switching back to Japanese.

Miho flinched, brows knitting, and Kara felt an immediate flush of guilt. The question had to have made it sound like she was less interested in Miho's presence than Sakura's absence.

"Sorry. Come in," she said, stepping aside. "I'm just worried about her, you know?"

"You should be," Miho said, entering the house and immediately removing her shoes, setting them by the door.

Professor Harper came out of his office, summoning up a welcoming smile. "Miho. I'm pleased you could make it."

The girl bowed stiffly. "I am honored to be invited, sensei," she said in English. "And I hope you will speak English with me. I would like more practice."

"You seem to be doing very well, but as you wish." Kara's father frowned and looked first at the shoes Miho had just left by the door and then at the door itself. "What happened to your roommate? You didn't walk here alone, did you?"

Miho gave a slight bow. "I did, sensei. Sakura is"—she paused to find the right phrasing—"not in the mood."

Kara started to ask for an elaboration, but Miho gave her a look that suggested she might want to hold off until they were alone. Her father waited a moment, but when it became plain their greetings were over, he put his hands up.

"Well, I wish you hadn't come by yourself after dark, but I'm glad to have you here. Why don't you girls go talk about boys or whatever it is you do while I make dinner?"

Miho blushed, but Kara laughed.

"Are you sure you don't want help, Dad?"

"No. Go ahead, honey."

With a look of quiet conspiracy, Kara and Miho went into Kara's bedroom. Any other time, what ensued would have been exactly as her father predicted, yet another conversation about boys. But Miho's obsession with American boys seemed to have waned in the shadow of murder and the terrifying notion that something inhuman might be lurking in the dark.

An awful feeling had been brewing inside Kara from the moment she opened the door to find Miho alone. As soon as she closed the door, she turned to the other girl.

"What's going on?"

"The police take Sakura . . . ," Miho began, then shook her head in frustration and switched once more to Japanese. "The police talked to her for over an hour, and then took her to Miyazu City, to the police station. They brought her back only a little while ago, and she won't talk to me about what happened there. I'm sure they must have accused her, but—"

"If they can't explain how Chouku died, they can't charge Sakura with anything," Kara interrupted.

"Exactly. And now she is acting so strangely."

Kara raised her eyebrows. "More strangely than this morning?"

"Yes. She barely spoke to me. She wanted the lights off in

our room and stood by the window, like she was waiting for something. I wish we hadn't told her about seeing the cat last night."

Kara thought about that. If Sakura really thought the cat was Akane, or had anything to do with her, it seemed all too plausible that she was waiting for her sister to come back.

"I was afraid to stay there tonight, but also afraid to leave her alone," Miho went on. "But then she told me I should go. It . . . hurt me. She's my best friend, Kara, and she doesn't want my help. It's as if some other girl who looks just like Sakura has moved in and is sleeping in her bed. She is so cold now."

Kara went to her window. The chill of the spring night made her shiver and she closed the window all but an inch or two. She stared out at the night. Off to the left, across the street, lights burned in a small house where there lived an old couple who always smiled when they saw her. It made her feel a little better knowing they were awake and alive in there, living their lives.

Which led her mind down a narrow lane to a hidden corner, where there lurked a terrible thought.

"What if it's just a cat?" she asked without turning.

"How could it be?" Miho said.

Now Kara did turn. She lifted her hands to her mouth and chewed on the tip of her left thumbnail, thinking. Then she dropped her hands.

"There's a little ledge out there. Not much, but I guess it could be possible that the thing came from another room, or another part of the building. I'm not sure I believe it, but let's just say that's all it is. If we're going to believe something crazy, wouldn't you rather believe that a cat could walk around out there than that there's something . . . that it isn't a cat at all?"

Miho stared at her, eyes hard behind her glasses. "I believe in ghosts, Kara. I always have. But I never even considered that there might really be evil spirits or demons or anything like that. I wish I'd never seen that cat. I wish I'd stayed asleep. I wish Chouku and the others were still alive. But let me ask you this, if that thing is just a cat, then who killed Chouku?"

Kara took a deep breath. She slid her hands into her pockets. "Well, it wasn't Akane."

Miho narrowed her eyes in sudden understanding. "You're saying you think the police are right?" she asked, face clouded with anger. "That Sakura—"

"No!" Kara said, hands becoming fists in her pockets. She shrugged her shoulders. "I don't really believe that. I mean, how would it be done, bleeding her like that, and with her roommate sleeping right there? And she'd have to have gotten out of *your* room without waking either of us, which we both know didn't happen. But the way Sakura's acting . . . look, you know you've considered it, too. I just thought one of us should say it out loud, just once."

Miho swallowed her anger, averting her eyes for a moment. The shy, giggly, boy-obsessed girl seemed someone else entirely now.

"All right. But let's not say it again."

"Deal."

Miho sat on the edge of Kara's bed. "There's more bad news. I'm going home."

Kara blinked. "Your parents are coming to get you?"

Miho nodded, forlorn. "In three days. My father can't get away from work until then."

Sadness and a bit of disgust tinged her voice. Other students had parents who were showing up tonight, and many more would be gone tomorrow. But with three students dead, at least one of them murdered, her parents couldn't make the trip for three days.

"Yeah, but they're coming," Kara said.

Miho glanced up in surprise. "You want me to go?"

"No way. I'm terrified. I want you here with me. But I'm happy that your parents are coming. What about Sakura's parents?"

Miho gave a slow shake of her head. "Out of the country. Sakura said the school hasn't even been able to reach them."

Kara sighed. "They're disgusting. Don't they care at all?"

"Maybe they don't."

The ugliness of the statement gave both girls pause, but then Kara sighed and flopped down on the bed beside Miho.

"I'm really glad you're here."

"Me too. It's strange to be in a teacher's house, though."

"When you're here, he's not a teacher, he's my father. Okay?"

"Okay."

Kara propped herself up on one elbow. "Well, we can't talk about this stuff all night. We need distractions. Why don't you let me fix your hair?"

Miho looked horrified. "Fix? What's wrong with my hair?"

"No, it's just an expression. Let me do something different with it. Just for fun. And after dinner, we can watch a movie. Something with explosions. Always a good distraction."

Miho touched her hair and gave her a doubtful look.

Kara got up and grabbed her hand. "Trust me."

A sound sweeps into Kara's bedroom on the chilly air, a tinkling noise like wind chimes, but there are no wind chimes hanging outside the little house.

The chimes become cries, and at first she thinks it is a baby, but then she knows the sound is adult. Sobs of grief, carried on the breeze, slipping through the gap between window and frame.

Her eyes flutter open. She shivers, so cold, and for a moment she only wants to burrow deeper under the covers, but the cries grow more plaintive, tugging at her heart.

Kara climbs out of bed, listing like a drunken sailor, feeling as though the thinnest sheet separates her from total wakefulness. She staggers to the window and peers out. The moon is limned with an icy white corona, as though it has frozen over. Its gleam illuminates a lonely figure, naked, seated on the ground with her legs drawn up to her chest, hugging her knees.

She knows that figure. Knows the knife-edge cut of her hair. Sakura.

Kara blinks. It feels like a dream, and yet her room is her room, just the same as always. In a dream, she knows, you're not supposed to be able to see your hands. But there's another kind . . . lucid dreaming, where you can control the outcome. If she can see her hands, either she's not really dreaming, or it's a lucid dream, and she can change things. She can be in control.

She tries to look down, but her body will not obey her mind.

She leans her forehead against the glass, squinting to get a better look out there, and the glass is cold and damp with condensation and solid against her skin. So real.

Sakura . . . if that is Sakura . . . weeps outside her window. Kara blinks. The little house where the sweet old people live is not there. Instead, her view is of the slope leading down to the bay. She can see the ancient prayer shrine and the modern shrine of anguish, the one created in Akane's memory. The place where she died.

Sakura rocks back and forth, hugging her knees against her chest. Is she cold?

Go out there, *Kara tells herself.* Hold her. Comfort her.

But fear skitters down her spine and her body flinches backward. She needs to pee. Needs to pee and then get back to bed. Needs to turn away from the window.

She knows that hair, though, and she knows it is Sakura out there on the bay shore, crying—there is something very wrong.

Sakura's back is to the window. And though Kara tries hard to will the girl to turn toward her, to give her a glimpse so she can know it really is Sakura, the girl does not turn.

The cries grow louder. Guilt squeezes Kara's heart. But fear closes her throat, and slowly, she begins to turn her head away.

She turns from the window, taking shallow breaths. Kara

closes her eyes and presses the heels of her hands against them. When she opens them again, she is staring at her bed.

Only then does she remember, in the shifting reality of dreams, that Miho is in her bed. The girl lays there, just at the edge of the bed, not wanting to take up more space than she requires. Her back is to Kara, and that gives Kara pause.

Another back. Another face she cannot see.

But she smiles, forcing the serpent of fright that twists in her gut to uncoil. For a moment, Miho's hair was straight, silken black. But now Kara blinks and sees the girl's hair is done in a thick braid, and laced through the braid is a bright red ribbon. Kara had spent over an hour working on it, and Miho had laughed and posed like a model in front of the mirror.

Miho.

The room feels fluid . . . liquid . . . and Kara wades through it, the edges of her perception melting as she climbs onto the bed.

"Miho," she says. Or thinks. Loudly.

She kneels on the bed and reaches for the girl.

Miho lolls toward her, tipping toward the weight Kara has added to the mattress like a corpse disturbed. Her head tilts, turns—

She has no face.

Kara jerks away, stumbles, and bangs her knee, and for a moment her vision clears. But then she glances up and sees the no-face girl, and in her bedroom there comes a soft, chuffing, insinuating laughter, like two girls sharing secrets, sweet and innocent and yet cruel all at the same time. And Kara opens her mouth to scream—

Only nothing comes out, and she knows why. She's been here before. Doesn't even have to reach up to feel the smooth skin covering the place her mouth ought to be. She has no mouth, no face, no scream. No voice.

Her heart races, searing its own scream into her. Her chest burns as she tries to find air.

She can only stare at the no-face girl, whose hair is braided with a red ribbon the way Miho's should be, and she wants to scream more than she has ever wanted anything in her life. Her whole body tenses, heaves, tries to scream, and her eyes burn with tears of frustration and terror.

In the moonlit shadows of her bedroom, she hears a cat begin to purr.

Kara runs, shaking, out into the short corridor.

The cats are black and white, ginger and gray, fat and starved. They sit on tables, on chairs, on tatami mats. One sits so still beside a lamp that it looks carved from wood. She wants her father, wants to go into his room and wake him, but three of them sit, barring his door.

As one, they follow her with their eyes as Kara weaves through the living room.

As one, they hiss.

As one, they begin to follow, stalking her.

Kara backs up to the front door, reaches behind her and finds the knob, fumbles it open, and then she is running.

Outside, the bay is gone. Her street has returned. The lights are off in the sweet old couple's home, and for a moment she wonders if they are dead.

On the sidewalk, the naked girl moans and sobs, her face still turned away. Kara's stomach churns. She moves to one side, takes three steps closer. Moves the other direction, trying to get a look at the girl's face, but cannot. The air seems to shift around her, obscuring her features, turning her at the last second, always only the back of her head.

The cats hiss, and again she hears the secret laughter of faceless girls, and she turns and sees that she's left the door to her house open. Figures move inside, and at first she thinks they are cats, but she blinks and they are dark silhouettes, tall figures with long, black hair, faces lost in darkness.

And then another laugh, just beside her, in her ear.

Kara squeezes her eyes shut. She doesn't see, but she knows—the girl she thought was Sakura is so close. She can feel the weight of her attention, knows that she has turned to look, and all Kara has to do to see her face is turn . . .

And suddenly it is the last thing, the worst thing, that she should ever do.

A soft purr in her ear. A laugh. A mewling hiss.

Pain stabs her palms and Kara looks down. In her fear she clutches her hands into fists so tight that her fingernails slice bloody crescents into the flesh of her palms.

Her hands.

She can see her hands.

No. I don't want to see, she thinks. But the presence is there, and then she feels something soft, a cat's tail, brush her leg.

A glimpse is enough. The jaws, open wide, the eyes glittering like flame, lithe and hunched, claws reaching for her.

She had no face, but now, at last, she screams . . .

. . . feels fur against her bare arms . . .

. . . feels claws puncture the skin of her back . . .

"Kara! Kara, stop!"

She felt herself shaking, felt the grip on her arms and then a light slap on her face.

Blinking rapidly, she drew a deep breath, as though she'd forgotten for a moment how to breathe. Kara found herself staring into her father's eyes and took a step back.

He let her go, but reluctantly. Miho stood beside him in her pajamas, shivering in the cold night air. They both stared at Kara, fear in their eyes. Or just concern. The three of them stood in the small yard in front of the house, pale in the moonlight.

"Dad?" Kara managed.

"Jesus, honey, you scared the crap out of me. You were breathing so fast, and you looked . . . you were having a nightmare. Sleepwalking and having a nightmare at the same time. You've never sleepwalked before. What if Miho hadn't woken me up?"

Kara stared at him. "I don't know." She still felt the tug of sleep. Of dreams. But she knew that wasn't the only thing pulling at her. She hadn't been sleepwalking. She'd been drawn out here in her dream. Lured with nightmare.

The night air hung heavy with the scent of cherry blossoms. Kara shuddered.

"I don't know," she repeated. Then she looked at Miho.

The braid remained in her hair, and the red ribbon, but her face was crinkled with concern. "Thank you."

Kara put as much feeling into those words as she could, wanted Miho to know she meant them.

Miho pointed at her hands. "You were hurting yourself."

Kara looked down, but even as she did, she knew what she would see. The night air stung her skin badly where her nails had dug crescent wounds into her palms.

"Dad," she said, looking up at him. "This isn't normal. There's something bad here. The place is poisoned somehow, and . . . there's this evil spirit . . ."

It sounded foolish when she said it aloud. Crazy. What did she expect her father to say?

He pulled her into his arms. "Sssh. I know it feels like it can't be real, honey, and I understand why it all feels wrong to you now, here. Seeing you like this, well, I guess I didn't realize just how much it was affecting you. I'll fix it. We'll figure it out, I swear. But you've been having nightmares for a long time, and now this, and I think what you really need more than anything else is real sleep. Do you think you want to take something to help you?"

By something, he meant Ambien. Kara was tempted by the thought of unbroken, dreamless sleep, but what had happened tonight had been more than just a nightmare, and it scared her to think about how vulnerable she would be if she took drugs to keep her asleep. Chouku hadn't been lured outside by nightmares. She'd been killed in her bed, in her own room.

"I'm okay, Dad. The nightmares never come twice in one night," she lied. "You're right, I think. I really just need sleep."

"All right, honey," her father said. "Just . . . I know it's hard, but try to get some sleep. We have a lot to talk about tomorrow." He looked at her, sensing that something remained unsaid, but when she did not elaborate, he kissed her on top of the head and escorted her back inside.

Kara locked her bedroom window while her father stood in the open doorway. As the two girls were climbing into bed again, he thanked Miho.

"I'm glad I was here," Miho said.

"So am I," Kara's father said.

When he left, the two girls looked at each other, sharing their fear without a single word, wide awake, unsure of what it all meant or what would come next.

12

卍

Monday morning, a light rain began to fall shortly after dawn, the sun struggling to peek through a thin layer of clouds. Miho had fallen asleep first, and might have gotten three hours of sleep after the sleepwalking incident. Kara had managed less than two—perhaps four hours total, separated by the most terrifying experience of her life.

By mid-morning, the rain slowed to barely a trickle, with shafts of sunlight reaching down through breaks in the clouds. It looked like the gloom would burn off, delivering another picturesque spring day on Miyazu Bay, perfect for the tourists visiting Ama-no-Hashidate. But it felt as though all of that existed in some parallel world now, a busy, happy reality blind to the dread and death that stalked the halls of Monju-no-Chie School.

"Dad, Miho wants to get back to the dorm. I'm going to

walk her, all right?" Kara asked, standing framed in his office doorway.

He looked at her, eyes narrowed. "Are you sure you want to go over there?"

Kara had shrugged. "There'll be plenty of people around. And I want to check on Sakura."

At his desk, Rob Harper stared at her, tapping a pen against his computer keyboard. "How do you feel? Did you get up again last night?"

His nerves were frayed. When she laughed, she knew she sounded frayed as well. There was no hiding it.

"Not as far as I know. If I did, I didn't go anywhere." But Kara knew she hadn't gotten up again. "And I'm okay," she went on. "Just really, really tired. If there's not going to be school, I think I'm going to try to sleep a little after lunch."

Miho came out of the bathroom then, lost in a hooded sweatshirt much too large for her. Kara's father glanced at Miho, then back at his daughter. "All right, go ahead. But unless you're coming back right away, after you go to the dorm, come by the school. I'm headed there shortly to help deal with the parents. There'll be a lot of activity later today with so many people coming to collect their kids."

Moments later, the girls were out the front door and walking briskly toward school, a silent but mutual urgency propelling them. Kara had brought her camera, but she uncapped it only once for a quick picture of the school in the distance, shafts of sunlight dappling the pagoda-style roof in splashes of golden light and gray storm shadow.

"Why did you bring that?" Miho asked in English.

Kara glanced at her. They'd spoken very little this morning, each keeping to her own thoughts. Kara's eyes burned with exhaustion and her head felt stuffed with cotton, the way she'd felt the one and only time she'd ever drunk enough beer to wake up with a hangover. And Miho might not have been suffering from nightmares, but she had to be exhausted this morning as well.

"When I'm upset or freaked out," Kara explained in English, "there are two things that make me feel better, taking pictures and playing guitar. I'm not some strolling troubadour, and I figured we didn't have time to hang out and sing Jack Johnson surf tunes. So, the camera."

Miho nodded slowly as they walked, listening, trying to take it all in. Her English was decent, but not as accomplished as Kara's Japanese. Miho didn't have a father who'd been teaching her a foreign language basically since birth.

"What does 'troubadour' mean?" she asked.

Kara smiled. She switched to Japanese. "Like a traveling musician."

Miho shot her a sharp look. "Don't do that," she said, resolutely sticking to English, irritable from sleeplessness. "Don't be so . . . Don't be . . ."

The girl grew frustrated, sighing because she could not find a word in English to express her feelings.

"Shit," Miho said.

Kara tried to hide her smile, and then laughed instead, raising a hand to hide her face. Miho shot her a fierce, withering look, entirely different from her usual shy, amiable demeanor.

"No, no," Kara said. "Okay, English. I'm not laughing at you. It was just . . . you don't have any problem learning English swear words."

Miho shrugged. "Profanity is useful and it makes you feel better. It's an . . . what is the word?" she said, throwing up her hands in frustration. "My brain is not working right today. Profanity is a very expressive part of any language."

The girls walked on another half a dozen steps in silence, and then Kara bumped Miho gently. "The word you wanted was 'condescending.' It means to treat someone like they're not as smart as you are, or something like that. And I'm sorry. I wasn't trying to be condescending. It's just easier to talk to you in Japanese."

Miho bumped her back, a little harder. "But I need to speak better English."

"Your English is freakin' amazing. You speak English better than most Americans."

"Really?"

"Really. No shit."

Miho smiled. "See? Profanity is useful."

"Oh, I can teach you all kinds of profanity you probably haven't heard yet."

"I would like that."

The drizzle had picked up a bit, and Kara snapped her camera case shut, keeping it close to her body. As she and Miho walked, they continued to bump each other every few steps.

Pretending they had nothing at all to fear.

As they stepped up onto the curb and then onto the lawn

in front of the school, Kara felt words coming up from deep within her, felt her mouth opening to ask a question to which she did not want an answer. She rubbed at her itchy eyes.

"Did you smell the cherry blossoms last night?" Kara asked.

"I was just thinking about that," Miho said, looking at her oddly. "I looked around this morning, but there are no cherry trees near your house."

"No. There aren't."

Kara expected Miho to pursue the point, to want to talk about what had caused the smell, but instead the other girl fell silent. But Kara couldn't bear silence right now.

"Did you see it, Miho? Last night, when I was outside?"

Miho glanced at her for a fraction of a second, obviously reluctant to meet her gaze. "I don't know."

Kara stopped. "What do you mean you don't know?"

Miho went on two steps further, then turned. Her gaze kept dropping, shifting from Kara to the ground and then up again.

"When I came out, for a moment I saw something," she said, then shifted into Japanese, pointing to Kara's camera. "If someone takes a photograph with a bright flash, sometimes it makes you blink, and there are colored lights that linger when you close your eyes. It was like that. I had only a glimpse of something that seemed only barely there, like I was looking out of the corner of my eye, but instead it was right in front of me. And as soon as your father yelled for you, I blinked and it was gone."

The two girls stared at each other. Kara had a hard time

catching her breath. The damp, gray day enveloped them. Sleep deprivation had made the whole world surreal and dreamlike to her, so that there on the grounds of Monju-no-Chie School, she felt as though she were no longer in the world she had always known.

"I saw it, for just a second. I came out of a nightmare, but I'm not sure I was ever really dreaming," she said, sticking to Japanese now, needing to be understood. Her voice was barely a whisper. Her father had put ointment on her palms last night but the little cuts still stung. She forced herself not to make fists of her hands. "Last night, as long as I stayed awake, I could still sort of picture it. But then I slept a little, and now all I have is the impression of it in my head, like the whole thing was a dream."

Miho hugged herself, looking like a tiny little girl in that voluminous sweatshirt. "It wasn't, though. It isn't a dream."

"No. It isn't."

"I'm sorry I snapped at you."

"That's okay," Kara said. "We both need a peaceful night's rest. We need to get away from here."

"What about Sakura?" Miho asked.

Kara pressed her lips together a moment. "I don't know," she said. "I don't think she'd want to leave."

Miho blanched, looking like she might be sick, but she didn't argue the point.

"Let's go talk to her," Kara went on.

When they started toward the school again, they walked a little faster. Several unfamiliar cars were in the lot to the left of the main school building. They went around, cutting across the field that separated the school from the dormitory. Other vehicles were parked beside the dorm where several mothers were gathered outside, and two boys were loading suitcases into car trunks.

Kara and Miho ignored everyone. A couple of boys tried to stop Miho to talk to her, but she brushed them off. Some of the doors were open on the corridor; the rooms were empty of students and any personal belongings. It was still early, but some parents had already come and gone, collecting their children. More boarders would depart over the next day or so. By tomorrow night, Kara had a feeling, the dorm would be empty except for a handful of kids, Miho and Sakura included. And then Miho would leave, and Sakura would be alone with her grief and obsession.

When Miho unlocked her door and pushed it open, they both saw Sakura sprawled, half-tangled in her sheets, un-moving. Kara gasped and from the visible jolt that went through Miho, she knew the other girl had made the same as-sumption.

But then Sakura moaned and stretched and rolled over. Her jagged, short hair stood up in tufts and wings. Bleary-eyed, she gave them a soft smile.

"Do you have to be so loud?"

"Sakura!" Miho said, hurrying toward her. "You scared me. For a second, I thought you were dead."

The smile drained from Sakura's face as she sat up, blan-ket around her waist. "That would be helpful. Then the police wouldn't think I had Chouku's blood on my hands."

"Oh, no," Miho said. "They don't, really."

Sakura nodded, rubbing her hands over her face. "Yeah. They do."

"But they talked to everyone," Kara said. "They asked me and Miho if you'd left the room during the night, and we told them no."

"How do you know?" Sakura asked bitterly.

Kara blinked. "What do you—?"

"You were sleeping," Sakura said. "You don't know if I left or not."

"We would've heard you," Miho argued.

Sakura gave a short, humorless laugh. "I'm sure the police were totally convinced by that argument."

She'd made a mess of the room, with dirty clothes strewn on the floor and piles of manga on Miho's bed. Now she seemed to notice the condition of the place.

"Sorry about this. I couldn't sleep, so I tried reading."

But Kara had stopped listening, stopped paying attention to her. The window stood wide open and the temperature in the room was a good fifteen degrees colder than out in the hall. She went over and closed the window tightly, locking it.

"Why are you so quiet?" Sakura asked.

Kara looked at her. "We need to talk."

"About what?"

"You know what," Kara said. She glanced at Miho, but the quieter girl only sat, waiting for her to speak. Miho and Sakura were best friends as well as roommates, but their dynamic had long since been established. Sakura was the wild one, the bold, outgoing one, and though Miho seemed more talkative with Kara, around Sakura she chose to play the part of modest mouse.

"Fine," Kara went on, sitting down on the edge of Miho's bed, locking eyes with Sakura. "You think Akane's come back, that she's giving us these dreams, that she's the one who killed Chouku and Jiro, and made Hana jump off the roof, because they were all involved in her murder. Maybe they were. And maybe you're right and Ume really did have something to do with it, too."

Sakura's nostrils flared, her expression cold. "And you think I'm crazy."

Kara and Miho exchanged a look.

"Not entirely," Kara said. Her heart raced and she felt her face flush. *God, it's so hard to say this stuff out loud*, she thought. "Okay, a lot of people would think the whole thing was nuts. Ghosts? Spirits of murdered girls back from the dead? That's pretty crazy. But Miho and I . . . we've been talking about it. What's going on here isn't normal. There's something awful at this school. I feel like a total idiot using the word 'evil,' but I know what I feel."

This last bit felt to Kara like a plea, and emotion welled up in her. Fear and desperation made her voice quaver.

"You're talking about vampires again, aren't you?" Sakura said, crossing her arms almost petulantly.

"Not exactly," Kara said.

Miho took a breath before speaking. "You know the legend of the ketsuki?"

Sakura rolled her eyes, but instead of humor, a grim anger

emanated from her. "Seriously? That's so much easier to believe? I've seen the looks between the two of you, I know what you think. I'm losing my mind. I miss Akane so much that I'm wishing for this to be true. But I don't wish it! I wish she was still alive, not a thing, not a spirit killing people! But she was my sister, and if she can't rest because the police are such fools they don't know how to make her killers pay, then she *should* rise! She should make them pay!"

Kara nodded. "Maybe she should. But I don't think it's Akane."

Sakura threw up her hands, then turned away, wiping tears from her eyes. "How insane is this whole conversation? They'll lock us all up if they hear us talking like this."

Miho went to sit beside her, pulled her into an embrace. For a while, Sakura wept into the soft fabric of Miho's sweatshirt. At last she steadied her breath and pulled away, looking up first at Miho and then at Kara.

"What makes you so sure it's a ketsuki?"

Kara hesitated, running her tongue over dry lips.

Miho answered for her. "It came for Kara last night."

Sakura's eyes widened. "What?"

Kara nodded. "If Miho hadn't woken my father, I'd probably be . . ."

She couldn't say *dead*, but she did not need to. Miho and Sakura both knew what word she had left out.

Sakura sat a moment, taking that in, and then she shook her head.

"No. It's Akane."

"Sakura?" Miho said in surprise.

"You imagined it," Sakura said, simmering with anger. "Akane's back. I know it. I can feel her when she's near. She wants justice. The police wouldn't give it to her, so she's taking it in blood, the way the old spirits always did."

"You're wrong," Kara said, shaking her head, trying to get through to her friend. "I saw it. And even if I hadn't, why would she come after me? I never even knew her."

"Maybe she was there to frighten you because you don't believe," Sakura said, lips curling into cruelty now. "Or maybe she just doesn't like you."

"That's not fair," Miho said, reaching for her hand.

Sakura pushed her away. As they stared at her, she stood and pulled on pants and a sweater, slipped into shoes, and went to the door.

"Wait, Sakura," Miho pleaded. "Don't go."

She didn't even hesitate, slamming the door as she went out.

Miho turned to Kara, eyes pleading. "What are we going to do?"

Kara gnawed on her lower lip. "She's having the dreams, too. If the ketsuki comes for her, she'll go willingly, thinking it's Akane. We can't let her be here by herself anymore."

Miho stared at the closed door. "We're going to have to stop it, aren't we?"

"Someone has to."

"How?" Miho asked.

Kara shrugged, troubled but no longer confused. She felt strangely awake now. "I'm not sure. Nobody else will believe us. You're leaving in a couple of days. But we have to . . . Wait a second." Kara turned to Miho, mind racing, forcing herself not to succumb to the powerful temptation to pretend none of it was real. They both knew it was real. Denying it might cost Sakura her life. "You said there was a Noh play about the ket-suki. We should ask Miss Aritomo about it."

Miho thought about that a moment, then nodded. "She might be busy dealing with parents, like your father, but let's see if we can find her."

A ripple of anticipation went through Kara. They might be crazy, but it felt good to be taking some kind of action.

"I should go tell my father I might be a while," she said.

"Okay. I want to take a shower anyway. I'll meet you on the school steps in half an hour?" Miho suggested.

Kara stood up. "See you there."

The new school term had barely started, really, and already it was coming to a close. Boxes and suitcases and trunks were being carried out of the dorm. In a way, that seemed fitting to Kara. It felt like many weeks had passed since school had begun—since she had walked so nervously toward Monju-no-Chie School—instead of a comparative handful of days. She remembered vividly how anxious she had been and how Sakura and Miho had set her at ease.

She left the dorm and strode across the field, going toward the trees that lined the opposite side. Sakura had taken off quickly, and Kara expected to find her in the arch of that recessed door on the east side of the school, smoking a cigarette, hiding out. That first day she'd had her uniform jacket inside out, all of those badges and patches on the inside, and

Kara had thought Sakura was so cool, that the girl had it all together.

But even back then, she'd been falling apart.

How did you not notice? she wondered now. *If not then, when you found out about her sister? How did you not know how broken she was inside?*

Kara couldn't blame herself, though. Miho hadn't noticed either, and they were roommates. And Sakura hadn't really begun to fray at the edges until the nightmares came and Jiro died.

If all of this was real—if she and Miho weren't completely freaking out and seeing things that weren't there—then they had to be so careful now. The ketsuki had come after Kara, but at least she knew it wanted to hurt her. Sakura felt righteous and invincible. She needed help desperately, and her parents weren't even returning calls from the school.

When she walked around the side of the building, she peered past the small trees up against the wall, into the deep shadows of that recessed doorway, in the shadow of the overhanging pagoda roof. So certain had she been that, for a moment, she thought she saw a figure there. But the little alcove was empty. Only cigarette butts, stubbed out in the dirt, remained.

With a sigh, Kara continued on. The ancient prayer shrine to her right loomed in the shadows of the trees, damp with rain and unattended. No candles burned there today. Students had been busy this year building shrines of a different sort. The one in memory of Akane still remained down by the bay. A second one had been established for Jiro just a few yards away, with photographs and candles and T-shirts, pins and bits of school uniforms, stuffed animals and toys left as little mementos, offerings from those who missed him. At the back of the school, where Hana had struck the ground after leaping from the roof, a third shrine had been created.

But the students were all leaving now. It appeared Chouku's spirit would have to wait for her own shrine.

As Kara came around the front of the school, she looked down along the tree line toward the bay and faltered. Coming to a halt, she stared at the lone figure who knelt not far from the water, just at the edge of the shrine of remembrance that students had built for Akane. For just a moment she thought it might be Akane herself, that Sakura was right. But she pushed the thought away. Death had taken Akane. It couldn't be her.

Narrowing her eyes, Kara realized who it was who knelt there, as though in supplication.

Ume.

Maybe she's asking for forgiveness, Kara thought. If Ume believed what Sakura had said, that Akane had come back for her killers, her going down to the shrine seemed like a foolish thing to do. And if Ume wanted people to believe she had nothing to do with Akane's death, hanging around the shrine looking guilty wasn't going to convince anyone of her innocence.

Kara took a step toward Ume, thinking she should try to talk to her. But whatever Ume's role had been, Kara had come to believe that Sakura was right about her involvement in Akane's death, and she decided that she didn't have time to waste on sympathy for a murderer. She hoped no one else would have to die, but if Ume was haunted by guilt or fear, Kara had no interest in alleviating her torment.

Turning away, she went up the steps and into the school. She kept her street shoes on. It felt odd not to stop in the genkan to change into uwabaki. But right now, no one would be paying much attention to the rules.

Kara found her father in his homeroom, talking to two couples who had come to retrieve their children. He came out into the hallway to tell her he thought it would be hours before he could leave and that she should go back without him.

"I'll be home before dark," he promised.

She wondered if the words sprang from something he saw in her eyes or his own fear for his daughter.

"I just have a few things to do with Miho, and then I'll be headed home," she promised. "Have you seen Miss Aritomo?"

He shook his head, too distracted by the impatient parents waiting in his classroom to wonder why she would ask. "I assume she's in her room."

Kara kissed his cheek and thanked him, then went down to the front door to wait for Miho.

"As much as I love Noh theater," Miss Aritomo said, giving them a curious look, "this is certainly not the time for club discussions."

In the art teacher's office was a bookshelf laden with hardcover Noh plays and books on the staging of such productions. Several crude masks hung on the wall above the bookshelf, unobtrusive, as though the display itself was an apology for its own existence.

"I'm not even in the Noh club," Kara said. "We just wanted to ask you a few questions."

Miss Aritomo glanced at the clock on her desk, then at Miho, who looked away a bit guiltily. The teacher settled her gaze on Kara.

"I know you must be aware of the crisis the school faces at the moment," the teacher said. "You girls are really not even supposed to be in the school building right now—"

"Yeah, like it's so much safer in the dorm," Kara scoffed.

Miss Aritomo flinched and then her expression went slack, closed off completely. Miho gave a sharp intake of breath.

Kara realized her mistake immediately. She stood stiffly and executed a deep bow, not raising her eyes. "Sensei, please accept my apology for interrupting you, and for the disrespect with which I spoke. It brings dishonor to me and to my father."

The woman visibly relaxed, brushing the words away with a wave of her hand.

"You are nervous and afraid and frustrated, Kara. Under the circumstances, much can be forgiven."

Kara gave a second, shorter bow.

Miss Aritomo bowed in return and continued. "A staff member is working with those boarding students who are not leaving today, making certain that we know who will still be in the dormitory tonight. Miho should be there. And Kara, your father must be wondering where you are."

Miho bowed her head and murmured an apology, ready to leave.

"Wait," Kara said to her.

Both of them looked at her in surprise.

"Miss Aritomo, Miho and I are going to have a few days before she leaves and wanted to do something to distract ourselves. I'm not a member of the Noh club, but I'm interested. We've talked about taking a Noh play and trying to write it as a comic book. Miho's roommate Sakura loves manga and she would draw it. So if we could just ask you a few, quick questions, I promise we won't keep you for very long."

She had come up with the explanation on the spur of the moment, but she warmed to the lie even as it left her lips. Miho blinked, staring at her.

Kara smiled and bowed her head briefly yet again. "Of course, if you'd rather be dealing with terrified and angry parents, I'm sure we can find some other way to occupy ourselves for the next few days."

Miss Aritomo's nostrils flared as though annoyed, and Kara worried that she had miscalculated. But then the art teacher smiled.

"All right. Five minutes. What Noh play were you interested in?"

Miho perked up, blinking in surprise. She smiled softly and then, as though remembering the real purpose behind their visit, grew serious once more.

"When I was younger, I remember seeing part of a Noh play about a ketsuki, a cat-demon that drank the blood of its enemies. At least, I think that was what it was about. I saw the mask once, too, at a Noh museum in Tokyo. My parents took me there three years ago."

Miss Aritomo began to nod even before Miho had finished her first sentence.

"Yes, of course. I know the play you mean," the teacher said. "And it would make a perfect manga. But I think it's in incredibly poor taste for you to ask about it now."

Kara flinched in surprise. "What do you mean?"

Miss Aritomo crossed her arms, studying them with obvious disdain. "You saw Chouku's body, Kara—I know you did—all those little bite marks on her. And I'm sure you've heard that she and Jiro lost a lot of blood. So the two of you start thinking something supernatural—"

"There's no such thing—," Miho began.

"Of course there isn't!" Miss Aritomo snapped, glaring at them. "But suddenly you're thinking about the ketsuki and now you want to do a manga story. Students are dead, and you want to use that for manga?"

Kara took a deep breath. Miss Aritomo had already made the connection to the ketsuki legend. Of course she had, with her knowledge of Noh theater. For a moment, Kara had thought the art teacher believed the ketsuki had killed Jiro and Chouku, but it was clear she didn't believe the creatures were real. She considered trying to convince the teacher but suspected that would only lead to Miss Aritomo telling her father and the principal that the girls were losing their grip on reality.

"It isn't like that, sensei," Kara said.

Miss Aritomo raised an eyebrow. "No?"

"No," Miho said. "It's true that what happened to Jiro and Chouku made me think about the ketsuki, but we mean no disrespect. We've been talking about doing a manga of a legend from Noh theater, and once I thought about the ketsuki, I knew it would make a good one. It would be a faithful retelling of the story."

The teacher seemed to relax a little. "Nothing to do with what's happening at school?"

Kara shook her head. "We would never disrespect Chouku and the others like that. We knew them, sensei."

Miss Aritomo hesitated, apparently trying to decide how much she trusted them. In the end she nodded, giving them the benefit of the doubt.

"All right. But I want to see every page as you create it."

"Of course," Miho said, giving the teacher a small bow of her head.

"The story *would* be perfect for a manga," Miss Aritomo said. "But it is somewhat different from what you remember."

"Could you tell us, please?" Kara asked. "Different how?"

"The story is not about a ketsuki," Miss Aritomo said, reaching back to pull a book from her shelf. As she continued, she flipped pages, searching for something. "Well, I suppose in a way it is. In the play, a woman named Riko is murdered by her husband, who has taken a new lover. Her children mourn for her, and her parents make a shrine at her grave, and there is so much grief that the demon Kyuketsuki senses their rage and grief and comes to their village.

"Kyuketsuki is only spirit but can work terrible evil on

the world through surrogates. Kyuketsuki influenced Riko's family, luring them to the place where her husband spilled her blood. Her father killed a cat on the spot, offering it up to Kyuketsuki. The demon takes all of the sadness and rage and collects it in a bowl, then pours it into the dead cat, transforming it into a blood-drinking monster, forged in the image of Kyuketsuki herself."

Miss Aritomo stopped flipping pages, then slowly went back several pages to something she had missed.

"There," she said, pointing to the page. She turned the book around for them both to see. "That's the mask of Kyuketsuki."

Miho leaned over for a better look. Kara felt frozen in place. The pointed ears and sharp little horns, the black lips and bloody red teeth, the bright orange eyes. The feline qualities of the *tengu* were noticeable, from the shape of the nose to the hissing mouth and sharp, tiny fangs. But the face was distorted and gruesome.

Kara closed her eyes so that she would have the strength to look away.

She'd seen it before.

"It's a rare play, almost never performed anymore," Miss Aritomo said, not noticing Kara's reaction. "So many Noh plays are lost to time and become unfashionable. If you really mean to take it seriously, it would be a service to the theater and to Japan for you to create a manga of this story. I'm sure I could give you credit for it in class, as well."

The teacher said this with a tiny smile, but the girls did not smile in return.

Kara looked at her. "So, the Kyuketsuki legend is older than this play, right?"

"Yes, very old. Most Noh plays are just retellings of older stories."

"Is it always someone sacrificing the cat? Are there other ways to call the demon? To create a ketsuki?"

Miss Aritomo cocked her head, studying them more closely now, her prior suspicions obviously returning. "There are different versions of the story. Most of them begin with a cat walking over the grave of a murder victim and Kyuketsuki taking the cat that way. But it's so coincidental, it would never work in the play."

Kara nodded slowly, mind racing.

"Unless it's not coincidental," Miho said quietly. She turned to Kara. "If Kyuketsuki has a bond with cats, maybe she can summon them. Maybe they come when she calls them, and she fills them with all that hate and makes them monsters."

Kara's pulse throbbed in her temples. Her chest ached with the pounding of her heart and she took a deep breath. Then she noticed the way Miss Aritomo was staring at them, and she knew they'd gone too far.

"Perfect," she said, faking a smile. "That's just the twist we need for a manga version."

A look of utter disapproval replaced the confusion on the teacher's face. "You just told me you were going to be faithful to the original. If you are going to adapt a Noh play, you should respect the material enough to tell the story the way it is meant to be told."

Miho bowed. "Thank you, sensei. You're right. We will discuss it."

Kara bowed her head as well. "Of course. But one more thing, sensei. The play? How does it end?"

"In tragedy," Miss Aritomo said. "The ketsuki kills Riko's husband and his new lover, but its bloodlust and need for vengeance are not sated. It decides that the woman's parents and children could have prevented her murder and so kills them as well. Only the youngest daughter, a little girl, survives. She lights candles and kneels on her mother's grave and prays for mercy. The sun rises, and the ketsuki vanishes.

"It's all very dramatic, if you like that sort of thing."

13

卍

Kara and Miho hurried back across the field toward the dorm. For the moment, at least, adrenaline had overridden Kara's exhaustion. Her eyes still burned from lack of sleep, but her racing heart kept her moving.

"Is your father going to be angry?" Miho asked.

"I'm sure he's not going to be able to leave school any-time soon," Kara said. "I'll still make it home before him."

Her skin prickled with foreboding. The whole world seemed to have changed around her, the slant of light some-how ominous, the air itself heavier. How had her perceptions been altered so completely that she could believe, even for a moment, that the demon out of some Noh play might really exist? The girl she'd been when she'd left the United States would never have believed such a thing.

But she had changed since then. Japan had changed her.

The dark events unfolding at Monju-no-Chie School had forced her eyes to perceive things she had never imagined.

She and Miho had left Miss Aritomo's room in silence, not daring to share their thoughts about what she'd said until they were on their own. Even now, walking alone across the field toward the dorm, they avoided the subject, and Kara knew why. She and Miho were both struggling with their fear.

Kara looked up at the sky, tried to gauge how much of the day had already passed. It must still be morning, but how many hours did that give them until nightfall? And were they really safe during the day? That was a presumption they'd made based on too many vampire stories, but did it apply to demons?

Her heart beat so fiercely that it hurt her chest. *Calm down*, she thought to herself, *or you'll be no good to anyone*. And Kara couldn't afford to let that happen. For whatever reason, the ketsuki had inflicted its nightmares upon her just as it had upon Akane's killers.

"Why . . . ," she began, then faltered.

"What?" Miho asked.

Kara swallowed, her throat dry. "Why do you think it's after me, too? I didn't do anything."

"I thought about that while Miss Aritomo told the story," Miho said, as they walked across the grassy field. In the dorm parking lot ahead, more students were packing their things into their parents' cars. "You were there. You saw the cat disturb Akane's shrine."

"But I didn't sacrifice it!" Kara said.

Miho shushed her. "Let's talk about it inside."

Now that she'd begun the conversation, it was hard for Kara to hold her tongue. But they were coming up to the dorm where there were students and parents about, and she knew Miho was right. She took a deep breath and forced herself to wait.

"Look who it is," Miho whispered, nodding toward the parking lot.

A small SUV sat at the edge of the parking lot. A father closed the tailgate while his wife looked on. But Miho had been drawing Kara's attention to the other two people near the vehicle. Maiko, the sleepless, frayed, brittle girl who was in Mr. Matsui's class with them, stood near her parents' SUV, talking quietly with Ume. The two girls' faces were pictures of worry and regret. Maiko held Ume's hands, nodding some kind of assurance they could not hear from that distance. Ume nodded, but more slowly, and then the girls hugged.

Maiko's father snapped at her to get into the car. With a last look at Ume, she obeyed her father. Ume waved and turned away, hurrying back to the front steps of the dormitory. If she'd looked up, she would have seen Miho and Kara coming toward her, but her thoughts were obviously elsewhere.

They entered the dormitory twenty seconds after her, just as Maiko and her parents drove away.

"Do you think the ketsuki knows they're leaving?" Kara whispered.

Miho looked around the foyer of the dorm to make sure they weren't overheard. She tucked her hair behind her ears.

"If it does, it's going to want to hurry to get as many as it can before they're all gone."

Kara turned the words over in her mind and found she didn't like them at all. Whatever they were going to do about this, if there was anything at all they really *could* do about it, had to be tonight. Otherwise there would be more blood, more death—and it might be her own. They had to find a way to stop the ketsuki, so she could finally rest. She badly wanted sleep, but the nightmares had to stop.

On the stairs between the second and third floor, they encountered Ren, who was on his way down.

"Miho, hey!" he said, smiling. "I was just looking for you."

"Really?" Miho asked, lowering her eyes and seeming almost to shrink into her own shyness, hiding behind her glasses. "Why?"

Despite her tension, Kara smiled. Miho had such a curiosity about and fascination with boys, but talking to a boy she obviously liked made her squirm. Kara hadn't had the heart to tell her Ren was gay.

Ren shrugged. "Just wanted to say good-bye."

Miho's disappointment was plain. "You're going home, too?"

"My parents are coming this afternoon. It's all so weird, isn't it? And a little scary. To be honest with you, I'm kind of glad to be going, at least until they catch whoever killed Chouku."

Miho seemed to be searching for something to say.

"Hopefully it won't be long," Kara said, to fill the silence.

Ren smiled. "I don't mind missing school. Anyway, I went up to say good-bye to you and Sakura, but nobody was there. I'm glad I got to see you before I left."

"Me too," Miho said.

"Are you going to be okay? When are your parents coming?"

"Not for a few days. But I won't be alone. Sakura will still be here, and Kara too. And we're going to have some teachers with us, I think, until we're all gone."

"Okay. Well, I'll see you soon," he said, hurrying past them down the stairs.

Miho watched him go, and then the girls continued up the stairs.

"So Sakura's still out," Kara said as they reached the third floor and moved toward Miho's room.

"She has to come back eventually," Miho replied. "I hoped we both could talk to her, but I can do it myself. Hopefully she'll listen."

Kara shushed her. They were passing by Ume's room and slowed to a stop. In the otherwise silent dormitory, they could hear Ume's voice very clearly.

"You don't understand," came the slightly frantic voice from the other side of the door. "I'm afraid. I don't want to wait until tomorrow. I need to come home today. You've got to come and get me. I'll meet you in the city if I have to. I could leave my things here until I . . . No, please listen . . ."

Miho tapped Kara on the arm and gestured for them to

continue walking. Kara was reluctant to go, but she didn't want anyone to see her eavesdropping, so she continued down the corridor.

Though it had occurred to her that Sakura might simply not have answered Ren's knock, Miho's dorm room was empty. They entered and Miho locked the door behind them and turned on some music. Given how clearly they'd been able to hear Ume, this seemed a very good idea.

"She must have been talking to her parents," Kara said.

Miho nodded, brow furrowed in contemplation. "Yes. And she seems much more frightened than the other students we've seen."

"You don't think she knows about the ketsuki?"

"I can't imagine it. But Ume knows what really happened to Akane. She had to have been there. She knows the connection between the people having the nightmares—"

"Except for me."

Miho nodded, leaning against her desk. "Yes. Except for you. Anyway, she knows Akane is the link between Jiro and Hana and Chouku, too. She's afraid she's going to be killed."

"She's a bitch," Kara said, "but she's not stupid."

"Agreed," Miho said. "All right, back to you. What I was saying outside is that Kyuketsuki . . . I mean, let's just not bother talking about whether Kyuketsuki is real, okay? I think we have to believe right now, and if it turns out we're crazy, at least we'll be crazy and you and Sakura will be alive."

"I'm with you," Kara told her. The room felt awfully cold and she rubbed her hands together, then slid them into her pockets. The light, hooded blue sweater she wore under her jacket was not thick enough to warm her, but right now, it was possible nothing would do the job.

"If the folktales about Kyuketsuki come from something real, let's think about the story. Maybe Kyuketsuki could be summoned in those days by sacrificing a cat, but she doesn't just prey on the killer or abuser, she also kills the ones who summoned her. In the story, they share the blame, but maybe that's part of the price of calling her up. Part of the sacrifice."

"But I didn't call her up!" Kara protested.

Even as she said the words, though, she could picture the cat slinking through the photos and flowers that comprised the shrine for Akane.

"You were there," Miho said. "I guess that was enough."

Kara saw it all unfold again in her mind, the red and copper fur of the cat emerging from the shadows and the flowers. She went to the window and gazed out.

"The shrine's the key," she said. "Think about it. Kyuketsuki gathers up the grief and anger of people who are mourning a murder victim and creates a ketsuki out of it. All of those notes and pictures and flowers, the stuffed animals, what are they except grief? Add Sakura's grief and her rage . . . I mean, that's the spot where Akane died. The shrine drew Kyuketsuki there."

"Yes. It all makes sense," Miho said, in a way that made it clear that she wished it didn't.

"But what about the cat? I mean, I didn't sacrifice it. The thing just walked across the shrine and dropped dead. Okay, maybe Kyuketsuki has the power to reach through and kill it, but the cat just happened to be nosing around the shrine while someone was standing there?"

"It could be coincidence," Miho said. "Or maybe not. Most people don't believe in demons anymore. Not really. Not even in Japan. They don't even perform this Noh play anymore. Maybe Kyuketsuki has to find other ways to fulfill her purpose. Maybe she influenced the cat, drew it to her so she could create a ketsuki."

Kara was about to argue, but then she thought of the other cats she'd seen, of the dreams she'd had in which so many gathered around the dead one, the ketsuki.

"Maybe," she allowed.

The two girls were lost in thought for a few moments. Then Kara pulled her hands from her pockets and turned to Miho.

"How do we make it go away?"

Miho took a breath and then shrugged. "Take away its power? If grief and anger drive it, we've got to make those things go away to weaken it."

Kara stared at her. "Meaning we have to get Sakura to let go of those feelings? That's not going to work."

"If we can't figure something out—"

"You don't have to convince *me*," Kara interrupted.

"We could start by destroying the shrine," Miho said. "Sakura would be so hurt, but if it means her life and yours, I'll risk it. That might weaken it a little."

Kara nodded. "Maybe enough for us to hurt it."

"We have to do it just after dark. Hopefully no one will see us."

"My father is never going to let me out, even if I'm with you," Kara said.

Miho paled, face slack with sudden fear. "I can't go alone. I just couldn't."

"I'm not asking you to. I'll find a way. I'll sneak out. But then I have to go back. He'll know if I'm not there at bedtime."

"Which leaves me to watch over both Sakura and Ume tonight."

Kara frowned. "Ume?"

"I don't like her either, Kara, but we can't just let the ket-suki kill her."

"You're right. I just wasn't focused on her." Kara pushed her fingers through her hair, thinking. She knew what this all meant but didn't want to admit it to herself. "I don't know what to do. I can't leave you to do this alone."

"You can't sneak out all night," Miho chided her. "Your father would notice. Not only would you be in trouble, but he'd come looking for you, and then he'd be in danger, too. No, we need someone else to help."

Kara threw up her hands. "Yeah, that'd be nice. But can you think of even one person who wouldn't think we were both insane?"

"Miss Aritomo?" Miho suggested.

"You saw her today. It's only a story to her."

"Ren might have believed me, or at least gone along with it because he's a good guy, but he's leaving."

Kara smiled.

"What?" Miho asked. "This isn't the time to tease me about guys."

"I'm not," Kara said. "But you just made me realize there is one person who might not think we're crazy."

Hachiro opened the door to his dorm room looking like he'd just woken up. He held his iPod in his left hand, one ear bud in place and the other dangling past his cheek. His Boston Red Sox cap was perched on his head, somewhat askew and a little too small for him.

Kara smiled. He looked ridiculous and adorable at the same time.

"Took you long enough," she said. "Did I wake you up?"

The big guy gave her a sheepish grin. "I was listening to music. I didn't hear—"

"Can I come in?" Kara interrupted.

Hachiro blinked. Girls weren't allowed in boys' rooms, but the school faculty had more things to worry about these days than kids breaking a few rules. Apparently, Hachiro felt the same way as Kara because he stepped back to allow her to pass him.

When she went in and sat on the edge of his bed, however, he left the door open. Apparently his sense of rebellion only went so far. But she needed the door closed.

"I'm glad you're here," she said, getting up again. "I thought you might have left."

Kara glanced into the hallway and shut the door, then turned to him. Hachiro raised his eyebrows curiously.

"My father is coming tomorrow. I think the teachers are going to make those of us whose roommates have already left double up tonight, so nobody is alone," he said, studying her, obviously wondering what she had in mind. "But I wouldn't have left without saying good-bye to you, Kara."

Despite her fear and nerves, she felt a few butterflies in her stomach. The sensation was very pleasant.

"I'm glad."

"I wish you didn't have to stay here," he went on, then shrugged. "I'll worry about you."

Her smile faded and she took a deep breath, trying to figure out how to begin to explain why she'd come.

Hachiro saw how troubled she was, and his face narrowed with concern. "What is it?"

"It's everything," she said. Kara sat back down on the edge of his bed and Hachiro seated himself opposite her on his roommate's bed. "I need your help."

He opened his hands like a magician releasing a dove. "Of course. Just tell me what you need."

Kara only wished it was as simple as he made it sound.

"First, I just need you to listen, and keep an open mind. And I need you to try not to be as terrified as I am."

Hachiro blinked, taken aback. And despite her warning, he did look a bit frightened. But his eyes filled with resolve as he nodded.

"Go on," he said.

"Okay," Kara began. "I guess it starts with Akane."

And she told him everything, all that she and Miho thought and suspected, all of her dreams and nightmares. When she related the details of the Noh play, she shivered as she recalled the image of Kyuketsuki's mask. But it was her account of her sleepwalking the night before, of being lured outside, half-awake, and the glimpse she'd gotten of the real thing, that made Hachiro's eyes widen.

When she finished, she took a deep breath and gazed expectantly at him. He seemed to be waiting for more.

"That's it," she said, throwing up her hands.

They exhaled together.

"You're sure it isn't just the sleep deprivation getting to you?" Hachiro asked, the question earnest rather than mocking. He asked as though he truly hoped she had been hallucinating.

Kara shook her head. "Miho's been sleeping fine, mostly. Until last night."

Hachiro took off his Red Sox cap, clutching it in his hands, working his fingers across the brim. He stared at the floor, brow furrowed.

"You don't believe me," Kara said, already trying to figure out how she and Miho could manage tonight without him. "I don't blame you. If I were you—"

"I didn't say that," he interrupted, lifting his gaze. "It sounds like a story, not real life. But Jiro did tell Akane he loved her. And I know how furious Ume was, how much hatred she had in her. I'd never have thought Chouku and Hana and the others would go along with her, but her hold over them was strong. They probably just . . ."

He put aside his cap and ran his hands through his hair, emotion welling up in his eyes and making his voice hitch. "They probably didn't mean to kill her. I won't believe that."

Kara didn't share his sympathy. "Whether they meant it or not, Akane's just as dead."

Hachiro nodded. "I know. Just like I know they've all had these nightmares and that Ume's terrified. Hana killed herself to make them stop. And Chouku . . . if her blood was gone, like Jiro's . . . I don't know if I believe you or not. I guess I need to see it with my own eyes. My mother says I'm stubborn that way."

"But you'll help?" Kara said hopefully.

"You knew I would," he said, his voice dropping a bit. "Even if you're wrong, it sounds like Sakura's going a little crazy. Someone should keep an eye on her. And if you're right . . . well, if you're right, I may scream like a little girl"—they both laughed—"but if you're right, that means you're in danger. And I won't let anything happen to you."

Kara and Hachiro stood at the same time.

"You're the best!" she said happily. On impulse, she moved forward and gave him a quick kiss.

Hachiro blinked in surprise, but Kara thought she might be even more stunned than he was.

She got over it.

Her smile faded and she swallowed, her throat dry, feeling suddenly nervous and more than a little shy. But she stepped closer to him, tilting her head back to search his eyes.

This time when Kara kissed him, Hachiro kissed back.

As night began to settle over Miyazu City—its lights glittering and the black pines of Ama-no-Hashidate like a scar across the bay—Kara, Hachiro, and Miho stood in the darkness of the woods that bordered the school grounds.

"We have to be quick," Kara said, glancing anxiously over

her shoulder among the trees. "I promised my father I'd be back by now. He's going to be worried and angry."

"And we're supposed to be in the dorm," Hachiro reminded her.

"I know, I know. All right," she said, glancing at Miho. "Let's get this done."

They crept along the tree line toward the bay, watching the looming monolith of the school—only a few lights burned inside—and the driveway that ran out to the main road. Monju-no-Chie School sat slightly askew, facing northwest toward the neighborhood where Kara lived. Its northeast corner jutted toward the bay, and the eastern wall faced the woods. Unless someone looked out from the school itself, or came across the grass from the street, they would not be seen.

Or so Kara hoped.

Her skin felt flushed and her heart raced. A host of childhood images flashed across her mind, walks in the woods with Tammie Bledsoe and Jim Orton when they'd been sure they were being watched from the upper branches or from behind stone property marker walls; heading home after dark from Tammie's house, cutting through neighborhoods of darkened houses and backyards. At eleven or twelve years old, she'd been certain that *things* waited in the dark to grab her. As she got older, she had realized how foolish such thoughts were.

Yet now that old certainty had returned.

"This is wrong," Hachiro whispered.

Kara and Miho exchanged a glance. They were frightened and disturbed enough without Hachiro's second thoughts.

Kara reached out and took his hand, held it in hers as they kept walking.

"It is," she agreed. "But it has to be done."

"If you're right," Hachiro said.

Kara glanced at him. She really liked him, and it seemed important that he believe her for several reasons. As crazy as she knew all of this must seem, it hurt her to hear the edge of doubt in his voice.

"You don't have to believe," she whispered. "But unless you can come up with a better explanation for everything that's happened . . ."

She let her words trail off, and Hachiro glanced away. They kept walking through the deepening darkness along the tree line, and at last he squeezed her hand. Kara looked up at him.

"What if you're wrong?"

"Then we'll have to live with this for the rest of our lives."

Miho let out a long, shuddery breath. Her eyes glistened wetly in the dark.

In the distance they could hear cars on the street that led away from the school. Kara thought about her father, back at their little house. He'd be looking at the clock now, wondering where she was. Her cell phone felt heavy in her pocket; she'd turned it off, anticipating his call. If she took too long, he might even start wondering if he'd lost his daughter the way he'd lost his wife, and Kara couldn't let it go that far. She hated the idea of hurting him like that, felt sick to her stomach. But chances were good before the sun rose again, she would have put him through worse.

Unless she and Miho were just crazy.

But Jiro and Chouku had been drained of blood, and that didn't happen on its own. Mysteries all had solutions; some of those simply weren't acceptable to the people hoping to find them.

None of them spoke as they approached the shrine to Akane. No candles burned tonight on that small patch of grass, set against the trees by the bay. They stood in respectful silence for several very long moments. A girl had died there. Been murdered there. People she knew, some of whom she must have laughed and gossiped with, sat next to in class, had killed her, all because another girl's boyfriend had fallen in love with her.

They stared at the yellowed, curling photos and the wilted flowers—no fresh ones had been placed there in a while—and the messages and stuffed animals. A Hello Kitty had turned brownish gray from the elements.

"Sakura will never forgive us," Miho said, barely able to get the words out. "I don't know if I can do this."

Kara thought she had it all together. She thought she had conquered her own fears and ghosts, the grief that lingered in her heart and in all of the darkest corners of her mind. But as she stared at the shrine—so much like a grave marker—and then turned toward Hachiro and Miho, her chest ached and her breath hitched.

"Do you think I don't understand what you're feeling?" she asked. Tears sprang from her eyes, shocking her, and her hands shook as she wiped them away. "I look at this spot and I think of someone doing this to my mother's grave. My mother, Miho. I didn't know Akane. That makes this harder for the two of you than it is for me. But Sakura talks about her sister coming back to life, and I wish she were right because if she were, that would mean that my mother could come back, too. It doesn't work like that. This is a shrine to Akane. She died here, yes, but something terrible was born here."

She covered her mouth with her right hand. Hachiro started to speak but she dropped her hand and continued.

"I know how awful what we're doing is. But we're not doing it to hurt Sakura. We're doing it to save her and to keep anyone else from dying."

Miho and Hachiro both stiffened.

Hachiro reached for her hand again. "I told you I wouldn't let anything happen to you."

"Tell that to Chouku. Her roommate was right there. Slept through the whole thing. The ketsuki gets what it comes for."

Kara wiped her tears away and managed to stop more from coming. She steadied her breathing, but her heart still fluttered in her chest.

Hachiro glanced back toward the school and the road, then looked out toward the water, making absolutely certain no one was watching them. If anyone noticed them from the windows of the school, they would be caught and vilified by other students disgusted by their actions.

Miho stepped forward first. She dragged her feet the way Kara always did when her father raked leaves in the fall, moving through the candles and dying flowers and pictures in a path of destruction. With her heart in her throat, Kara joined her, and at last Hachiro helped out as well.

Quickly and quietly, they scattered the pieces of Akane's shrine along the grass and among the trees. It took less than two minutes and when they were done, Kara felt sick.

"We have to get back," Miho said to her.

Hachiro looked at Kara. "*You* have to get back."

"I'll be fine."

Miho shook her head. "No. Hachiro has to walk you."

"Yes. If it's . . . I mean, the ketsuki has already come after you at least once," he agreed.

Kara frowned at Miho. "What about you?"

"It hasn't visited my dreams. I'll be fine."

"I hope you're right."

"Go," Miho told them. "Hurry."

Kara nodded. Hachiro took her hand and she liked the way their hands fit so easily together. Miho started across the grass back toward school and the dormitory beyond it. After a few steps, she broke into a light run.

"Come on," Hachiro said. "She'll be all right."

Kara watched her go, then glanced one last time at the wreckage they had made of Akane's shrine, sick with guilt.

A cat's eyes stared out from the darkness of the woods. She flinched, let out a tiny gasp, and stepped back.

"What is it?" Hachiro said, and he turned to look.

She counted seven pairs of gleaming yellow and green eyes, not moving, only watching. Not the ketsuki, then, but its friends, its creatures, its familiars.

"We need to go," she said, tugging Hachiro away.

They ran for the road, crossing the grassy slope that

separated the school from the bay, glancing back to be sure nothing followed.

"It's true," Hachiro said, more to himself than to her. "God, it's really true."

But the fear of those words only lasted a moment. He shook himself, clutched her hand tighter, and looked around with grim, dark eyes, determined to keep his word, to protect her.

Kara wished Hachiro could have made her feel safe. But the night had just begun.

14

The windows were closed and locked and the air in Kara's bedroom felt stale and close. Glass would not keep the ketsuki out if it tried to come for her, but the sound of it shattering would wake her father. The demon might be pure emotion, rage and grief and dark hatred, but it had been clever thus far as well. She banked on it not coming after her first, prayed it would not. In the Noh play, the ketsuki killed the summoner last, after it had sated its lust for vengeance.

Which meant Ume would die next.

But the ketsuki had drawn Kara out of her house last night, so all bets were off. The Noh play existed only as a story, and the thing that stalked her now was real.

So she lay in her bed, staring at the ceiling, ready to scream for her father if there came so much as a scratch on the window.

Back home in Massachusetts, Kara had friends who were

party girls, but she'd never been the rebellious type. When her mother was still alive, both of her parents had been open and honest with her, and after her death, Kara and her father had survived their grief by joining forces, making decisions together, and maintaining that honesty. One girl she had grown up with, Paige Traficante, had first been grounded for sneaking out of the house after hours at the age of twelve. Time hadn't tamed her. If there was a party, Paige would be there. The previous summer, she had stayed out all night several times, making sure her parents knew she could not be controlled.

Kara could never do that to her father.

But now she lay on her bed, fully dressed under the covers. When her father had gone to sleep, she had tugged on jeans and a sweatshirt and slipped into sneakers. In her right hand she held her cell phone, which was set to vibrate.

Waiting . . .

Every minute that passed, she felt more awake. Her eyes still burned with that constant sandpaper feeling and her bones felt too heavy for her flesh. She felt as though she had deteriorated into a kind of empty, brittle shell of Kara, as if her real body had been swapped for some slow, aching, papier-mâché sculpture.

Part of her hoped the phone would never vibrate, that she would still by lying there come sunrise. But mostly she just wanted it to be over, so she wouldn't have to be afraid anymore.

She lay there, heart thrumming in her chest, imagination painting shadow-puppet shows on the ceiling, too keyed up to even consider the possibility of sleep. Yet her eyelids began to droop and she blinked in surprise, glancing down at her cell phone before once more staring at the ceiling, not daring to look at the windows, fearful of what might be outside.

And then she drifted, eddying down into a dreamless sleep. At the edges of her unconscious mind, something crept on cat feet, nightmares lying in wait, preparing for the moment when she would begin to dream.

Her brow creased and she murmured softly in her sleep. Troubled, she turned over and settled more deeply into her pillow, drawing her knees up into a fetal position.

Girlish laughter, almost a purr, infiltrated her subconscious. The flicker of a nightmare began . . .

Kara frowned and snapped her eyes open. Moonlight cast a gauzy glow over her bedroom, every detail of that space sharply outlined. Panic rippled through her as she feared what might have happened while she slept.

But then she felt the vibration against her ribs. With a blink, she realized the purr she thought she'd heard had been the vibrating of her cell phone. She'd rolled over on top of it while she'd slept; otherwise it would never have woken her.

She sat up in bed, flipping the phone open as she whipped the covers back. Her eyes darted around the room. She could feel her heart beat on every inch of her skin.

"What's happening?" she whispered.

The light from the display on her cell seemed weirdly bright. The sound of her own breathing echoed back to her from the corners of the room and she wondered if her father could hear it, if he'd heard the vibrating of the phone, if the creak of her bed had disturbed him.

"She went out, Kara," Miho said, her voice a tiny, frantic rasp over the phone. "Oh, God, she went out."

Kara tried to picture where Miho might be now, crouched in the hall or at the top of the stairs. Hachiro would be waiting on the second floor, watching for Ume to pass by.

"You got out without waking Sakura?" she asked as she unlocked her window. With the phone clapped to her ear, she managed to ease the window up a few inches with one hand.

"What? No. I'm *talking* about Sakura. She got up. She left the room."

Kara froze. "When? Just now? What about Ume?"

"I have no idea."

"What are you doing?"

"What do you think I'm doing?" Miho whispered. "I'm following Sakura."

Kara shot a glance at her bedroom door, mind racing, fearful that she'd been too loud, made some noise that would bring her father at a run. He'd be sleeping lightly tonight, worried for her, and if she woke him, he'd come running into her room and there would be no way she could get out past him, and then Miho and Hachiro would be on their own.

"I'm coming," she whispered.

"Don't hang up," Miho said. "Stay on the phone with me."

"Hang on."

Silently sliding the window as wide as it would open, Kara slipped one leg out. The neighborhood seemed abandoned save for the occasional light in some of the houses further down the street. In the other direction, the school loomed darkly atop the slope of its grounds. Between houses across the street, she could see the dark expanse of Miyazu Bay. It did not look beautiful tonight, but vast and forbidding.

Sitting on the windowsill, she swung her other leg out, then dropped the few inches remaining to the ground.

Then she ran, rubber soles padding on the soft earth as she fled the safety of home. She risked a glance back and only then realized that she'd neglected to lower the window. An image of her father's face sprang into her mind, of the terror that would strike him when he saw her window open and feared the worst, that someone had stolen her from her bed.

Her heart faltered, but her feet did not. Her sneakers touched pavement and she plummeted forward, toward Monju-no-Chie School and the cruel, vengeful secrets that had been born there.

"Kara?"

"I'm here," she said into the phone. "I didn't want to talk until I was away from the house. Tell me what's going on. Where are you?"

"The third floor of the dorm," came Miho's whispered re-ply. "There are still a few other girls here. I don't want to . . . wait, I hear music."

Kara ran past the corner where some of the girls at Monju-no-Chie School congregated in the morning before classes began.

"Probably just someone who can't sleep," she said as she ran across the road. The main street turned right here, but straight ahead was the driveway that led up to the parking lot on the west side of the school.

Kara could have run faster, but with every step she glanced around, keeping watch on the shadows. Phone clapped to her ear, she dashed up the driveway, searching the darkness for the lithe motion or glowing eyes of a cat, or the prowl of something worse.

"Keep talking," Kara said, breathing hard. If Miho went silent, she would be too scared to go on.

"The music," Miho said immediately. "It's coming from Ume's room. The door's open. I'm going to . . . Hello?"

In her mind, Kara could see Miho stepping into Ume's room. She couldn't stop images of Chouku's naked, scraped-up corpse filling her mind.

"Be careful—"

"Oh, God, Kara. She's not here. The room's empty."

"I thought she was supposed to have a roommate for tonight. You all were," Kara said quickly.

"Nobody would share with her," Miho replied, her voice very small.

In frustration, Kara nearly wept for Ume. She couldn't imagine being abandoned with her own fear that way. But the girl didn't deserve her tears.

The line sounded like it went dead for a second, and Kara knew it had to be Hachiro, calling Miho.

"That's the signal," Miho said. "I'm going downstairs."

Kara reached the small school parking lot and ran past. She glanced up at the darkened windows and felt as though they were dark eyes, watching her pass.

"Be careful," she whispered.

Seconds passed, just a few steps, and she heard Miho say, "Hey." Over the phone she could barely hear a whispered conversation between Hachiro and Miho. She tried to picture them together on the second floor landing, tried to make out what they were saying, but they spoke so quickly and quietly that even her Japanese wasn't good enough to understand.

"What is it?" she asked.

"Hachiro says Sakura went out first and he was about to call when Ume came down the stairs. He was standing right there and she didn't notice him."

"Like she was sleepwalking," Kara whispered, remembering the previous night. "The ketsuki's luring her out in dreams."

"But what's Sakura doing?" Miho asked.

"You don't think—"

"I can't. I can't think that."

"Then there's only one way to find out," Kara told her. "I'm coming. But how are they going to get past Mr. Matsui?"

Kara's father had said that her homeroom teacher had the midnight to four a.m. shift at the front doors, making sure no one entered the dormitory who wasn't supposed to. The police were also supposed to drive by twice an hour, but she hadn't seen any sign of them so far.

"I don't know, but it's very quiet downstairs. We're going down."

A night bird cried, startling Kara, and she nearly tripped. She passed the school, continuing up the drive toward the dormitory. But the road led to the dorm parking lot, so she left the pavement and started across the grassy field toward the front doors. The wind picked up and she could hear it rustling in the trees from all the way across the field.

Her heart pounded in rhythm with her feet.

"Miho, talk to me before I totally freak out."

"Sorry, sorry. I'm just . . . I don't want to be here, Kara. I want to go hide. I want to go home. Does it make me a baby if I want my mother?"

Hachiro said something that Kara could hear in the background. It sounded like he was agreeing, that he wanted his mother, too.

"We all do," she told Miho.

"Oh, Kara," Miho said quickly. "I wasn't thinking—"

The dorm loomed ahead, a dark, two-dimensional silhouette against the indigo sky. Kara slowed down, studying the windows, only a few of which showed a glint of light within.

"Where are you?" she asked.

"First floor, coming up to the . . . Shit."

Kara felt her throat tighten. She looked around as she strode toward the dorm's front doors. If Ume and Sakura had come out, where were they? Why hadn't she seen them?

Then she noticed something odd, even as, over the phone, Miho put voice to it.

"The door is open," the girl said. "The glass is cracked."

"Where's Mr. Matsui?" Kara whispered, gaze darting

around. The wind seemed to whisper, and suddenly she felt sure there were eyes upon her. Someone watched her, even now. She stopped short and did a slow circle, searching for some sign of her observer.

"Gone," Miho said. "No sign of him."

In the background, Hachiro said something that sounded like, "There's blood here."

"Kara," Miho said.

"I heard," she whispered.

Kara started for the school again, tentatively. After only a few steps, she saw something on the ground ahead, a dark, undulating shape. Two small shadows darted from it and she uttered a tiny, frightful squeak.

"What?" Miho asked, her voice sounding close in Kara's ear.

The shadows raced low across the field, heading for the trees on the far side, first two of them and then a third and fourth. As Kara approached, slowly, dread coursing icily through her, the last two fled from the figure sprawled on the grass.

Her free hand fluttered up to cover her mouth, though to stifle a scream or attempt to prevent her from being sick, she couldn't have said.

Mr. Matsui had been slashed badly. There were tiny scratches like the ones on Chouku's corpse, but other claws had been at him. Deep gashes had flayed his face and chest and opened his abdomen. Through the tatters of his shirt and jacket, she saw glistening black things that had to be organs.

Cats hadn't done this.

Ketsuki, she thought. *The ketsuki killed him and left him to the cats.*

Breathing through her mouth to keep from throwing up, she started to scream but cut herself off. Turning away, she clutched the phone and spun around, searching for the demon that had nearly taken her from her own house the night before.

"Kara, what—"

"He's dead," she whispered.

"Who?" Miho asked.

But by then she could hear them coming and turned to see Miho and Hachiro running across the grass toward her, pale in the moonlight, almost two-dimensional themselves against the black silhouette of the dorm.

Hachiro carried an aluminum baseball bat.

"Oh no, oh no, oh no," Miho said, running toward Mr. Matsui.

Stupidly, both girls still had their phones against their ears.

"Don't look," Kara warned her.

Miho faltered, looked at her. They both closed their phones and stashed them in their pockets as they hurried toward each other.

"Are you okay?" Miho asked.

"Not even close."

Hachiro stood by the corpse, staring down. Then he backed away as if afraid it would jump up and follow him. When he'd nearly bumped into them, he turned, and the three of them huddled together.

"Did you see anyone?" Hachiro asked.

Kara shook her head. "Just a bunch of cats."

"Where'd they go, then?" he went on.

Miho and Kara exchanged a knowing glance.

"The shrine," Miho said.

"Or what's left of it," Kara replied, nodding.

Hachiro slung his baseball bat over his shoulder as the three of them turned and started to run.

They followed a path that had become so familiar to them, diagonally across the field toward the east side of the school and the woods that bordered the grounds there. Over the years, generations of feet had worn a trail right down to bare earth, like the running path of a baseball diamond.

Instinctively, they kept off the dirt track, their footfalls quieter on the grass. Running felt good and right, and it allowed Kara to chalk her rapid-fire heartbeat up to exertion rather than the terror that had nestled inside her.

None of them spoke. Their chuffing intakes of breath sounded so loud in her ears—her own most of all. Far away, a car horn blared. Something rustled high in the trees off to the right and she glanced up, telling herself it had to be some silent night bird. Cats couldn't climb that high. Still, she scanned the branches and the tree line for the slinking shapes.

Hachiro glanced at her and Kara picked up her pace. But when they came to the back corner of the school, Miho slowed down, and they quickly followed suit. The three of them stalked hurriedly alongside the building, wary of the woods.

Miho stopped, staring at the ancient prayer shrine that abutted the woods on the right, just ahead. Hachiro looked around, holding the bat with both hands, ready to swing.

At least a dozen white candles were burning on the altar of the ancient shrine, ringed in a carefully arranged circle and surrounded by freshly picked cherry blossoms. The smell of the flowers wafted to them on an errant breeze.

Kara peered past the old shrine into the woods, then looked ahead, toward the front lawn of the school and the bay beyond. Who had done this, and what did it have to do with the ketsuki? With Akane? With any of this?

In the darkness at the lee of the school, someone struck a match.

Kara turned to see Sakura's face illuminated in the corona of light as she put fire to the tip of her cigarette and drew in a lungful. She shook out the match, but the cigarette glowed orange in the dark.

"Sakura—," Miho started.

"What are you guys doing out here?"

Hachiro didn't lower the bat. "We were worried about you," he said.

Sakura had her fuku uniform on, the jacket inside out the way she'd worn it the first day Kara had met her. All of her patches and pins were showing. Her hair was feathered and jagged at odd angles, fresh from the pillow, and though she wore socks, she had no shoes on. She looked more than a bit crazy, like she'd been in a trance.

No, Kara thought, *she looks like something out of one of my dreams. Or a nightmare.*

A terrible thought occurred to her.

"You know this isn't a dream, right? You're awake. This is real."

Sakura stared at her, taking a long pull from her cigarette and then exhaling, letting it plume in twin streams from her nose.

"That's the stupidest thing I've ever heard. I know I'm not dreaming. I wouldn't dream this."

"Where's Ume?" Hachiro asked.

"Having a chat with Akane," Sakura replied, gesturing north toward the bay, down the slope to where they had ruined the shrine the students had built for the dead girl.

"That thing isn't Akane," Kara said.

"How can you be so sure?" Sakura asked.

"Because we knew her," Miho said. "And she wouldn't have done this. Not ever."

"Maybe not before they killed her," Sakura sneered. "I'm pretty sure being murdered might change your attitude."

"Sakura, listen," Kara said. "You can't let this happen. It's wrong."

The girl curled her lips in disgust, about to argue.

"Yes, I know, she killed Akane," Miho snapped, and Kara had never heard her speak to Sakura that way before. "Or you think she did. But if you don't do something, you're just as bad."

"And when Ume's dead," Kara said, pleading with her to understand, "it's going to come for us. You're the one who brought this thing to life! Your grief, your rage. Just like in the story."

Hachiro took a step away from them, headed down the slope for the ruined shrine to Akane.

Sakura blocked his way, flicked her lit cigarette at him.

"You're wrong. I know you're afraid, but you don't need to be. She won't hurt you, or me." Emotion contorted her face and Sakura shook her head, looking at each of them. "Don't you get it? What's going to happen *has* to happen so Akane can finally rest."

Miho hesitated. Kara saw in her face how difficult this was for her. They were roommates, and Miho struggled with her love for Sakura. But Kara hadn't known them as long. She couldn't just stand there.

"Get out of the way, Sakura," Kara said, starting forward.

Sakura shook her head, her mouth a tight, expressionless line.

"You can't stop us," Hachiro warned.

Sakura swore and spit at him. Then her calm broke and she began to cry, balled her fists up and shook them like a toddler having a tantrum.

"Please," she said, looking from Miho to Kara, ignoring Hachiro now. "Don't interfere. This has nothing to do with you."

Miho hesitated. Kara looked at Hachiro. She didn't want to hurt Sakura, but she was ready to force her way past the girl.

A cry of terror rose into the night, startling all four of them and rousing an owl, which took flight from a tree and vanished over the roof of the school.

The cry became a scream.

Ume had woken from her sleepwalking dream into a nightmare.

15

🔩

As they started to run toward the sound of that scream, Sakura grabbed Miho's arm.

"Leave her alone, please!" Sakura said. "This has to happen!"

Miho struggled, and Kara and Hachiro both faltered, starting to go back for her.

"You're hurting me!" Miho snapped.

Sakura must have seen something in her eyes then that jolted her out of her grief and obsession, must have remembered this was Miho, her roommate and best friend, who'd always stood by her. She let go, pulling her hands back as though burned.

"I'm sorry," Sakura said. "But—"

"No," Miho said. "Wake up! It's not Akane!"

Then she ran to catch up to Kara and Hachiro and they

raced down the slope toward the bay and the ruin they'd made of Akane's memorial.

More screams tore at the darkness, cries for help and for forgiveness. Kara's thoughts grew darker. For Sakura's sake, they'd been fighting the idea that the bloodthirsty thing killing their classmates could be Akane. *But maybe it is*, she thought now. *In a way*.

Maybe part of what Kyuketsuki used to create the ketsuki was the murdered spirit of the dead girl, weaving Akane's anguished ghost into the fabric of a nightmare, right along with her sister's grief. The story from the Noh play was just a version of the tale, like all legends. The reality might be more complex. Kara knew it was only a theory, but if it held any truth, that meant Akane might be part of the ketsuki, but a tainted, awful version of herself that the dead girl never would have wanted.

But Sakura had tortured herself enough over her sister's death. Kara wouldn't make it worse by suggesting such a thing.

Sakura hesitated only a second before sprinting after them.

"Kara, stop," she begged, in English.

"You helped create this thing, Sakura. You have to let go of your hate and grief or more people are going to die." She stopped and spun to face Sakura, who nearly collided with her. "And I'm going to be one of them."

Sakura only gaped at her, shaking her head in denial.

Kara swore in frustration and turned to run. The screaming had stopped and that frightened her. Hachiro and Miho had gotten ahead of her, and as she looked past her friends, down the slope toward the bay, she saw two moonlit figures at the water's edge.

The ketsuki stood like a tiger on two legs, seven feet tall at least, even with its back arched. Its tail rose up from the bay, casting off diamond droplets of water as it dragged Ume along beside it, one clawed hand hooked through her clothes. It had the face of the Noh mask Miss Aritomo had shown them, but terrifyingly real.

The grief-forged thing threw back its head and cried out, and its voice reminded Kara of the terrible sounds she'd heard sometimes at night, when animals had fought in the woods behind her house. It was a scream, but nothing like Ume's.

The air was thick with the scent of cherry blossoms.

"Do you smell it?" Kara called to Miho.

Wide-eyed, staring at the demon, the other girl only nodded.

"Be careful. Don't all approach at once," Hachiro said, waving her and Miho back with one hand as he raised the bat.

"We destroyed the shrine and that did nothing," Miho said. "How do we fight it?"

As she spoke, Kara glanced over at the memorial the students had built for Akane. Her eyes widened. "Look."

The shrine had been restored, but only partially. Bits of letters and photos had been carefully arranged. A single red candle burned in the center. Rain-soaked stuffed animals and moldy beanies sat together the way they might on a little girl's pillow.

Kara shook her head. Had the ketsuki done that?

"Akane, it's all right," Sakura called, walking past them, headed for the revenant, the monster. "You can rest now."

It yowled that terrible, spine-raking noise again and tossed Ume onto the shore. The girl lay there, unmoving, and Kara hated herself in that moment. They were too late. Sakura had slowed them just enough that it had cost Ume her life. The ketsuki had drowned her. Kara wondered if Ume had done the same to Akane.

And then it hit her.

The rebuilt shrine. The candles at the ancient prayer site.

"Jesus, Sakura, you did this!" Kara said. "We took its power away, and you gave it back, on purpose!"

Sakura ignored her, not even turning now. She kept walking toward the ketsuki, hands out as though the thing might embrace her. But Kara didn't need a reply; she knew it was true. *You can rest now*, Sakura had said. She thought she was doing this for her sister.

"No more," Miho said, running for the rearranged shrine. "It has to stop now."

Kara bolted after her, knowing what she meant to do.

The ketsuki cocked its head, long ears perked up, and it hissed at them. In that moment, jaws wide, lips curled back from its gleaming red teeth, Kara thought it looked nothing like a cat, except for the green, feline eyes.

"It's okay, sister," Sakura said softly, in a small, little-girl voice. "She was the worst one, and she's gone now."

Kara and Miho tore into the shrine, first with their hands and then kicking and shouting and dragging their shoes through the wreckage of it. Miho cried out prayers to God and her ancestors and Kara could hear in her voice that she was weeping with fear and panic.

The ketsuki lunged across the ground, dropping onto all fours and springing toward them. Sakura shouted at it, tried to grab for its tail, but missed and was left staring at her empty hand.

"No, Akane, stop!" Sakura shouted. But she didn't move, only stood there, such a strange figure in the moonlight, almost like a ghost herself.

It would have barreled into Kara, ripped her open like it had Mr. Matsui, but Hachiro took three sure, firm steps to intercept it, cocked his arms, and swung the bat with such force that he let out a yell. Kara could hear the aluminum whistling through the humid air.

The ketsuki tried to dodge, but not quickly enough. Hachiro struck it in the side of the head with a terrible crack and the dream-walker, the vampire, lost its footing. Its momentum drove it forward, tumbling into a mass of limbs and flashing claws.

Miho screamed, paused, and then kept kicking at the ruins of Akane's shrine. If the ketsuki wanted to stop them, their instincts must have been correct. Kara felt something soft underfoot and looked down. There was the Hello Kitty she'd seen before. She picked it up and tugged at it, fingers searching for the seams.

Sakura still shouted for her sister. But if the beast had anything of Akane within it, she ignored Sakura's pleas.

The ketsuki rose, shook its head, and hissed at Hachiro, stalking toward him.

Kara tore the head off the Hello Kitty beanie.

The ketsuki flinched, staggered, and turned to glare at her.

Kara blinked. The whole world seemed to tilt beneath her and she found herself looking not at the feline vampire but at a slender girl with long, silken hair and no face. Soft laughter came from the faceless girl.

Hachiro swung the bat.

When it struck, Kara blinked again, and the illusion had gone. The bat cracked into the thing's shoulder and it staggered backward again.

The night wavered. The air shifted.

The ketsuki yowled again, but now a different sound came from its throat, a hiss like the breath of hell that made Kara remember all of the hurtful words she'd ever overheard, made her feel the pain and humiliation accumulated in a lifetime, and made her relive the crippling heartsickness that had destroyed her on the day her mother died and on so many days thereafter.

That, too, passed, and then her skin prickled with revulsion and fear and she could barely breathe. Tears slipped down her cheeks and a sliver of vision passed through her mind, an image of her imminent death, the ketsuki on top of her, fetid breath in her nostrils, its tongue darting into the cavity where her heart had been before it had torn open her chest and gnawed her bones.

She saw it so clearly.

Knew she'd join her mother in the grave.

And Kara screamed.

A shadow moved behind the ketsuki, in and around and

enveloping it, much larger than the vampire-thing, the essence of its bloodlust and insidious heart.

The demon. Kara felt the truth of it, knew what she saw. *Kyuketsuki.*

"I see you," Kara whispered to the night.

Down by the water, someone began to scream. At first she thought it was Sakura, but a quick glance revealed Ume, rising unsteadily to her feet. A choking cough interrupted her scream and she began to shake, walked two steps and collapsed. But she still lived.

The ketsuki turned toward her now, confused and torn by too many distractions. But vengeance had molded it from rage and pain and vengeance commanded it. It took a step toward Ume.

Sakura stood in the way, studying it, searching its cat eyes.

"Akane?" she asked, pleading and pitiful, hopeful and heartbroken.

Hachiro, breathing quick, terrified breaths, steadied himself and went after the dream-killer again. The ketsuki did not like to be hurt. It had learned. As he swung the bat, it shifted so that it seemed almost to flow around the bat, and then it leaped at him.

With a cry of fear, Hachiro swung again, but too late. The ketsuki lashed out, talons raking his chest. If Hachiro hadn't pitched himself backward, attempting to escape the attack, the ketsuki's claws would have flayed him open to the bone.

Swiftly, it stalked after him, picked him up, and flung him

toward the trees. Branches snapped and leaves shook as Hachiro fell among them.

A dozen sleek, stealthy cats darted from the woods, scattered by the intrusion. They kept a distance from the ketsuki, prowling at the edges of the unfolding scene like vultures waiting for a meal.

Miho and Kara moved as quickly as they could, scattering bits of the shrine far from the spot where Akane had died. Kara picked up a small poster of some J-pop band and began to shred it in her hands, then scattered the pieces on the light breeze, making sure they were strewn across the grass away from the memorial. Once again the shrine was ruined, but they continued to drag their feet through the debris, kicking and spreading the pieces.

The ketsuki seemed smaller as it turned to them. In the woods, Hachiro did not stir, and so step-by-step, almost wary, it started toward Miho and Kara. It picked up speed, beginning to lope.

"Miho!" Kara shouted.

Both girls screamed. But Kara knew who it came for. She had been here to see it born. Her dreams had been poisoned by it, tainted by its hideous intentions.

When it lunged, she tried to move, to hide behind a tree, but was too late. It snatched her, claws puncturing her clothes and flesh, drawing blood and screams. Terror ripped through her like nothing a nightmare could inspire. Every breath came out a scream and she wailed, blind with fear, and beat at its arms as it lifted her toward its face. Those slit cat eyes gleamed with pure hatred and anguish, and it opened its jaws wide, breath stinking of rot and death.

Kara heard the laughter of faceless girls.

The ketsuki let out that bestial, primal cry of pain and rage it had yowled before, and there among the trees it drove her to the ground so hard that her screams went silent. The breath went out of her. Sakura had summoned it unknowingly, and the ketsuki had made Kara its witness. Now she couldn't even speak. She tried to breathe, tried to scream, and as it pressed its weight on her chest she knew she was going to die.

The baseball bat smashed into its feline snout. Someone screamed. The ketsuki whipped its head around to see its attacker when the bat struck again, crashing down on its neck.

Hachiro! Kara thought.

But as the vampire-thing shifted atop her, she saw Miho holding the bat, terror contorting her features but determination in her eyes.

A nighttime shadow moved in the darkness of the trees, and Hachiro appeared. With a strength driven by fear, he thrust forward a thick, splintered branch, jabbing it into the ketsuki's chest like a spear.

The ketsuki shrieked, faltered, staggering away from them. It shook itself and stood up on two legs. Its cat eyes locked on Kara, and for a moment she sensed the presence she had seen before, the rotted, voracious aura of evil that lingered behind it.

Then it took one hate-filled step toward her.

"Akane, stop!"

It whipped its head around. When it saw Sakura coming toward it—and two steps behind, a limping, wounded Ume following her—it lay back its head and let out the most hideous, sorrowful wail yet.

Kara studied it, waiting for another glimpse of the demon that had created the vampire-thing, that had let it insinuate itself into dreams. But of Kyuketsuki, there was no sign.

"Why would you hurt them?" Sakura asked, shaking her head. Her tears glistened in the moonlight. She held something in her hand, some scrap that had blown away from the ruined shrine. "I don't understand."

In her uniform, with her jacket reversed and badges showing and with her edgy, jagged haircut, she didn't look like a rebel anymore. She looked like a little girl playing dress-up in her sister's clothes.

The ketsuki started toward Sakura and Ume.

"Sakura!" Kara yelled. "You've got to let it go. Ume murdered Akane, but your hate's going to kill us all."

Ume fell to her knees and hung her head. "Please, no. I hated her so much. Nobody meant for her to . . . I did not come out here to kill her. Things just got out of hand."

Her wet, matted hair hung in curtains that blocked the moonlight, so it almost seemed that Ume had no face. The illusion made Kara shiver.

"I'm sorry!" Ume wailed, lowering her head further as though waiting for the executioner. "Please, I'm so sorry."

Miho and Kara's destruction of the shrine had scattered

scraps of letters and photos all over the place, and the breeze had blown them across the slope, down toward the water. The ketsuki stalked toward Sakura and Ume, carefully choosing its path so that it did not step on a single scrap.

"Sakura, please!" Miho cried.

Kara and Hachiro and Miho all fell silent then, staring as Sakura stood defiantly in the path of her own heart's vengeance.

Sakura closed her eyes and raised up the scrap she had been holding. Its glimmer revealed it as a photograph, but they were too far away to see the image.

"I can't forgive Ume," Sakura said. "I never will. I do wish she would die, and if you were Akane, I would not stand in your way." She sobbed and her hand shook, but she did not lower the picture. "But my sister would never hurt the people who care about me. I knew the truth when Jiro died. She didn't want to be his girlfriend, but he meant so much to her. She would never have hurt him. But I didn't want to know it. I wanted so badly for you to be her."

The ketsuki took another step toward her but then only crouched, watching her, shivering. It seemed much smaller than before.

Kara thought Sakura would destroy the photo, tear it in half and cast the pieces to the wind again. Instead, she turned and walked the few steps back to Ume. Sakura reached down and picked up Ume's hand, forced the girl to take the photo from her.

"You gave me this pain, Ume. Now I give it back to you, and you can live with it. I'll go on, for my sister, and I'll have her with me always. And you go on with your guilt, and I hope it's with you always. I pity you."

The ketsuki screamed and collapsed. It struggled to stand, limping back toward the place where the shrine had been but was no longer. It fell in the spot where Akane had died, mewling and writhing.

When at last it went still, all that remained of it was the cold, dead body of the red and copper cat that Kara had watched die there weeks before—Kyuketsuki's first victim at Monju-no-Chie School, and its last.

Hachiro limped up beside Kara, blood weeping from a scratch on his face, one hand clutched against the slashes on his chest, and put an arm around her.

"You all right?" he asked.

She nodded, amazed by this guy who'd been brutalized but who seemed concerned only about her own welfare. Kara stood on her tiptoes and gave him a quick, soft kiss. The punctures in her side and back bled, but she'd live.

Miho went to Sakura. They'd been best friends, but just watching them now, Kara could see the distance all of this had put between them. And yet, with just a few steps and open arms, Miho closed that distance. She put her arms around Sakura—the shy girl now strong, the rebel now tender and broken—and hugged her close.

Just a few feet away, Ume still knelt on the ground, sobbing quietly. She had her arms wrapped around her knees and her face buried there, hidden. In one hand she still clutched the photograph that Sakura had given her, tilted in the moonlight so that at last, Kara could make out the image.

The picture was a shot of Akane and Sakura in their school uniforms, arms around each other, heads leaning together. The sisters had the same smile.

"Is it over?" Sakura asked, hopeful.

"Yes. It's over," Miho said.

As one, Miho and Sakura, and Kara and Hachiro, turned their backs on Ume and started to walk toward the school and the dormitory beyond. The police would drive by soon. Twice an hour, they'd said. They would notice the open door of the dormitory and find Mr. Matsui's body. Eventually they would find Ume, crying, and the girl would confess . . . or Kara and her friends would tell them of her confession.

What would happen then, she had no idea. But for the moment, Miho was right. It was over.

Yet even as the thought entered Kara's mind, the wind picked up.

The breeze eddied and swirled and whipped at her clothes and tugged at her hair, and the torn bits of notes and pictures danced and skittered across the grass, moving in tighter and tighter circles. It grew stronger still, dragging pieces of cotton and the cloth skins of stuffed animals into its inexorable pull, and the gathering fragments began to build something.

A silhouette. A shape. An effigy.

At first Kara thought the fragments were constructing the image of the ketsuki, but then a sick feeling clenched in her gut and she felt the wave of grief that she'd felt before, and terror stole her breath away. She felt the presence of the demon, even as the wind finished sculpting it out of the remnants of Akane's life.

"Oh my God," Sakura whispered.

Miho said its name. "Kyuketsuki."

Its hideous face looked very much like the Noh mask they had seen, but uglier, more massive, and when it opened its papier-mâché mouth, the long knifelike fangs within did not look like paper at all.

Nor did its eyes, when they opened. They were cat's eyes, like the ketsuki's, but they gleamed a sickly, putrid green.

Hachiro held Kara tightly, braced as if to run, to carry her away if need be.

And the demon spoke.

"Fortune has smiled upon you," it said, voice a flutter of torn paper in the breeze. "I can only reach my hands into the world by chance, on those rare occasions when a window is opened. You have closed that window. I swear to you that if I should ever find a door, you would all suffer such agonies as even your nightmares cannot contain.

"But the doors have all been closed since the world was young, and I cannot touch you as I would like. Still, you must be punished for your interference, so I put my curse upon you. Little remains in the world now of the darkness of ancient days . . . but what there is will come to you, and to this place. All the evil of the ages will plague you, until my thirst for vengeance is sated."

And the air went still, and the debris fell and fluttered to the ground. A moment later, the wind kicked up again, but it was only the natural breeze from across the bay, and the torn pages and photos began to disperse again.

But the scent of cherry blossoms lingered.

EPILOGUE

On a chilly, crystal blue morning, eight days after the darkest night of her life, Kara Harper sat on a stone wall in view of the Turning Bridge and strummed her guitar. Her fingers moved along strings and bounced from fret to fret with little conscious thought. She'd run through all sorts of songs that her hands knew so well, they didn't really need her mind or her voice to participate. "Normal Sea" by Common Rotation, "Waiting for the World to Change" by John Mayer, a handful of Beatles and James Taylor songs that her father loved, and even the acoustic version of Pearl Jam's "Evenflow" that she'd been playing for years.

Now she just strummed, idly, watching the people who waited for the Turning Bridge to swing back into place so that they could cross over onto Ama-no-Hashidate. But playing the guitar was like singing for her. When Kara thought she was only humming tuneless notes, a song would come out of her mouth as though the radio in her head had been playing all along and she had just turned up the volume. Likewise, her hands surprised her by discovering that they were not simply strumming, playing the opening notes of The Frames' "When Your Mind's Made Up."

Quietly, under her breath, she sang along.

When she first spotted the thin girl in the blue skirt and long gray coat, with her white socks and black shoes and the white bow clipped in her hair, just above her right ear, she did not even look at her face. In those clothes the girl, all alone, seemed to have wandered away from some kind of church tour group. Only when the girl kept walking, away from the Turning Bridge and up the path toward the stone wall, did Kara look curiously at her face.

Her eyebrows went up, and then she smiled.

"Sakura?"

With a shrug, Sakura paused and presented herself like some actress on the red carpet who'd just been asked what fashion designer had made her outfit. Sakura actually spun around once.

"Total transformation," she said in Japanese. But she continued in English. "My mother thinks clothes can change a girl. She thinks we are what we wear. Good girl clothes means good girl Sakura."

Kara strummed quietly, studying her friend. "How's that going?" she asked in English.

Sakura sat down beside her, reached inside her long coat

and withdrew a packet of cigarettes. She tapped one out and flicked open a lighter Kara hadn't even seen her produce, putting flame to the cigarette's tip.

"I'm still Sakura," she said. "If the school uniform did not change me, why should this? First my mother wanted me to be more like Akane, and now she wants me to be more like her. I told her it was hard enough trying to be like me without trying to learn to be someone else. She didn't understand. Thought I was trying to make a joke."

Kara put her fingers over the guitar strings, stilling the music. She gave Sakura a sad smile and switched back to Japanese.

"I'm going to guess she didn't think it was funny."

Sakura pointed the cigarette at her. "You're not as dumb as you look."

Kara laughed. "You're not as paranoid as people say you are."

Eyes mock-wide, Sakura looked around. "People? What people?"

They grinned at each other and then fell into an easy companionship. Kara played and Sakura smoked. It occurred to Kara that they must look very odd together, the proper Japanese girl in her pristine clothes and the blond gaijin girl in blue jeans and a Boston College sweatshirt. People would look at them and wonder. Kara liked that.

They had spoken on the phone and via instant message regularly throughout the days since Mr. Matsui's murder, but they had not seen each other even once in that time. Furious with her and terrified for her, Kara's father had not let her leave the house for the first three days unless he was with her, and by the time she had been free to go anywhere on her own—during the day, of course—Miho and Hachiro had both been taken home by their parents.

Sakura had never gone home, but the principal had restricted her to the dormitory and Miss Aritomo had stayed with her whenever she wasn't at the police station answering questions. That arrangement had lasted for two days, and then her parents had finally arrived. They had been out of the country, out of contact, but had become miraculously findable when, instead of merely being in danger, their daughter had been arrested for assault.

So many times, Kara had wanted to say, "At least they came." But the words never made it as far as her lips, mainly because she knew they would be hollow and bordering on deceit. Though who she was trying to deceive, herself or Sakura, she was not quite sure. Sakura's parents had come to be with her, that much was true. But neither their daughter nor anyone else involved—even Kara's father—thought for a moment that they had come for any reason other than to save face. They defended their daughter because if she was indeed guilty of a crime, that would be an embarrassment to them.

It had apparently never occurred to them that their neglect of their surviving girl did more to dishonor them than anything Sakura might have done, or would ever do.

"Are you officially innocent, then?" Kara asked.

"As innocent as I'll ever be," Sakura said. "Thanks to you and Miho and Hachiro, they don't have any reason not to believe my version."

Kara cringed inside. She had hated to lie, but no one would have believed the truth, and so they'd all had to manufacture a version of that long, terrible night to account for its events without any hint of the supernatural. Given her troubled history and school record, neither the police nor the school board had any difficulty believing that Sakura had snuck out a first-floor window that night.

Sakura had wanted to visit her sister's shrine, as she had nearly every night, to say a prayer for her. There, she discovered that the memorial put together by so many students had been destroyed, nearly every scrap of paper and every photo torn up. Furious and anguished, she had searched the site for a picture of herself and her sister that she had left at the shrine. She did not realize that Ume had followed her, out the window and down to the bay, until she heard the other girl laughing.

Sakura claimed Ume had admitted destroying the shrine and gloated about it. To give the story the ring of truth, Sakura confessed to the police that she had attacked Ume, that she had been the one to throw the first punch, but that she had no doubt that Ume had come there to harm her. They fought on the shore and then in the water. Ume had tried to drown her and had confessed in the ferocious heat of that moment that she had murdered Akane.

And then they had heard screaming from the direction of the school.

Sakura told the police she had left Ume there by the water and gone running back up to the school and then around to the field, where she had found Miho, Hachiro, and Kara frantically screaming for help and using their cell phones to call the police after having discovered the torn, bloody corpse of Mr. Matsui.

Kara had snuck out of her house and gone to meet Hachiro, desperate to say good-bye to him before he left for home the next day. They had feelings for each other, and she had been unable to sleep, thinking that she might never see him again. Discovering Sakura missing from her bed, Miho had gone in search of her and run into Hachiro, and she agreed to try to distract Mr. Matsui so that he could sneak out and say good-bye to Kara.

In the foyer of the dormitory, Hachiro and Miho had been surprised to find the door open and Mr. Matsui gone.

At the same moment, as she walked across the field, Kara had found the bloody remains of Mr. Matsui. She had screamed and then heard a roar. A black bear had charged her from the trees. She had run toward the dorm but not been fast enough, and it got its claws into her.

Hachiro had grabbed an aluminum baseball bat that he and his friends had left near the door the day before and rushed out. He had struck the bear several times, and it had raked his chest with its claws before finally retreating. He told the police he believed he had injured it badly, that it had been staggering.

Then Miho had seen Mr. Matsui's body and begun to scream, even as Kara called the police.

As far as Kara was concerned, the whole thing sounded like the biggest pile of bullshit she had ever heard. Mainly because that was exactly what it was. But they had certain things working in their favor.

Ume confessed to murdering Akane and gave the names of the other students who had been there that night and taken part. In defending themselves, those girls—the ones still alive—had all agreed on one thing, which was that Ume's confession was one hundred percent true. She had murdered Akane.

So when Ume told the truth about what she had seen that night—the demonic beast that had tried to drown her before being driven off by Hachiro and the others—what else could people think but that she had witnessed their skirmish with the bear and her mind had twisted it into something worse? The girl had admitted to murder and that she'd been unable to sleep, haunted by nightmares and guilt.

"She snapped, I guess," was how Kara's father had expressed it.

The police were still calling Jiro's death a suicide. Hana had jumped off the school roof, but she had been there the night Ume murdered Akane and it seemed obvious that guilt had consumed her and driven her to take her own life. As for Chouku, when questioned, one of Ume's soccer girls—who had also been present for Akane's murder—had recalled Chouku saying she thought they should all go to the police and tell the story. They couldn't prove it, but with that scrap of information, the police suspected that Ume had murdered Chouku as well to protect herself.

No one ever mentioned that Jiro and Chouku had been drained of blood. Hachiro, Miho, Sakura, and Kara had compared notes over the phone, and none of them could recall anyone putting forth a theory as to *how* Ume was supposed to have killed Chouku. As absurdly unlikely as the official version of that night's events might be, it was a puzzle in which all of the pieces fit together. The absence of blood in the bodies of two dead teenagers was an extra piece, and the puzzle had no room for it, so the police had discarded it.

The police had told Miss Aritomo, who told Kara's father, who told Kara, that a black bear had attacked two men on Takigami Mountain and that their dog had killed it. The story had to be either a massive coincidence or an outright lie on behalf of the police, perhaps an attempt to calm fears at the school and in the town.

At first, Kara had been amazed that anyone would accept such a story and chalked it up to the Japanese sense of order, the need to have an explanation for something that was inexplicable. But the more she thought about it, the more she realized that the police in American cities and towns also probably concocted stories on a regular basis to set people's minds at ease. How many times had she seen something on the news about some suspected serial killer, where it seemed the cops had known for ages that the murders were connected and the guy was out there hunting people, but hadn't bothered warning anyone? Murders went unsolved all the time, and nobody was panicking about killers living among them.

Of course, when the cops back home invented stories to explain something they could not understand, it didn't involve the supernatural. At least, Kara didn't think it did.

And then there was Sakura.

Despite Ume's confession to murder and Sakura's tale about the girl ruining her sister's memorial shrine, the police had wanted to press charges against her for assaulting

Ume that night. But Sakura's parents were influential people. Their eldest daughter had been murdered and the police had not had a single suspect, and now the murderess had confessed and their younger daughter—defending her sister's memory—was to be charged with assaulting the girl who had killed Akane?

Embarrassment and fear of public humiliation had taken their toll. After days of hesitation, the police had dropped the charges.

Incredibly, it was over.

"So, you're leaving, then?" Kara asked.

Sakura took a long drag on her cigarette, blew a smoke ring, and smiled. "Well, *they* are. Tomorrow."

Kara gaped at her. "They're letting you stay? How did that happen?"

"Easy. I told them I wanted to come home, that the teachers at Monju-no-Chie School expect too much and are too strict. They decided that I would be too free in a public school, that I would get into even more trouble. It really wasn't that difficult. It isn't as though they wanted me to come home with them."

Despite the smile on Sakura's face when she said this, it gave both girls pause. Kara started to play something soft and slow, not paying any attention to the music or even aware of what song it might be.

This was her moment to say something encouraging or reassuring—something like *I wish I could stay with you*. But she didn't want to lie and feared that those words might not be the truth. How could Sakura want to stay? Yes, this was her school, and Miho would be back tomorrow, and in a few days classes would start again. And from Kara's perspective, leaving would probably mean never seeing Hachiro again. But still . . .

"Aren't you afraid?" Kara asked, looking down at the guitar, watching her fingers move along the neck as though she needed to focus in order to play, when really she just did not want to see Sakura's eyes when she asked the question.

"Of what?" Sakura said. "The curse?"

Kara nodded without looking up.

"A little. But it's been six days and nothing has happened. The world Kyuketsuki came from is dust now, Kara. You heard what it . . . she . . . said. The old darkness, the things people in Japan used to believe in, are nearly all gone. They're weak things. We don't know if Kyuketsuki's curse will really affect us, or if other dark things still exist to do anything about it. You know that story about how these guys caught this giant prehistoric fish that everyone thought had been extinct for thousands of years? Maybe Kyuketsuki's like that fish, out there alone."

Sakura paused to puff on her cigarette.

Kara looked up at her. "Maybe. But maybe not."

Sakura nodded solemnly. "All right. I admit I was scared at first. But nothing's happened yet. Nothing may ever happen. I'm afraid to be out after dark alone, and I'll probably be jumping at shadows for my whole life. But I can't run away when there might not be anything to run from. And all of my friends are here. I don't have anywhere else I'd rather be."

Kara played a few more chords, and then her hands went

still. She stared out at Miyazu Bay and at the black pines that lined Ama-no-Hashidate. This was truly one of the most beautiful places she had ever seen.

"How have you been sleeping?" Sakura asked.

Kara turned to her, studied her face. "Fine. Really well, actually. No more bad dreams."

Sakura smiled. "See? No restless nights. No nightmares."

"You're trying to get me to stay."

"Of course. I'll miss you if you go."

Kara sighed. "I have to go. It's all arranged."

Sakura raised her eyebrows. "You don't really want to live with your aunt."

No, she didn't. But her father had a contract to teach for the school year and could not leave without fulfilling that contract. At first he had planned to do just that, uproot them and take his daughter home. But the school board had expressed their extreme displeasure with the merest mention of that plan, and friends in the U.S. had warned that it could damage his career. So they had decided that Kara would live with her Aunt Julie—her mother's sister—in Maine until her father completed his contract.

"You know I don't," Kara said. "The school year's almost over back home. In the fall I'll probably have to repeat this whole year. I won't even be home with my friends. I'll be at a high school in the middle of nowhere in Maine, starting all over again."

"So why are you going?"

Kara watched a sailboat slice the water out on Miyazu Bay and breathed in the cool, pure spring air.

"Because I'm afraid. And my father's afraid for me."

"You don't even know if there's anything to be afraid of!" Sakura said, stubbing out her cigarette on the top of the stone wall.

Kara glanced at her sharply. "Don't we?"

"Kyuketsuki's gone. Look, we've been over this. As far as your father's concerned, whatever danger you might have been in is over now. There's no way he wants to send you back to America while he stays here. He was so worried about being able to keep you out of trouble—to keep you safe— here! How's he going to do it when you're seven thousand miles away?"

The words hung between them. Kara felt angry with Sakura but knew it was only because she was right. About all of it. The terror of that awful night felt fresh to Kara, and though she had pleasant dreams when she slept, when she was awake, the fear often came back. Like Sakura, she didn't want to be out alone after dark, and shadows made her nervous.

Like Sakura.

Kara looked at her. "You think I want to leave? I don't. I'll miss you guys, and I'll miss Japan. My dad and I dreamed about doing this for so long and when my mother died . . . It was supposed to be our new beginning. We knew she'd have been so proud of us. We both promised her we would take care of each other. And now I'm supposed to leave my dad behind? I'm scared to stay, but I don't want to leave without him."

Her eyes burned a little and she felt them welling up with emotion, but she blinked and wiped at them, refusing to cry.

"So why do you think he's sending you home, then?" Sakura asked, her voice gentle.

Kara swallowed hard. "Because he thinks it's what I want."

Sakura lit another cigarette. She glanced away, as though the conversation meant nothing to her.

"But it isn't?"

Hiding the truth about what had happened from her father had seemed the only sensible thing to do. He would never have believed her, and if he did, it could have gotten him killed. And now that it was over, telling him the truth served no purpose except to make him think she was crazy, or make others think he was crazy, and get them all in trouble. But keeping secrets from her father had put distance between them that had never been there before, and she hated it.

She couldn't tell him the truth, but if she left now, they might never be as close again. And she'd never forgive herself.

"I just told you I don't want to go," she said.

A family walked by on the path in front of them, two little girls racing ahead of their parents, laughing.

Sakura blew a smoke ring and turned to Kara. "You should probably tell him that, don't you think?"

Kara strummed her guitar, another song emerging from her fingertips unplanned. "One more thing I'm afraid of."

"Are you afraid he'll still make you go, or afraid he'll let you stay?"

It occurred to Kara that she had started playing "When Your Mind's Made Up" again, and the irony made her laugh.

She thought Sakura might ask what Kara found funny, but instead she just looked at her, waiting for an answer.

"A little of both, I guess."

Frustrated, Sakura sighed. "So what are you going to do?"

Kara slid off the wall, a smile stealing over her face. She slipped her guitar around behind her so it hung there from its strap like a hunting rifle.

"I'm going to do what I promised my mom I would do—look after my dad."

Sakura brightened. "So you're going to stay?"

Kara shrugged. "I'm going to talk to him. And then we'll see."

The girls said their good-byes and Kara headed for home, leaving Sakura sitting on the stone wall smoking. She'd be fine there on her own. Night was a long way off.

Kara sang softly to herself as she walked, her spirits lifted. She didn't have to tell her father the truth about Akane's shrine and Kyuketsuki in order to be honest with him about how she felt. They had both made promises to her mother, and those vows had to be kept.

As for Kyuketsuki's curse, Sakura was right. Nothing had happened yet. On a day such as today, with the sky so blue and the bay calm and clear and the distant sound of a little bell ringing on a child's bicycle, the curse held little power over her—and far less magic than did the music of her guitar or the shyness in Hachiro's eyes when she caught him looking at her.

When the sun set, she knew she might feel differently. A curse had more power then. After dark, the edges of the world seemed to blur, so that anything might be possible. Nowhere felt safe then, and nothing could be trusted.

The thought made Kara pick up her pace. She needed to have a conversation with her father, and it would be best if they could have it while the sun still shone. Once night fell, fear might get the better of her, and she couldn't allow that.

She had promises to keep.

AUTHOR'S NOTE

Though Miyazu City is a real place, and I certainly recommend that you visit it someday and take in the beauty of Ama-no-Hashidate, I have taken certain liberties in creating its fictional counterpart for The Waking. Shh. I won't tell if you won't.

ACKNOWLEDGMENTS

I would like to thank Melanie Cecka, Elizabeth Schonhorst, Margaret Miller, and everyone on the Bloomsbury team for their support and enthusiasm. Thanks also to Jack Haringa for his keen eye and helpful feedback, and, as ever, to my family for their love and laughter.

All the evil of the ages will plague you,
until my thirst for vengeance is sated . . .

The WAKING

Spirits
of the
Noh

Read on for a sneak peek!

PROLOGUE

Demons covered one entire wall of Yuuka Aritomo's class-room. At least, that was how other people would have seen her collection of Noh theater masks. Some were monsters, some evil spirits, and others merely distorted representations of gods, crazy people, and fierce warriors. Most of them were tragic figures, and many were hideous to behold, but Miss Aritomo thought them all quite beautiful.

A shiver went through her, a sudden feeling of dread that spider-walked up the back of her neck. She turned to stare at the shadowed corner of the room, troubled by the certainty that something had just darted out of view. For a moment, it felt as though the masks were staring at her.

Stop. You're frightening yourself.

Alone in the room, the school so quiet, it was easy to get spooked—but this was more than nerves. Something made her uneasy. Something had flitted through the shadows in her peripheral vision.

No. Stop.

"You're a grown woman," she said aloud, and the sound of her own voice comforted her. She might be an adult, a teacher, but at heart she was still the little girl who had been afraid of her own shadow.

It's just the murders, she thought, and shivered. Several students and one teacher had died on the campus of Monju-no-Chie School this past spring, and another girl had been drowned the previous fall. They hadn't all been murders, at least according to the police, but she could not help feeling claustrophobic there, alone in her classroom, with the echoes of those deaths—the cruelty, the malice, the evil—lingering in her mind.

She could only imagine how the students must feel. Which was why she had decided to do something to take their minds off such grim reality. The summer term was about to begin and she had just come from a meeting with the school's principal, Mr. Yamato, who had approved her request to give her students a once-in-a-lifetime experience—they would put on a Noh play, complete with actors, musicians, and traditional dance. The club would build a Noh stage and create costumes and props and masks.

Miss Aritomo looked at the masks again and smiled. They were just masks, after all. She had loved Noh theater since the age of nine, when her father had taken her to a performance of *Lady Aoi* and told her that, in an earlier era, commoners had been forbidden to learn the music and dance of the Noh.

Now, while she loved teaching and enjoyed all forms of art, her greatest pleasure came from her role as faculty advisor to the Noh theater club.

She studied the various masks on the wall and felt nine years old again, studying the faces of gods and monsters.

Should they perform a realistic *genzai no*, or a more fantastical *mugen no*? After the tragic deaths of the last year, it seemed more respectful to choose a genzai no. But her Noh club would doubtless prefer some wild fantasy. It was a difficult decision.

Miss Aritomo let her gaze wander over the masks. There was Satokagura, a furious red devil with white hair and a beard, and Torakumadoji, whose ivory devil face was made almost comic by the huge brushes of his bristly eyebrows. There were long-jawed gods with golden faces, dragons and elementals, and several versions of the fox-mask of Kitsune.

From the bookshelf by her desk, she plucked a thick volume that listed every Noh play included in the modern repertoire, as well as older variations that had gone out of fashion. There were fewer than three hundred to choose from, and it would be a simple matter to narrow it down now that she had decided on some parameters.

She started to riffle the pages, glancing casually through them. She intended to wait until the second week of the summer term to reveal her plan to the Noh club. That way, the few students who were transferring in would have time to adjust to the club and decide if they wanted to remain before she sprang the surprise.

A contented smile settled upon her features as she turned

pages and thought about the effort and dedication it would require of her students. Yet she knew they would love every moment of it, just as much as she would.

Perhaps not just as much, she corrected herself, *but nearly.*

Rob would love it, though. When she had discovered that Professor Harper shared her interest in the arts, she realized they had the potential to grow into a real relationship. Yuuka had no desire to compete with the memory of his late wife, but Rob was still a young man. He had a future to look forward to and, though she knew it was much too early to be thinking seriously, she could not pretend that she had not wondered if they might share that future together.

Don't get ahead of yourself, she thought. No matter how strong her feelings for Rob were growing, his lingering devotion to his wife created a barrier between them, and the powerful bond he shared with his daughter, Kara, meant that she would always be foremost in his mind.

That's as it should be. He's her father, Miss Aritomo reminded herself.

And yet she could not help feeling at least a little jealous.

The book fell open to *Lady Aoi*. She had read and reread the description of that play dozens of times, so it was no wonder that the binding naturally opened there. It would be wonderful to do that one, but it was too grim and too fantastical, and the disturbing presence of the Hannya made it everything she didn't want for this first production of the Noh club.

First production? Her smile widened as she realized she had already begun thinking of it in this way. But she told herself to slow down and focus. So much would be involved in this performance that it would be foolish to assume she would be able to do it again, or that Mr. Yamato would allow it.

A clatter came from behind her. Frowning, she turned to see that one of the masks had fallen off its hook.

"Oh, no," she said, hurrying to pick it up.

She put a finger into the book to hold her page and crouched to reach for the mask. As her fingers brushed its surface, she realized with a shudder that it was the Hannya mask. Knees bent, she turned it over and stared in astonishment when she saw that it was unharmed. There were no cracks, the reddish paint was not chipped, and—even more surprisingly—the horns and metallic fangs were intact.

Yet what she felt was not relief. Her brow knitted with an unease she did not understand and, as she began to rise, a wave of disorientation swept over her. She felt cold and unsteady and her vision began to blur, and Miss Aritomo fell, book and mask both dropping from her hands.

It might have been minutes or merely seconds later that she opened her eyes and found herself sprawled on the floor. Her head ached from the impact of her fall and she felt strangely thirsty. Blinking, breathing steadily, she moved carefully into a sitting position, afraid she would faint again. She had passed out only once before, on a hot, humid morning when she had been a schoolgirl.

Shaken, she glanced around. The Hannya mask lay on the floor a few feet away, still unharmed, staring up at the ceiling with what she'd always thought of as gleeful malice. The book had fallen open a few feet from the mask, and now Miss Aritomo reached out to retrieve it.

Curious, she glanced at the pages and saw that the book had fallen open to *Dojoji*, a horrific play that, like *Lady Aoi*, also featured the Hannya. *Dojoji* concerned the spirit of a young woman who had been spurned by her lover and transformed into a demonic serpent—the Hannya—to take her vengeance.

Miss Aritomo smiled and reached for the Hannya mask. A small voice in the back of her mind objected, but she forced those concerns away and they were instantly forgotten. *Dojoji* seemed like the perfect choice for the Noh club.

Just perfect.

1

ㅈ

To Kara, the best part of summer had always been the long, golden twilight of early evenings, when the day had come to an end but night had not yet arrived. On that Friday night, as the heat of the day began at last to break, she sat on a fence across the road from the tiny house she shared with her father, playing her guitar and softly singing along. It was a song about tragic romance and, though Kara had never had the kind of relationship the song depicted, she could imagine heartbreak all too well. Perhaps for that very reason there were times when the idea of falling in love terrified her.

Or maybe you're just sending a message, she thought.

A tiny smile played at the corners of her lips, but then guilt drove it away. Her father and Miss Aritomo were inside the house and surely could not hear her singing. Even if they could, they wouldn't be able to make out the words. Still, she faltered, losing interest in the song, and moved on to another.

Kara had plenty of homework and she wanted to get as much of it done tonight as possible because she had plans for tomorrow. But hitting the books could wait awhile, especially since Miss Aritomo was inside cooking dinner with her father. The two teachers had been getting closer over the last couple of months. Though her dad kept insisting they were just friends, it was obvious to Kara—and anyone else paying attention—that they liked each other a great deal. What was going on was more than friendship. Dating, at least. Maybe other things that she refused to think about.

At first Kara had encouraged it. Miss Aritomo taught art at Monju-no-Chie School and was the faculty advisor to the Noh theater club. While Kara and Sakura had been working on their manga, she had been a huge help.

Pretty and petite, with gorgeous eyes, Miss Aritomo had seemed to take to Rob Harper immediately. Kara wanted her father to be happy, to smile more, and she had seen him *noticing* Miss Aritomo. She'd smiled and teased her dad to let him know it was all okay with her, and she told him her mother would never have wanted him to be alone.

Those sentiments had felt true at the time. But now that her father and Miss Aritomo were getting closer—maybe a lot closer—Kara was having a difficult time with it, and she refused to let her father see that it bothered her. He didn't deserve that.

So she sat on the fence across from the house and looked out over Miyazu Bay below and played her guitar. It didn't hurt that the view was considered one of the two or three most beautiful in all of Japan. A spit of land thrust out from the shore, a two-mile sandbar that had been there long enough for eight thousand pine trees to grow along its length. Ama-no-Hashidate—this finger of land—was a major tourist attraction, and Kara always smiled to see people coming to view it in the traditional way. From various vantage points, they would turn their backs to Ama-no-Hashidate and bend over, looking at it upside down through their open legs. It looked ridiculous, but she had tried it, and from that angle the spit did indeed look like a bridge in the heavens, which was a rough English translation of its name.

Her fingers lost their way on the strings, moving almost of their own accord, jumping from note to note before finally falling still.

With a sigh Kara stood up, holding her guitar close, and stepped over the low fence. Off to her left, in the distance, she could see Monju-no-Chie School and the welcome arch at the edge of its grounds. As she started across the street, her father opened the door of their squat little house and blinked in surprise when he spotted her.

"Perfect timing," he said with a smile.

"My stomach is psychically attuned to the precise moment of dinner's readiness," she said in English.

Her father raised an eyebrow as he stepped aside to let her in. "Hey, I thought we were supposed to stick to Japanese."

Kara laughed. "You think I can say 'psychically attuned' in Japanese? You aren't *that* good a teacher."

His mouth gaped in false astonishment and then he glared

with equally invented anger. "My dear," he said in Japanese, "I am an exceptional teacher."

"And modest, too."

As they walked into the dining area, Miss Aritomo was pouring ice water from a pitcher into the glasses. She smiled.

"You have a very pretty singing voice," she said.

Kara bowed her head in thanks. "I didn't realize I was singing so loud."

"Not very loud," Miss Aritomo replied. "But the window in the kitchen is open, and we could hear you while your father cooked the pork."

Kara stared at her, forgetting for a moment to put on a smile for her father's benefit. Miss Aritomo had sounded so much like a parent that it freaked her out. Part of her wanted to act out, to vanish into her bedroom and not come out, but that would be juvenile and unfair to her father.

Instead she smiled. "Everything smells delicious."

Miss Aritomo blinked, a flicker of doubt shading her eyes. She'd sensed Kara's hesitation, though Kara's father seemed clueless. Before the situation could become awkward, Kara hurried to sit down. Dinner had been served, and the shiitake mushroom rice and orange-simmered pork really did smell wonderful.

"How was your day, Kara?" her father asked.

She smiled. "Hot."

That started the three of them on a conversation about the terrible heat of the week, combining misery with the relief that the forecast brought. It had cooled off significantly in the last few hours, and a thunderstorm was due to sweep through overnight, taking the last of the heat wave out to sea. They talked and ate, and her father and Miss Aritomo had some plum wine, and soon any awkwardness Kara had felt dissipated. She was glad, for her father's sake. But she couldn't stop the little twinge it gave her heart to see the two of them smiling intimately at one another, talking sweetly, and just generally behaving like a couple-in-the-making.

Get over it, she told herself time and again. *It's what Mom would want.* And maybe that was true—she thought so—but for once, what her mother would have wanted didn't seem to have much influence over her. Getting over it would be easier said than done.

"Tell me about your day," her father said. "Did anything interesting happen?"

"Not really," Kara replied.

"Good," her father said, momentarily serious before his smile returned.

Swallowing a bite of pork—it was truly delicious, lean and suffused with orange flavor—she gestured to him and Miss Aritomo both. "Actually, at the calligraphy club meeting, Ren asked me and Sakura what our next manga was going to be."

"Next?" her father said. "You just finished the first one."

Kara nodded. "I know. Sakura's been drawing like crazy for months. I'm sure she's not in a rush to get started on another."

"I don't know about that," Miss Aritomo said, taking a sip of plum wine. "She's such a talented artist, and the manga has given her focus. I'm sure Sakura is already wondering the same thing. What is next for you two?"

Kara shrugged. "I have no idea. I've barely thought about it. Another Noh play, maybe. Something else creepy."

A thin smile appeared on Miss Aritomo's face and she studied Kara over the rim of her glass. "I know just the thing."

"Really?" Kara's father said.

Miss Aritomo nodded. "I haven't told the Noh club yet, but I've decided that this term, we're going to perform an actual Noh play."

"Seriously?" Kara asked, intrigued. "Miho will love that!"

"I think they all will," Miss Aritomo said. "And it really would be perfect as a manga for you and Sakura as well. The story is gruesome and full of evil, just the way you seem to like them."

Kara forced a smile, trying to hide a shudder. Such tales did make for excellent manga, but she thought "like" might be the wrong choice of words.